Pilgrimage

A Post-Apocalyptic Survival Story

Tom Abrahams

A PITON PRESS BOOK

PILGRIMAGE

Cover Design by Hristo Kovatliev
Edited by Felicia A. Sullivan
Proofread by Pauline Nolet
Proofread by Patricia Wilson
Interior design by Stef McDaid at WriteIntoPrint.com

tomabrahamsbooks.com

FREE PREFERRED READERS CLUB: Sign up for information on discounts, events, and release dates:

eepurl.com/bWCRQ5

Works by Tom Abrahams

THE ALT APOCALYPSE SURVIVAL SERIES

ASH

LIT

TORRENT

THE TRAVELER
POST APOCALYPTIC/DYSTOPIAN SERIES

HOME

CANYON

WALL

RISING

BATTLE

LEGACY

THE SPACEMAN CHRONICLES
POST-APOCALYPTIC THRILLERS

SPACEMAN

DESCENT

RETROGRADE

MATTI HAROLD POLITICAL CONSPIRACIES

SEDITION

INTENTION

JACKSON QUICK ADVENTURES

ALLEGIANCE

ALLEGIANCE BURNED

HIDDEN ALLEGIANCE

To Courtney, Sam, and Luke

For whom I would cross mountains and valleys

AUTHOR'S NOTE

This novel is the combination of three previously published novellas loosely based on the The Perseid Collapse series of books written by author Steven Konkoly.

This is a stand-alone story in which new characters experience the same catalyzing event that begins Konkoly's series.

For more about Steven's genre-defining Perseid Collapse Series visit:

StevenKonkoly.com

Part 1

Crossing

CHAPTER 1

EVENT +30:56 Hours
Acton, Maine

James Rockwell wrapped his lips around the barrel, still warm from the last time its owner pulled the trigger. It tasted like a mixture of fireworks and the sensation one gets when testing a battery with his tongue. His fingers were linked behind his head. He was on his knees, a rock buried in the thick grass digging into his left shin.

His wife, Leigh, knelt beside him. She was sobbing, tears streaking down her face. James could tell she was on the verge of hyperventilating. He tried to reach for her, hoping to offer some small comfort, but the psycho with the gun jammed the barrel past James's teeth, gagging him.

He could not see his children, Max and Sloane, but he could hear them whimpering. They were on the other side of their mother, forced into the same awkward positions.

They've already been through so much, James thought. *After everything...the pain and growth of the last six years...the life-altering chaos of the last day and a half...this is how they will die?*

"You don't need to kill us," offered Max, his voice sounding like the strong young man he was becoming. "You have our car. You have our food. Just let us go."

"Shut up, runt," said the would-be executioner. He was dressed in military camouflage fatigues and a matching boonie hat. An AR-style rifle was slung across his back. The strap was pulled tight under his chin. His face was drawn thin, his eyes deep set. "You're not going anywhere. This is where your road ends."

"What are you waiting on?" a voice bellowed from behind the Rockwells. James could hear the man's boots marching through the wet grass. "If you don't have the stomach for it, I'll handle it."

"I got this," replied the executioner. "I'm just deciding how I want to do it. Handgun or rifle."

"You use that nine millimeter, you're gonna get blood all over that nice new MultiCam uni you're wearing." The jackbooted thug walked around James and stood next to the executioner. He was older, thicker in the middle. And though he wore the same fatigues and hat as his younger comrade, his rifle and tactical gear were different.

"I just figured." The executioner slid the barrel out of James's mouth and held it up, the gray gunmetal wet from the rain.

"You're an idiot," said the thug. "Plus, you can't do it out here in the grass. We need to get them into the woods."

The rain had started again. It was loud, slapping against the canopy of trees and the pavement nearby. The executioner grabbed James by his elbow and forced him to his feet. The thug went to grab Leigh, but James stepped in front of him.

"Don't touch her," he snapped. "And don't touch the kids!" James helped his wife to her feet as he coughed. Both kids jumped up and wrapped their arms around their parents.

"You're not in a position to demand anything," the thug snarled before swinging the butt of his rifle into the side of James's head, knocking him back to the ground.

"Don't hurt him!" cried Leigh, huddling with the children. Sloane was knuckling the tattered shell of her stuffed bear, pressing it into her chest.

The thug glared at her, setting his jaw before inhaling and spitting onto her husband's neck. "Now get up." The thug kicked James in the gut with his boot. "We've got more important business."

James, dizzied by the hit and winded by the kick, pushed himself onto one knee. He wiped the spit from the back of his neck and looked up at the thug, keeping his gaze affixed on him as he stood.

"I said," James wheezed, his voice thick with mucus, "don't. Touch. Her."

"Stop it, Rock," Leigh pleaded, touching his shoulder. "Enough."

"*Rock*?" The thug laughed. "Did you just call him *Rock*? That is wicked awesome." The thug took his thick mitt of a hand and thumped it square in the middle of James's back. "She called him Rock." He laughed again for the benefit of the family and the executioner. "Like he's Dwayne Johnson or something. Like he's some big movie star."

"His name is Rockwell," answered the executioner. He pulled a brown leather billfold from his pocket and tossed it at the thug. "Says so on his driver's license. He's from Maryland."

The thug opened up the wallet and thumbed out the license. He flipped it over and slipped it back into place before shoving the wallet into his own pocket. "What are you doing here?"

"Vacation," James said, his hands on his knees. He couldn't catch his breath. "Family vacation." His voice rattled.

"Not the R and R you were hoping for, eh, Rock?" The thug snickered. "It's over now. Let's march."

The executioner holstered his nine millimeter and swung his rifle into his hands. Alongside the thug, the two of them pushed the Rockwells toward the woods fifty yards away.

James's mind, cloudy as it was from the rifle butt, was spinning for a solution. How could he save his family, even if it meant sacrificing his life in the process?

Their captors, armed as they were, seemed sloppy. The younger one was in over his head. The older one was power happy.

There has to be a way…

James looked over at his wife, his children. He swallowed hard.

"Pick up the pace, *Rock*," said the executioner. "Keep moving."

A wet breeze blew across James's face, a sign of the approaching fall. He could hear it whispering its way through the trees ahead of him.

Do something! They were telling him. *Save your family.*

He shook his head as he trudged forward, certain the blow to his head had him hearing things. It was that or the lack of sleep.

You can't let them die here.

They were twenty-five yards from the beckoning woods, crossing the pavement of a parking lot entrance, when James wondered if his eyes were playing tricks on him too.

Facedown in the trampled weeds marking the entrance to the woods were five bodies. Two big, three small. He couldn't make out whether they were men or women, boys or girls, but that was irrelevant.

James knew, hallucinations or not, they wouldn't be the first family to die here. They wouldn't be the last either, unless he acted quickly…unless he killed first. It was a notion to which the high school physics teacher from Maryland had grown alarmingly accustomed in the last thirty-six hours.

But he was running out of time.

CHAPTER 2

EVENT -06:00 Hours
Peaks Island, Maine

A brilliant orange streak arced across the sky, silently burning a path through the Earth's atmosphere. Another followed.

James Rockwell was perched on the edge of a weathered Adirondack chair, his children at his feet.

"What's a Perseid, Dad?" Sloane was nine years old. "And why is it called a shower? There's no rain."

"It's a *meteor* shower," answered twelve-year-old Max, "because it's like they're raining in the sky. They're called Perseids because they come from the Perseus Constellation."

"I couldn't have said it better myself." James rubbed the top of his son's head, tousling a mop of sun-bleached blonde hair. "Where'd you learn that?"

"Google," answered the rising seventh grader, who was a spitting image of his father, "and Wikipedia."

"You know Wikipedia isn't always right," James counseled his son. "You need to fact-check the sources."

"That's why I Googled Google." Max giggled. "It said the meteors are part of the Swift-Tuttle comet."

"Very good," said James. "And what is a comet?"

"Ice and dust mostly." The twelve-year-old shrugged. "Sometimes gas, like when it gets close to the Sun."

"Correct." James leaned back in his chair and looked back up to the sky. He took a deep breath and closed his eyes, savoring the moment. The pocket almanac he'd stuffed into his bag at the last second before leaving home had proven worth the purchase. Otherwise, he'd have forgotten the annual astronomical fireworks.

Still, renting a beach house on an island off Maine's coast was not his idea of a vacation. He craved adventure-filled, adrenaline-pumping, life-affirming excursions. But Leigh had insisted this year's getaway should take a sharp one-hundred-eighty-degree spin. She wanted time to relax.

They'd spent weeks debating the annual trip, going back and forth about what to do at the end of the summer. They were jogging on side-by-side treadmills at the local YMCA when she managed to convince him.

"We've hiked and biked mountains in Colorado," she reminded him, "and slung ourselves down zip lines in Costa Rica."

"Don't forget spending a night in the Alaskan Wilderness in a tent," James added.

"That too." She laughed in between deep breaths. "We need a break."

"A break from once-in-a-lifetime experience?" James questioned.

"C'mon, Rock," Leigh huffed, "that's not what I mean. I think the kids would like a nice, quiet trip too. We don't have to keep proving we're *alive*. No need to thumb our collective noses at Death."

That stung. But James understood. Everybody coped with loss differently. He'd forced his mechanism on the rest of his family. They'd acquiesced for six years. Now it was his turn to be pliable.

"Okay," he agreed, chugging the final push on the treadmill. It was elevating, spinning faster, challenging him in the final ninety seconds of the workout. "I'll go wherever you want to go."

Leigh, with help from the kids, chose this idyllic cottage on the beach. A ferry's ride away from Portland, Peaks Island was the most populated island on Casco Bay. "The Coney Island of Maine", Peak's Island was a tourist's dream, replete with ice cream parlors, a market, galleries, and restaurants.

The rental property sat on a curved narrow strip of sand along the western side of the island. Complete with a small kitchen, sitting room, a bedroom downstairs, and a loft upstairs, it fit the Rockwells. And Leigh was right. The ten days and nights they'd spent relaxing were rejuvenating. Enjoying the meteor shower was the perfect way to end the summer.

"What are you thinking about?" Leigh was standing over James, holding two cups of hot green tea. "I'll trade you this tea for your thoughts?"

James opened his eyes and smiled, sitting up in the chair as he took the steaming cup from his wife. "You," he said as she sat on his lap and leaned back with her head on his shoulder.

"Me?" She feigned flattery. "How so?"

"You were right." He shifted in the chair to give her more room. "This was a good vacation."

"It was, wasn't it?" She purred before taking a sip of the tea. "The kids enjoyed themselves."

James looked at his children on the sand and nodded. Max was growing up so fast. He was smart beyond his years with an interest in mechanics and science. He was a voracious bookworm, as was his younger sister. Sloane was the spitting image of Leigh. She was funny and inquisitive. James knew he'd need to add a shotgun to his armory as she grew older.

"There's another one, streaking left to right," said Max, navigating the sky for his sister. She sat next to him on the beach, clutching her stuffed bear, Noodle.

Noodle never left Sloane's clutch. He was worn, missing an eye, and was the patient to Leigh's surgical sewing kit more times than anybody could count. But he was Sloane's guardian angel. She'd told them that. They'd allowed her to believe it.

"Are we all packed?" Leigh asked her husband, rubbing his leg with her hand. "Ready to catch the early ferry?"

"Yep." James nodded. "If we get up at five thirty, we can probably catch the six-fifteen. If we miss it, no big deal. There's one an hour later."

"If we get up at five thirty," she countered, "it'll be the one an hour later. I'm not getting ready that quickly."

"No problem," he said. "But I don't want to get the kids up earlier than five thirty. They'll be cranky as it is."

"I'll miss this place." She sighed, taking another sip. "Maybe we should consider coming back next summer." She nudged him for effect.

"Maybe." He chuckled. "But only if they add a high-intensity obstacle course, a zip line, and somebody starts offering shark diving." He slapped her rear with the palm of his hand.

"Ha!" She laughed. "I'll look into that for you."

"You do that." He took a sip of his tea. It was hot and singed the tip of his tongue.

"Time for the kids to hit the sack?" she asked. "Then we'll have a few minutes to ourselves."

"A few minutes?" he replied, sliding the tip of his tongue on the back of his front teeth. "That's more than I'll need, right?"

"You're awful." She slapped his chest and sat up. "I'll put them down. You clean the kitchen."

"Deal."

It was the end of the vacation, the final moments of the world they knew. It was good they didn't know what was coming.

CHAPTER 3

EVENT -00:00 Hours
Peaks Island, Maine

James woke up to a bright red light engulfing the loft. He squinted, shielded his eyes as they adjusted, and sat up in bed. Leigh was still asleep, her head under a feather pillow.

The light seemed oddly hued for sunrise. It was intense too. Then James realized, his window faced westward. He shouldn't be seeing the sunrise in that direction. Every other morning had greeted them with a gentle orange light reflected off the blue of the bay.

This was very different.

He pulled off the sheets and walked to the window. The clock on Leigh's side of the bed glowed 5:01 a.m. Too early for sunrise, James thought.

At the window, his concerns were amplified by the throbbing, reddish glow emanating from the southwestern sky just above the horizon. As he tried to wrap his head around what he was seeing, the color morphed into a deeper red and purple hue. It changed shape and pulsed. He'd never seen anything like this before. But knowing a little bit about science, he had his suspicions.

"Leigh." He turned to his wife. "Leigh, get up." The clock next to her flickered and went black.

She groaned from under the pillow. "It's too early, Rock. Give me five more minutes."

"Leigh." His voice was stern. "Get up."

"What is it?" She shot up, tossing the pillow from the bed. "Are you okay? Wait. What is that light?" Leigh shielded her eyes with her hand as her feet found the floor.

"I don't know," answered James. "I mean, I'm not sure. But it's not good."

Leigh blinked against the hellish shimmer on the bay. "It looks like an explosion or something."

"I think that's exactly what it is," answered James. He put his hand on the small of his wife's back. "We need to move."

"What?" Leigh crinkled her nose, her brow arched with confusion. "Why?"

"If there was a big explosion of any kind"—James put his hands on his wife's shoulders and turned her toward him so he could look squarely into her eyes—"I mean of any kind, and it was in the water, we're in trouble."

"I don't under—" She shook her head, her eyes beginning to well.

"That explosion would be an impulsive disturbance, displacing the water column—" explained the physics teacher.

"In English, Rock!" Her lip was trembling.

"Tsunami."

"What do we do, Rock?" Her voice trembled with panic. "We're on an island."

"We find the highest possible structure and ride out the wave," he offered. "The car is packed. We need to go now."

"But I'm still in my—" Leigh was wearing thin cotton lounge pants and a loose-fitting tank top.

"Now!" He squeezed his wife's shoulder, pulled her in for a brief but loving hug, and then took her hand, leading her quickly down the narrow stairs to the first floor of the cottage.

"I'll carry Sloane," instructed James as they bounded through the kitchen to the bedroom. "You guide Max to the car. He'll be out of it, but he can walk."

"Got it," Leigh sputtered past the lump in her throat. She shook awake her son and pulled him from groggy sleep, through the kitchen, and out the open front door of the cottage.

James was buckling Sloane into the rear driver's side. It was still dark aside from the fading glow to the southwest.

Max found his way into the backseat behind his mother, and James jumped behind the wheel of their Jeep Cherokee. He cranked the ignition, the headlights illuminating the front of the cabin, and he slammed the Jeep into reverse.

"Wait!" cried Sloane. "What about Noodle? I don't have Noodle!!"

James cursed and slammed on the brake. Without even looking at Leigh for approval, he knew he couldn't leave behind the guardian angel of a bear. It was too important to his daughter. He ripped the gearshift into park and left the Jeep at the end of the driveway.

Guided by the headlights, he ran back toward the cottage. As he reached the front stoop, a strong gust of wind pushed him off balance. He recovered, bracing himself against the door frame, and lumbered inside the house.

James navigated the small kitchen back to the children's dark first-floor bedroom, banging his bare foot into the corner of the island. Biting his lip, he limped into the bedroom and fumbled around for a light switch. He found it, flipped it, and it did nothing. So he dove onto the bed to dig amongst the sheets and blankets, blindly feeling around for the kinked wool plush.

As he tore through the sheets, he heard a loud wail outside the home. It shook the house and was immediately followed by the whoosh and bang of the front door slamming shut and a loud crash.

James found Noodle at the same moment he heard his wife scream and call out his name.

CHAPTER 4

EVENT +00:05 Hours
Peaks Island, Maine

James threw open the door to find what looked like the aftermath of a tornado.

The blast wind.

From the glare of the headlights, he couldn't make out clearly why his wife had screamed. But as he darted to the car, he dodged fallen limbs and debris in the driveway. He slid to a stop at the passenger's side of the Jeep.

Leigh had the door open, one leg on the ground. Her chest heaving, James knew she was trying to keep from hyperventilating.

"What happened?" he asked and his wife pointed.

Then he saw it. So focused on her as he ran to the Jeep he'd missed the obvious. A two by six was lodged in the front windshield, its splintered edges just inches from his wife's headrest. It had punctured the bench seat back between their children. Both of them were crying.

James pulled his wife from the car and wrapped his arms around her. "It's okay," he told her. "It's okay." Leigh sobbed into his chest before pulling away.

"It was just," she said between deep breaths, "a big wind. We—I—it shook the car. Like a tornado. Or hurricane. I—it was so strong. I—"

"Shhh." James rubbed his wife's back, pulling her toward him again. "You're okay. It was a blast from the explosion. There won't be another one until the wave hits." He pulled away. "We have to move now. Quickly."

"But the wood—"

"I'll get it. Just get the kids out of the car for a second."

James let go of his wife and, as she and the children backed away from the Jeep, climbed onto the hood. He sat with his feet pressed against the windshield and grabbed the back end of the two by six. He made sure he had a tight grip with both hands and yanked on the board as he lay back on the hood. The board gave easily and released from the seat, pulling pieces of shattered glass with it as James pulled it onto his chest and past his head.

Leigh moved to the side of the Jeep and helped James finish the job, tossing the would-be spear onto the driveway. He rolled off the hood and told his family to get back into the vehicle.

"Be careful of the glass," he suggested. "We won't be in the car long."

"Where are we going?" asked Leigh, pulling her seatbelt across her lap.

"Battery Steele," said James, maneuvering the Jeep around obstacles littering the narrow road that ran along the western side of the island.

"How far is it?" asked Max.

"Less than two miles," answered his dad.

"How long do we have to get there?" Leigh had her hand on his thigh. "Will we make it?"

"Honestly?" James yanked the wheel to the right to avoid the remains of a charcoal grill. "I don't know the answer to either of those questions."

"Guess," insisted Max, using his mother's headrest to pull himself forward.

"Sit back, Max," ordered James. "It's not safe to sit up like that. Are you buckled?"

"Yes." Max slinked back to his seat. "Guess, Dad."

"Maybe an hour." James slowed and swung the wheel to the right. A chaise lounge was blocking half the road. "Maybe less. And yes, as long as the roads aren't impassable, we can make it."

James jinxed himself.

"Rock!" Leigh cautioned, pointing at the shattered windshield. "Watch out!"

James slammed on the brakes and swerved, fishtailing the Jeep around the marquis for a gas station. He took his foot off the accelerator and regained control in time to miss another large branch and a small wild turkey wandering around aimlessly on the edge of the road.

Leigh tugged on the shoulder strap of her seatbelt, adjusting it against her chest. She watched the locals as they drove past. Many of them stood in front of their properties, hands on hips, assessing the instantaneous damage to their homes and businesses. Some of them had their eyes on the horizon, pointing or waving their hands at the odd mixture of the civil twilight at the edge of sunrise and the fading purple and red aura to the southwest. Others still were scurrying about, picking up debris. Everybody was dressed in pajamas or shorts and T-shirts. They looked like ants emerging from a sneaker-kicked mound.

James was driving south along Island Avenue. Casco Bay and the mainland were to the right.

"Do you know where you're going?" asked Leigh. She pulled her cell phone from the center console to check navigation. The phone illuminated, but the satellite-driven maps wouldn't work. She had no signal, regardless.

"I think so," James said, leaning forward to better see through the spider web spreading across the windshield, obstructing his view. "I remember it's to the left of Island Avenue and on a main road. I don't remember exactly."

"Why Battery Steele?" she asked.

"When the wave hits," James answered, "there's no telling how high it's going to be. Whatever detonated out there was big. You felt its blast. We need to be as high off the ground as possible."

"Detonated?" asked Sloane. "What's that?"

"It means explosion," answered Max. "Dad, what exploded? There was an explosion?"

James didn't answer him.

"Is this your turn?" Leigh referenced an upcoming intersection with a left turn into the heart of the island.

"I think you're right." James slowed and spun the wheel. "Yeah, this is it." He accelerated out of the turn and for the first time noticed the small black compass mounted on the dash.

James knew they were headed due east. He was sure of it. But the compass was drifting. It couldn't fix on a direction. The explosion, whatever it was, had set off an EMP, an electromagnetic pulse.

"I can't believe the car is working," said James. "It's a miracle, really," he mumbled.

"What?" asked Max. "What did you say, Dad?"

"Nothing." James caught himself.

"You said the car shouldn't be working?" Max pressed. "Why? You didn't answer me about the explosion."

He glanced in the rearview mirror at his son and then over at Leigh. They shared the same puzzled looks on their faces, their brows pulled tight as they bit their lower lips.

"Are we going to die?" asked Sloane.

"Dad"—Max sat forward in his seat, pulling himself between his parents—"what explosion? Why aren't you answering me?"

"We'll be fine," answered Leigh, turning to reassure her baby. "Daddy's going to take care of us. He's very smart."

"Dad." Max huffed impatiently. "Answer *me*, please."

James hesitated before he answered, unsure how truthful he should be with his children or his wife. He took a deep breath, and with the sun rising in his face, he did his best to obscure the reality of their situation.

"So, Max," he began, pulling down the visor to help his vision of the road, "during certain kinds of explosions, gamma rays are emitted from the fission fragments. Those gamma rays transfer their energy into air molecules. It's called the Compton Scattering Process, and when that—"

"C'mon, Dad." Max wasn't fooled by the tech-speak. "I'm not one of your physics students."

"I'm not sure they'd understand him either, Max," Leigh added, looking over at her son. "Don't try to candy coat it, Rock. What's going on?"

James used to be a big believer in blissful ignorance. He was one of those lemmings who agreed, based on nothing more than a stupid colloquialism, that what he didn't know couldn't hurt him. Until it did. The worldwide flu outbreak commonly called the Jakarta Pandemic changed everything.

That's why he was blunt with his wife and his young children as they drove for their lives.

"I'm pretty sure that somebody, some country, exploded some form of nuclear weapon off the coast of the United States." Nobody interrupted him this time. "That detonation triggered what's called an electromagnetic pulse. That pulse, in turn, is capable of rendering just about every electrically powered device practically useless."

"Like our Jeep?" asked Sloane. The eight-year-old got it.

"Yes." James nodded. "Like our car, our phones, the alarm clock, satellite communication, televisions, you name it."

"Then why is our car working?" asked Max, gripping his small hand on his father's shoulder.

"I don't know," admitted James. "I've read studies that contend only one percent of vehicles are operable after an EMP. There are others that calculate the number much higher than that."

The Rockwells drove in silence for the next minute. Nobody knew what to say, where to begin, what questions to ask or how to answer them.

"How do we get off of the island?" asked Max. "If boats don't work, what do we do?"

"I don't have the answer to that yet, Max," James admitted. "But that's not my primary concern right now. My first priority is getting us as high off the ground as possible. There's going to be a lot of water on the island very soon. I mean, there will be water everywhere, and we don't want to be swimming in it."

"Like a flood?" asked Sloane "Like Noah from the bible?"

"Something like that." James sighed, reconsidering whether or not honesty was, in fact, the best policy, or if it was just another useless saying made up by the blissfully ignorant.

"I think we're there," said Leigh, covering her eyes from the sun. "That's Battery Steele over there!"

"Where?" James couldn't see through the bright light refracted in the spider web of cracks in the shattered windshield. He squinted and tried to score a quick glance out the passenger's side window. He took his eyes off of the road for just a moment.

That was all it took.

CHAPTER 5

EVENT +00:20 Hours
Peaks Island, Maine

The door frame lying in the road acted as the perfect ramp. The blast wind had ripped it like a Frisbee, a light pole pressing it in half en route to its landing spot. James tried, at the last instant, to avoid it, but he couldn't react quickly enough. The collision jacked the left side of the Jeep onto two wheels before launching it into the air. James tried to surf the two wheels but couldn't overcorrect enough before the family was flipped upside down, careening in a metal box that tumbled and slid for what seemed like forever.

As the steering wheel airbag exploded into his face, James instinctively swung his right arm across the space between his seat and Leigh's, catching Max in the chest just enough to knock the boy back into his seat and engage the seatbelt's automatic locking mechanism.

Leigh raised her hands above her, bracing herself against the roof. Her fingers dug into the fabric-covered foam headliner. She screamed out for Sloan and Max, praying aloud as she felt the shoulder strap dig into her shoulder, the lap belt press against her pelvis.

The children were remarkably quiet, stunned into silence as the Jeep tumbled, crunching with each ear-grinding maneuver against the asphalt. Sloane never lost her grip on Noodle as the Jeep came to a rest on its roof, teetering on the edge of the road's narrow shoulder and just inches from the thick trunk of an eastern white pine.

James pushed the deflating airbag from his face, wincing against the percussive burn on his cheek. "Everyone okay? Can everyone hear me?"

Still suspended by their belts, his family answered him. They were okay. Sloane was whimpering, explaining she was stuck upside down and scared. Max complained the shoulder belt was digging into his neck. Leigh revealed a pain in her left wrist, wondering aloud if it was sprained or worse.

James loosened himself from his belt first, dropping onto the headliner with a thud. He crawled to his wife, bracing her as she unlatched her belt and sank next to him.

"Get out of the car," he instructed. "I'll get the kids."

Without argument, Leigh tried pushing open her door. It wouldn't budge. She pressed her shoulder into it without any luck. "It's stuck," she explained. "I need to get out your side."

James slid into the backseat, between the kids, then turned around to pop open the driver's door. It was undamaged in the wreck and swung out without any problem. Leigh crawled past her husband and out onto the road. James helped Sloane first, laying his body underneath her as he unlatched her. The back of her head landed safely on his chest and she rolled over to face him.

"Thank you, Daddy." She blinked past tears and kissed him on the cheek before Leigh helped her out through the rear driver's side door. She told him her neck was sore but she was okay.

"Okay, Max." James turned to his son. "Your turn."

"It's about time," he replied. "This thing is *killing* me."

"Be thankful there aren't any rear airbags," countered James. "Then you'd really be hurting."

"I thought those were supposed to save lives." Max dropped on his hands and flipped over as his dad unlatched him.

"Yes," James answered, sliding feet first out of the Jeep. "But they can be painful. Mine singed my cheek a little bit. It's like a solid rocket booster, you know?" James found himself on the pavement, his arms extended to guide his son out of the Jeep.

"Really?" Max asked, distracted from reality by the science of an airbag. His neck was bleeding along the spot where the belt cut him, but it wasn't concerning to James given the seriousness of the wreck.

"Yep," said James as his son emerged from the vehicle. "When there's a collision, a sensor ignites an instantaneous chemical reaction. That reaction—"

"Are you kidding me, Rock?" Leigh, barefoot and still in her pajamas, stood with her arms folded across her chest.

"What?" James looked at her like a guilty puppy with his paws on the counter.

"We don't need a physics lesson right now." She rolled her eyes and grabbed her wrist. She winced when she touched it. "We need you to get our crap out of the Jeep and lead us, without further incident, to a safe place high off the ground."

James looked at her and smiled to himself. He couldn't believe how calm, how in control she was. In the midst of a life-altering cataclysm, seconds removed from a violent, acrobatic car wreck, she was keeping it together. Without saying anything, he took two steps to her and threw his arms around her, holding her tight and squeezing as her arms found their way around his back.

"I love you," he whispered into her ear before kissing her on the cheek and climbing back into the Jeep to grab a trio of backpacks and two rolling duffel bags.

"Love you too," she called behind him. "And I need my shoes out of one of those bags, now that we have to hoof it. We all do. I could use a bra too."

James emerged with the luggage, assigning a backpack each to wife and son. He gave Max the lighter of the duffels to roll. He took the heaviest pack and the larger duffel.

"Kinda strange, huh?" James observed as he slung the pack onto his shoulders.

"What?" Leigh was adjusting the waist strap on her pack. She was having trouble, so her husband helped her.

"Not a single person came to help us out of the wreck," he said, nodding his head toward the half-dozen people buzzing their way around their own properties. "You'd think that would be human nature."

"What does that say, then?" asked Leigh.

"It says we're on our own," James reasoned and pointed ahead to the north side of the road. "Everybody is on their own." He took a couple steps ahead of his family and looked back over his shoulder at them. "That's where we're headed. We need to move. If you get tired, Sloane, I'll carry you, okay?"

"I'm good, Daddy." She nodded, Noodles swinging back and forth in her hand. "Let's do this."

CHAPTER 6

EVENT +00:45 Hours
Peaks Island, Maine

The ten-minute hike was relatively flat, which made it easier on the Rockwells as they trekked north and east along an extension of Central Avenue. There was debris from the tall trees and brush lining both sides of the road that littered their path, however, which made rolling the duffel bags more challenging for Max and James. They passed a shop that rented kayaks, canoes, and fishing gear. For a moment, James wondered if he should grab one of the kayaks. They were fiberglass, looked light enough to carry, and might come in handy. He decided against it almost as soon as the thought dripped into his mind. They were already overloaded and there was no conceivable way they could manage with the awkward vessel as added weight. So they kept walking. It was more and more exhausting with every step.

But they managed until James told his family to stop. He dropped the duffel on the road, slipped his thumbs inside his pack straps and stepped off the asphalt and onto a dirt path leading south into the woods.

"Is this it?" asked Leigh, her wrist wrapped like a cast with a flesh-colored elastic bandage pulled from her pack.

"I think so," he turned and nodded, before stepping back to grab the duffel. "Max if you can't get the bag, I'll take it from here." He extended a hand to his son, who refused the help.

"You okay to keep walking?" Leigh asked Sloane.

"Yep," the eight year old was a trooper, well-seasoned from her annual adventures. A short walk was nothing.

"Okay," James took a deep breath and yanked the duffel onto the pine-needle-covered dirt path, tugging it through the leaves. "Let's find this thing."

The Rockwells wove their way among the trees for only maybe thirty yards before they saw it; a tall concrete structure rising above the canopy, its tower a full sixty feet in the air.

"What is that?" Max asked as they approached the base of the tower.

"It's a fire control tower," James explained, dropping the duffel. "I remember seeing there were two of these when we were looking at the GPS map for Battery Steele."

"That's the army thing, right?" Max asked. "The one with the graffiti?" They'd visited the historic military installation just five days ago, walking through its tunnels and admiring the artwork locals and tourists had painted on its walls.

"It is," James answered, looking up at the tower. "Max, help me check for an entrance to this thing. The doorway on this side is filled with concrete."

Max dropped his duffel and marched around the left side of the tower. Finding nothing, he circled the side opposite his father. "Dad!" he called. "There's a ladder!"

James jogged around to meet his son and, sure enough, there was an aluminum extension ladder leading to a small opening about fifteen feet off the ground. "Good job, Max!" James gave his son a thumbs-up and tousled his sweaty head. "Let's get Mom and Sloane up there first."

They grabbed the duffels and led Leigh, Sloane, and Noodle back to the ladder. James suggested Leigh go first. She reluctantly agreed and climbed the ladder to the opening before sliding herself headfirst into the narrow opening. She reemerged a second later, her head poking through what amounted to a small open-air window.

"Okay," she called down, "I'm good here. It looks like there's a staircase to the top."

"Your turn, Sloane," James told his daughter. "You climb up and I'll be right behind you." He turned to Max. "As soon as she's up there, I'll come back down. You're next."

Max nodded and tugged on his pack, adjusting it on his shoulders, before sitting down on his duffel. "I'm good," he said.

Sloane climbed the ladder like a monkey. James was two rungs behind her, making sure she didn't fall. She reached the top of the ladder and reached out to her mom, who pulled her through the opening and into the tower.

"So far, so good," said Leigh. But James couldn't hear her. A crack, the sound of snapping wood, was too loud. At first it was a solitary noise, coming from the distant south. But it was followed by another sickly pop. And another. It began sounding like popcorn. And it was getting louder.

"What is that?" Leigh asked, almost yelling above the growing din.

James didn't answer. He was already halfway down the ladder. "Max!" he yelled to his son. "Get up! Hurry!"

As he reached his son, Max could see the panic in his father's eyes. He jumped up, and without thinking about it, ran the short distance to the ladder, covering the final steps with a shove from James.

Max didn't understand what was happening as he grabbed the bottom rung of the ladder and began to climb. James did. The snapping of trees meant the water was coming.

CHAPTER 7

EVENT +00:53 Hours
Peaks Island, Maine

James was on Max's heels as they climbed the ladder. Max's pack bounced on his back as he moved as quickly as he could up the rungs.

"Start moving," James yelled to his wife, over the sound of trees yanked from their roots. "Get as high as you can!"

Leigh's head disappeared inside the opening just as Max reached the top of the ladder. James waited for his son to climb through the window and he turned to look back.

He couldn't see the trees falling, but he could hear them.

James was on the verge of pulling himself through the hole when he reconsidered. Against the growing roar of the water he knew was racing toward him, he slid down the ladder and hopped to the ground.

The fifteen feet between him and the larger duffel may as well have been a mile. But James covered the distance and ripped back the zipper at the top of the bag.

"Dad!" yelled Max. "What are you doing? Dad!" His scream was primal.

James ignored him and focused on the bag. He knew exactly where he'd stuffed a small pistol. Blindly, he found the weapon and a small box of ammunition. He stuffed the box in his waistband and launched himself back to the ladder.

"It's coming, Dad!" Max cried. "Ruuuuunnnnnnn!"

James grabbed the side rails and pulled himself up two rungs as a wall of water tore through the trees at the edge of the small clearing that surrounded the tower. A large pine, ripped from the ground, slammed into the tower wall. James shimmied up as quickly as he could, but a wall of water slammed into the tower as his right hand grabbed the opening.

"Dad!" Max said above the deafening surge. "Grab my hands!"

James felt his shoulder tug as the ladder was washed out from underneath him. His feet were underwater, being pulled in one direction and then another. He was losing his grip when Leigh appeared next to her son.

"Rock!" She reached out and grabbed onto his wrist with both of her hands, relieving the pressure on his wrist and shoulder. The water was rising. It was at his waist, swirling and tugging.

He felt something slam into the back of his leg. The sudden, thickening pain was almost enough to weaken his resolve. But he, somehow, managed to raise his left arm, the gun still in his hand, and reach his son's grip.

"Take the gun!" James grunted. "Get it out of my hand before you pull!" The water, halfway up his chest, was cold and angry. A surge slammed him against the concrete wall, knocking the breath from his lungs.

Max took the gun and checked the safety before putting it down and reaching to grab his dad's fingertips. He leaned as far as he could from the small opening, trying to grab farther up James's arm.

"Max!" warned Leigh. "Don't fall. Be careful." She was wedged between the edge of the window and her son, holding onto her husband's slipping arm. She looked past her husband at the surreal seascape a full thirteen feet above the island. A cascade of timber was bobbing along the bubbling, foaming surface. The roiling water wasn't rising anymore, she surmised, but it wasn't receding yet either. And with the branch-laden trees riding the tide toward her husband, she knew there wasn't much time before she'd lose him. She wasn't going to let that happen.

"Max!" she growled with renewed purpose. "When I get to three, pull as hard as you can. Got it?"

Her son nodded and waited for the count.

"One," said Leigh, affixing her grip with both hands, ignoring the growing pain in her wrist. "Two. Three." She pulled her husband, the love of her life, the father of her children, the man she knew she needed to keep them safe, with everything she could muster. Her stomach tightened, her thighs burned, her neck strained. She could feel the loss of oxygen in her head as she held her breath, tugging against James's weight. And then, with one last effort, she felt an instant of weightlessness and fell back, losing her grip.

She caught herself as she flew backward, stopping short of the interior concrete wall. On the edge of the window, his body draped across the opening, James was safe.

"You're bleeding, Dad!" said Max, his hand on the small of his father's back. He looked to his mom for help when James didn't respond.

Leigh looked over at Sloane sitting quietly against the wall next to her mother's pack, took a deep breath, and moved carefully to her husband. "Rock, are you okay? Can you move?"

James nodded, but he said nothing. His body was racked with pain, exhausted from the fight, he couldn't bring himself to talk. But he slid himself forward on the window ledge, his wife and son helping him inside.

He slunk to the floor, lying on his stomach. He knew the back of his leg was injured. He assumed that's where he was bleeding. Leigh confirmed it.

"You have a bad gash on the back of your leg," she said, gently stroking his cheek with the back of her hand. She was kneeling beside him. "I'm gonna have to dress it. I mean, under normal circumstances, you'd probably need stitches."

"There's a sewing kit," James managed. "It's in my pack."

"I'm not doing that," Leigh countered. "And since you can talk"—her tone shifted from compassionate to annoyed—"what the hell were you doing?"

"We needed the gun," he mumbled.

"The gun?"

"Nobody helped us when we wrecked," James said, wincing as he shifted his torso on the concrete. "Nobody's going to help us now."

"So? You were stupid to go after it. You could have died." She looked at Max. He was transfixed by what his father was saying.

"We're going to need the gun," he repeated slowly. "It was worth the risk."

"I don't see how—"

"This is just the beginning, Leigh," James explained, trying to roll himself onto his side. "It's going to get worse."

CHAPTER 8

EVENT +02:00 Hours
Peaks Island, Maine

The water was receding. It slipped to half its height, though that wasn't obvious to James as he stood atop the tower, some sixty feet above what used to be Peaks Island. He was looking west, toward Portland. There were boats of varying sizes dotting the bay between Peaks and the mainland. James couldn't tell, however, how many of them were upright, let alone seaworthy.

"How's your leg?" asked Max. He was standing next to his dad, his arms folded identically across his chest.

"I'm okay," James reassured his son. "Mom did a great job dressing it. I'll have a scar to remember this adventure. But I'll be good."

"Good." Max nodded.

"You did a great job down there, Max," James praised his boy. "You helped save my life. Don't forget that."

"I won't." A grin filled the space between two dimples on Max's cheeks. "Especially at Christmas time."

"That's a given." James laughed and then turned back to the horizon. "What's not a given"—he sighed—"is how we're going to get off this underwater island."

"We need a boat, right?" asked Max.

"That would be a good start." James turned toward the east, his back to the mainland, searching for an answer. He found nothing there but the muddied waters of the bay. What had been so clean, so blue a day ago was soiled and murky.

Leigh was a floor below, sifting through her husband's pack, reorganizing it after having used some of its contents to salve his wound. She chuckled to herself, remembering the heated discussion she'd had with James about the money she thought he'd wasted on the expensive survival gear.

"It's a great deal," he'd bargained. "It's the ultimate survivalist backpack."

"And we need to spend two hundred dollars on this?" she'd asked. "We take one big trip a year. We're not *preppers*, James."

"First," he'd explained, "I got two of them for two hundred dollars. Second, you say *preppers* like it's a bad word. There's nothing wrong with being prepared. We were completely flat-footed six years ago. If we hadn't been then maybe—"

"Don't go there!" she'd warned, her angry finger pointed at his chest. He'd pressed a button he shouldn't have. "Wasting money on a couple of stupid backpacks would not have saved her. She would not be alive because we now have a portable mosquito hammock, paracord, and a rubber tourniquet."

"Look," he'd said. "That's not—"

"She died because she got the flu, James." Leigh's fists were clenched tight, her arms straight at her side. "Our oldest child, your parents, my mother"—she'd suppressed the urge to scream at him—"they're dead because they got the flu. No amount of preparedness, no *carpe diem* vacations, none of it will bring them back."

This was an argument they'd suffered before. They blamed one another. They blamed themselves. They faulted the government and the local hospital. The arguments always escalated until James and Leigh couldn't stand the sight of one another.

They'd throw their hands up and walk away. He'd get in the Jeep and drive to the YMCA to burn off the anger. She'd start cleaning the house, ignoring him as she scrubbed and wiped.

It was a pattern that repeated itself over and again in those six years. Their therapist gave them tools to cope with the pain and with one another. Slowly, the *events*, as they were, lessened in intensity and in frequency. The therapist told them their relationship was like a muscle, and to make it stronger they had to work hard at it, suffer through pain and difficulty. Their marriage was growing stronger again. They were learning how to cope with the loss, with daily challenges, and with each other.

So instead of fighting her on the cost/benefit of the Yukon Outfitters Survivalist Alpha Backpack, he'd dropped the gear to the ground and wrapped his arms around her. She'd buried her head in his chest and sobbed. Six years of grieving, of coping, of trying to rationalize the guilt…

It was that argument that persuaded them to take the relaxing, stress-draining trip *she* wanted. And here they were, in need of these stupid packs. The irony wasn't lost on Leigh as she stuffed the two remaining eight-ply, three-by-three gauze pads back into the bag.

She looked over at Sloane. Her daughter was sleeping on the concrete floor, her head using Noodle as a pillow. She looked peaceful despite the chaos around them. Leigh hoped her daughter was having a good dream, momentarily escaping the nightmare in which they found themselves.

Leigh zipped the pack quietly and stood to walk over to the window. She pulled her head through the opening and looked out at the apocalyptic landscape. At fifty feet above the ground, she was at the height equal to where the forested canopy should have been.

Instead, the trees were few and far between. Those left standing were stripped of their branches and foliage below twenty feet. Beyond the smattering of trees was a filthy bay corrupted by the remnants of homes and businesses, their contents, and the bodies of the people who called the island home. Leigh wondered if anyone on the island, other than her family, had survived the tsunami. Had anyone else known what was coming?

She looked down along the length of the tower. The water was a good ten feet below the flood line on the tower's exterior. A collection of tangled branches was stuck against the side of the tower, likely grounded underneath the surface.

And trapped within those branches, another miracle. Two miracles.

Leigh twisted her body to look up toward the roof of the tower. "Rock!" she called, cupping her hands around her mouth. "Come here! You've got to see this!"

CHAPTER 9

EVENT +2:15 Hours
Peaks Island, Maine

The kayaks appeared to be in good shape. Both of them were stuck, side by side, in the branches scratching up and down against the concrete tower. A third kayak was barely visible, one curved end of it peeking above the water. Even more miraculous than Leigh's discovery was that both of the salvageable kayaks were two-seaters. And both had paddles strapped to them.

"They must be from that rental place we passed," James reasoned. "I think these'll work."

"How do we get down to them?" Leigh looked at the growing distance between the window and the water's surface and then back at her husband. "We can't risk jumping that far. Especially since there's so much junk in the water."

"I've got a rope," James reminded his wife. "Actually, we have two of them. The packs each have a hundred-foot paracord in them. They can handle plenty of weight."

"That's fine for Max, you, and me." Leigh glanced over at her daughter, still asleep. "But I don't know about munchkin over there. How is she going to Army Ranger her way down a rope into a floating kayak?"

James bit his lip and shrugged. "I'll carry her on my back."

"Right."

"Seriously." James's brow furrowed. He was bothered by his wife's lack of faith. "I'll go down and secure the kayaks, make sure they're not taking on water. Then Max comes down and gets into one of them. You follow. Then I climb back up and get her."

"I don't know—"

"The option, then"—James wasn't in the mood for a debate—"is staying here. We have enough cliff bars, water, and electrolyte packets to last us three days. That's it. Your call."

Leigh sighed. "You're right. The water is only going to recede more. We're better to risk it now."

"Good." James nodded. "I need your help."

Together they fastened one of the paracords to a rust-covered rebar handle sticking out of the interior concrete wall and strung it out the window. Leigh held the second cord in her hands. They'd use that for the kayaks once James was on board one of them.

"This should hold me, no problem," he told his wife and son and climbed onto the windowsill. He looped the cord loosely through one hand and backed through the opening, almost sitting on the exterior wall, and used his feet to walk himself backwards down the length of the tower. He felt the give in the cord as he inched backward. The back of his leg tinged with pain as he pressed his extended leg with each step.

"You okay?" Max called from the opening.

"I'm good." James looked up and smiled at his son. "No problem." He walked another few steps and checked over his shoulder. He was just a few feet from the tangled mess of branches at the edge of the tower.

James regripped the cord tightly with both hands and freed his left foot from the wall. Dangling his foot just above the water, he was able to toe one of the kayaks closer to him. He pushed with his right foot and jumped the short distance to the kayak, landing face first onto the neon green fiberglass. His weight shifted as he tried to maintain his grip on the kayak, but it tipped and he slid into the water.

The current was surprisingly strong under the surface. He could feel the debris slipping past his legs. His wound screamed with pain, but he maintained a hold on the kayak with one hand. James held his head above water, knowing that if he slipped underneath the surface and lost his grip, the ebb would carry him quickly away from the tower.

"Dad!" Max called. "You okay? Do you need me?"

"I'm good," James grunted, swinging his other arm out of the water to find a grip on the kayak. He pulled himself up slowly, trying not to capsize the fourteen-foot watercraft. It cooperated and he slid into the rear cockpit seat.

James looked back up at the window, some fifteen feet above the water. His wife managed a weak smile. Max gave him the thumbs-up with both hands.

"Toss me the other cord," he called up and Leigh threw one end of the paracord at her husband. She held the other end. James thanked her and then looped the cord through the small opening in the seat back in the front cockpit. Using a sailor's figure-eight knot, he secured the kayak temporarily.

Reaching out to his left, he grabbed onto a thick, leafless branch, and pulled his kayak toward the other. It was only a few feet away on the other side of the debris web.

"Be careful," Leigh yelled down to her husband. "Don't tip."

"Thanks." James waved up to his wife and winked. "I'll try to stay upright."

He gave the branch another tug and floated close enough to reach one of the paddles attached to the kayak at its stern. But the paddle slipped from the kayak, he lost his grip, and the long oar floated away from him. It was lost.

James cursed under his breath and, using a paddle aboard his kayak, swung the vessel around the other side of the debris, working to avoid catching the attached paracord in the sharp, broken branches reaching above the surface.

A small current caught the kayak and shoved James away from the debris, but he paddled against the ebb and worked his way close enough to the other kayak to reach out with his paddle and stab at it.

He caught the front cockpit and yanked, freeing the other kayak from the debris. Quickly, he dug against the other kayak, bringing it to the side of his kayak. Still holding the paddle in one hand, he reached out with the other and grabbed the side of the front cockpit.

He reattached his paddle to its onboard mooring and loosened the paracord on his kayak. He pulled on the slack, giving him enough length to run the cord through a seat back on the other kayak. With the two side by side, he climbed into the second kayak and tied another figure-eight knot. Now they were secure.

"Walk back," he called up to Leigh, "and pull on the cord! Get Max to help you!"

Leigh waved an acknowledgement and backed away from the window. The cord tightened, the slack disappearing, and slowly the kayaks moved toward the tower wall. James used his hands to manipulate the cord around the protruding debris until the kayaks were safely moored at the wall.

"Toss down the packs first." James stood in the cockpit, his feet spread into the narrow gaps between the edges of the seat and the frame of the kayak. "I'll catch them one at a time." He balanced himself against the tower wall with his hand, ready for the first bag.

"Here it comes." Leigh held the pack away from the wall and dropped it.

James let go of the wall and caught the pack with both hands. He wobbled and almost fell over, but caught himself and put the pack into the front cockpit.

Leigh tossed the second pack and James had no trouble with it. He slung it into the other kayak and then readied himself for Max.

"All right," James said. "Son, it's your turn." James steadied himself against the wall and held the climbing cord loosely at his waist. "I'm going to suggest that once you clear the window, you slide down hand over hand. Wrap your legs around the cord. Don't use the wall like I did."

Max nodded and grabbed onto the cord. He pushed himself from the window and did what his dad suggested. He reached the kayak without any problems.

"Okay." James patted his son on the back. "I want you in the front of the other kayak. Get in the front, put your mom's pack on your back, and then wait for your mom."

Max did as he was told. It was time for Leigh.

"Are you sure we shouldn't get Sloane down first, somehow?" She was leaning out of the opening. "I don't want to leave her up here by herself."

"She'll be fine," replied James. "Plus, I'd rather leave her up there alone than have Max out here by himself."

"Good point," she said and climbed out onto the window ledge. "I woke her up and told her you'd be back to get her. She seems okay with it."

"Come down the same way Max did," James instructed. "It's easier than the way I did it."

Leigh wrapped her legs around the cord and then grabbed with both hands. She took a deep breath and dropped from the window, bouncing slightly from the give in the nylon cord. She slid down, hand over hand, wincing each time her wrapped wrist bore any weight, and made it to her husband.

"You're in the kayak with Max," James told her. "He's got your pack. I'll give you one of my paddles. That way each of you have one. As soon as I get back down, you'll move over."

"Okay." She wrapped her arms around James's neck. "Be careful."

James kissed her on the cheek and grabbed the cord. He wrapped a small section of it around his hand and then tested the slack as he put his right foot on the wall. Then, hand over hand, he pulled himself up the wall to the small window. Sloane was standing there, tears welling in her eyes, Noodle suffocating against her chest.

"You're okay, baby," James whispered as he hoisted himself through the opening and into the tower. "We're gonna be fine."

"I'm scared," she whimpered and grabbed her father around his waist. "I'm scared we're going to die."

"Look." He knelt down and looked his daughter in the eye. "Mommy and I are going to keep you safe. If we can be okay after the stupid car crash, we'll be okay through anything."

"I don't want to leave here," she pleaded. "Can't we just stay here? Why can't we stay here?"

"Well"—James kept his voice calm and even, rubbing his daughter's shoulders with his hands—"we need to get home. We can't stay here. This is an island. Mommy and I know it's better for us to get off of the island."

"We don't have a car," she reminded him. "We can't take boats all the way home to Maryland."

"You're right," said James. "We don't have a car. But we'll find one just like we found the kayaks. Right now, though, it's important we get into the kayaks and start paddling away from the island. It'll be another adventure, okay?"

She sniffled and bit her lower lip before digging into the corner of her eye with her knuckle to wipe away her tears. She nodded.

James looked at the two cords affixed to the tower. He'd have to leave them. If he loosened the climbing cord, he'd be screwed. If he unloosed the one holding the kayaks, he risked them floating away from the tower as he descended. He turned back to Sloane.

"Here's the plan, Sloane," he told her. "I'm going to climb onto the windowsill and grab onto the rope. Then," he explained, "I want you to hop on my back and wrap your legs around my stomach and your hands around the top of my head. Then we're going to slide down the rope. Easy. Got it?"

She nodded.

James climbed onto the sill and faced out toward the bay. There were more boats out there now. Some of them looked like they were moving. That was a good sign, he thought.

Sloane hopped on her father's back and did as he instructed, her sweaty little palms flat against his forehead. He knew she was frightened.

"Do you have Noodle?" he asked.

"He's inside my shirt," she told him. "He's scared too."

"Tell him we'll be okay," he suggested and, without looking down, spun around slowly so that he was facing the inside of the tower. His daughter's grip tightened around his midsection as he swung her out over the water. "Here we go."

With a careful, slow motion he backed out of the window, his grip on the cord almost as tight as his daughter's around his head. Her face was pressed against the back of his neck. He could feel her shallow, nervous breaths against his ear. Her heart was pounding. But she said nothing as he began to lower them away from the window.

She was only forty pounds, but she might as well have been four hundred when she shifted against his back and moved her hands down his face and wrapped her arms around his neck. Sloane, whimpering from fear, tightened her grip, putting too much pressure on James's throat as he slid down the rope using only his arms. As he tried to stop her, he exhaled. It only exacerbated the danger.

Their feet were a good ten feet above the kayak when his vision blurred. His daughter was choking him, but he couldn't tell her to stop. He couldn't let go of the cord to move her hands. With little air in his lungs, he was on the verge of blacking out.

The pulse in his temple intensified, the veins bulging, as he worked to catch a breath. He tried pulling in air through his nose, but it didn't work. It was as if he was under the roiling water, dropping deeper and deeper into the blackness.

But he pressed on, gripping the rope as tightly as he could as they slid down. He grasped at her hand twice, but couldn't pull it from his neck. They were just six feet from the kayak.

James squeezed his eyes shut. His daughter slid up his back, her thighs pressing against his lungs. She didn't know what she was doing.

He could feel the strength in his hands weakening as he rushed to try to close the distance to his wife. He knew he couldn't make it. So with one push, he pressed his foot into the wall and spun them around to face the kayak.

Leigh saw her daughter's arms around her father's neck, his face purpling from the pressure. She reached up to grab at them and yelled at her daughter, "Sloane," she cried, "let go of Daddy's neck. He can't breathe."

The girl was too scared to understand what she was doing. She couldn't move.

James felt the panic of suffocation. His arms trembled, his legs twitched as his brain struggled to find oxygen. His grip loosened on the cord and they fell. Leigh caught Sloane as James tumbled onto the kayak and rolled into the water, unconscious.

His body slipped under the surface, caught in the tangle of branches. But Leigh grabbed at him quickly. With one hand she held onto his leg before putting Sloane into the rear seat. Gripping the back of his shoe, she jumped into the cold water, losing her breath as she kept her head above water.

"Max!" she called. "Help me!"

Max bounded to the kayak and leaned over its edge, holding onto his father's leg while his mother dove underwater. She resurfaced with James as Max let go of his leg and grabbed underneath his armpits to pull him onto the bow of the kayak.

Leigh, still in the water, held her husband on the fiberglass. "Move, Max!" she snapped. Max slid to the rear of the kayak so that his mother could pull herself into the front cockpit. She leaned over her husband, his legs still dangling in the water, and pounded him on the back repeatedly. It did nothing.

"Check if he has a heartbeat," Max told his mom. He'd taken CPR at school and remembered the basics.

Leigh pressed her fingers into James's neck and felt a weak pulse. She then rolled him onto his side, careful not to push him back into the water, and pounded on his back again.

"That's not the right—" Max started.

"Not now!" his mother yelled, each slap onto his father's back more passionate than the one before. Leigh was on the verge of giving up when James convulsed and coughed up water.

James coughed again and then sucked in a ragged breath as his eyes opened. He licked his lips and rolled onto his back, his chest heaving as he regained consciousness.

Leigh threw herself onto her husband, almost tipping the already overloaded kayak, and sobbed into his chest. "You're an idiot!" she told him and grabbed his face with her hands. She looked him in the eyes. "I can't keep saving you!"

James wrapped his arms around her back and held her. Staring up at the sky, clouds beginning to build against the blue morning sky, he knew she was right.

She couldn't keep saving him. Then there would be nobody to save her.

CHAPTER 10

EVENT +4:30 Hours
Casco Bay, Maine

James wasn't a metrosexual. He didn't get manicures and pedicures, use too much gel in his hair, or spray his body with the latest quasi-masculine scent. But he didn't work with his hands either. He was a teacher. The worst he might suffer was a paper cut or writer's cramp. After two hours of paddling across Casco Bay, toward Portland, his hands were blistered.

Each stroke to the left, to the right, was more painful than the one before. The blister on his right hand had popped. The skin was raw and had started to bleed.

There was a pair of gloves in each of the packs. He'd given them to Max and Leigh. It was more important they have them, especially with Leigh's wrist, James thought, though he didn't tell her it was probably fractured.

James was wheezing as he paddled west toward the shore. He knew the risk of pneumonia after a near-drowning was high. He'd already popped the first dose of the amoxicillin he had in his pack, hoping he could stave off an infection in his lungs.

The bay was littered with trash. There was a long, wide sheen of what James figured was oil or fuel from a boat or ship that didn't make it.

There was virtually no wind, but the water was still choppy.

Sloane was in the front of his kayak. She'd sat quietly for the last hour. Occasionally, she'd lean back in her seat to look up at the sky.

Paddling just ahead of them were Max and Leigh. They led by about thirty yards, occasionally resting to let James catch up. The trip was taking longer than James thought it would. He knew the ferry ride from Peaks Island to Portland was a little more than three miles.

And while that was from the western side of the island to the easternmost point in Portland, he didn't figure the distance to be much farther from the southeastern corner of the island to South Portland.

They'd swung south of Cushing Island, hugging what was now its coastline at Ottawa Avenue. James figured it to be the quickest shot, and if they ran into trouble, that small part of Cushing Island could serve as a temporary port.

From the position of the sun peeking out from behind the thickening clouds, he guessed it was around ten o'clock in the morning. They still had a good hour to go, he figured, before hitting the mainland. Then they'd have to reassess.

Max and Leigh were at the southernmost point of Cushing Island, floating with the paddles out of the water, when James heard what sounded like a high-pitched motor struggling to churn through the water. He looked around and didn't see anything. There was only post-tsunami flotsam and jetsam bobbing around them as he stroked closer to his wife and son.

The whining motor got louder, and as he approached the other kayak, James could tell Max and Leigh had heard it too. They both looked to the right, toward the bend in the island.

James was maybe twenty yards from them when he saw the boat. It was a skiff, maybe even a johnboat with a small outboard churning off the stern, emerging from the western edge of the island. There were three people aboard, but he couldn't tell if they were men or women. But they were headed straight for Max and Leigh's kayak.

"Who is that, Daddy?" Sloane twisted in her seat to try to look at her dad.

"I don't know." James felt a wave of nausea roll through his gut. He sucked in a deep breath of the humid air, coughed against it, and then dug deeper against the chop, propelling the kayak toward his wife and son. The dual-bladed paddle pushed against one side and then the other. The bow of the boat shifted to the opposite side of each pull as James willed the kayak to close the gap.

He saw one of the boaters wave at his wife as another pointed toward him. The two people at the stern of the boat seemed to be conspiring while the one at the bow was the greeter. As they drew closer it appeared the skiff sat awkwardly on the surface, as if it were taking on water.

Leigh waved back, but with Max's help, turned the kayak in a more southerly direction. She was still working her way toward South Portland, but was turned away from the boat. Her gut was warning her too.

James stayed his course. If he could speed up just a little bit, he'd be able to split the difference between his wife and the other boat, intercepting the path and serving as a blockade of sorts.

But the boat, despite its awkward position, chugged through the water at five times the speed of the kayaks. James was still a good ten yards from his wife's kayak when the boat pulled alongside her, the person in the front grabbing the side of her kayak.

James could tell all three were men. They looked haggard, worn from the morning's event. They were talking to her, saying something James couldn't hear. He dug deeper against the water, the lactic acid building the burn in his biceps with every pull. He was wheezing, having trouble breathing, as he chugged forward. He couldn't comprehend what he was seeing. How could this be happening? They were hours into…whatever this was…and people were acting as if the world had come to and end?

Or was it that bad people saw an opening and took advantage of it? Was this a violent crime of opportunity? Was the boat stolen? He couldn't know the answer to any of these questions as they raced through his mind. None of it made sense.

"Leigh!" he called as one of the men reached to grab his wife's arm. "The paddle!"

Leigh took her paddle, pulling it from the water, reared back, and launched the blade into the man's face. He fell back, cupping his hands over his nose and mouth. Leigh screamed as one of the conspirators in the back lunged forward, trying to grab her paddle.

Max pulled his from the water and swung it like a baseball bat, catching the man on his back between his shoulders. He fell forward onto the kayak, grabbing for it as he tumbled into the water.

James was closing the distance. He was five yards from his wife and he thought about jumping into the water and swimming to help. But he couldn't leave Sloane, who was now crying, calling for her mother.

Instead of comforting her, he stopped rowing, the boat slipping forward with momentum. James pulled his pack off his back and swung it in front of him, on the deck of the kayak between the two cockpits.

The man in the water was tugging at Max. Max was struggling, trying to fight him off as Leigh turned to punch the man in the head.

The first boater, the one who took the blade to the face, was back in play. Blood streaming from his nose, he jumped from the boat into the water and grabbed onto the front of the kayak. He started rocking it, trying to tip it over.

James unzipped his pack and pulled out the pistol. He calmly told his daughter to lie down as he aimed the weapon at the bleeding man on the bow of his wife's kayak.

POW! A single shot echoed against the water, ripping through the man's forehead, his neck snapping back with the force. He floated from the kayak and slipped beneath the surface as James turned the gun to the second man. He'd stopped attacking Max at the sound of the shot. That gave James the opening he needed. He leveled the pistol.

Pow! Pow! Two shots found their mark in the man's neck. He let go of the kayak, grabbing at his throat as he lost the ability to stay afloat, bubbling to the bottom of Casco Bay.

The man at the rudder tried to steer his boat away from Leigh's kayak, turning the handle on the lower power Evinrude hard to the left.

He heard the final shot from James's gun at the moment his world turned black. He slumped over to the right, and the skiff made a circle back for the kayaks.

"Hang on!" James called to his wife and son. Putting the gun back in the pack, he dropped his paddle into the water, and with four quick strokes he was aside them. The boat, motoring in a circle, just missed them as it swung north again.

"Take Sloane!" James ordered his wife. "Take her!" he repeated. Leigh was in shock, her gaze a world away until he told her a third time to grab their daughter and pull her into the kayak. Leigh shook herself from the daze and reached for her crying daughter.

"I'm getting that boat," James said. He handed the pack to Max. "Take this. I'll be back in a second."

James waited for the boat to circle back around and he jumped. His footing slipped from the wet fiberglass of the kayak, preventing him from making the leap he'd hoped.

Instead he landed in the water, his hands holding on to the left side of the boat, being pulled at ten miles per hour through the cold, salty water of the swollen bay.

Exhausted and having difficulty breathing in the spray bouncing off the surface, James gathered what strength he had in his upper body and kicked with his legs. Ignoring the sting of the salt in the wound on the back of his thigh, he managed to propel himself over the edge of the boat and onto its aluminum deck. He rolled over and, pulling himself to his knees, crawled to the stern. He grabbed the dead pilot by the lapels of his thin windbreaker and, without looking at him, heaved his body into the water.

James spun on his heels and sat on the thin bench in front of the tiller. He grabbed it and turned the propeller straight, moving parallel to his wife's kayak. When he got within ten feet or so, he killed the motor and drifted alongside the kayak.

He helped his family into the boat. Nobody said anything, and aside from his daughter's whimper, the only sound he could hear was the lapping of the water against the side of the skiff.

He set the choke and pulled the outboard to life. It smoked and hummed before whining to full speed. The boat did have water in it. But it wasn't sinking. Something was damaged somewhere. That accounted for odd list of the vessel's hull. Still it moved. They'd be ashore in minutes.

James wasn't sure whether or not that was a good thing. Less than five hours into some sort of cataclysm and people were already losing their minds, their sense of decency. He'd always read in dystopian books that the civilized world would peel away slowly, like layers of an onion. But as he motored toward shore, he reminded himself that nobody could know how fast those layers would slough off until the catastrophic really happened. Nobody could say how fast or slow things would devolve, how quickly everyone would revert to their primal survival instincts.

He wasn't so much worried now about a lack of help from others as he was about those base instincts. Civilized society always hung by a thread in the best of times. People were always a power outage or water shortage away from anarchy.

For a high school physics teacher, his was as basic a principle as atomic fission. It was science and sociology wrapped into one warped reality: natural selection. Only the fittest survive. The weak are picked off and devoured.

CHAPTER 11

EVENT +6:15 Hours
South Portland, Maine

The Rockwells had never been to South Portland, Maine. On their drive north from Maryland, Highway 9 and Interstate 295 took them west of the city. But even if they'd lived in the small coastal city their entire lives, they wouldn't have recognized it.

Much of the coastline was underwater. Even with the tsunami surge receding, there was muck and standing water a good mile inland. The family trudged through it, shirts pulled up over their noses to minimize the horrible odor of death and excrement.

James was wheezing, but kept walking. He knew if they worked their way west, toward the interstate, they'd eventually find dry land. They'd come across the occasional loner amidst cars and SUVs abandoned on the silt-covered streets. As best James could tell, there was no electricity.

They were walking southwest on Broadway when Leigh stopped walking. She looked behind her and then squinted back in the direction they were headed.

"What is it?" James asked. "You okay?"

"I'm fine," she said. "But I don't get it."

"What?"

"We've seen at least four cars of different makes and models on this street alone." She ran her uninjured hand through her hair, pulling it from her face. "They're dead. But then we saw that one Subaru circling around. The gray one. It was working just fine."

"You mean, why are some cars working and others aren't?" James took a step closer to his wife, lowering his voice and checking the pistol in his waistband. He didn't want to attract any unnecessary attention.

"We can't keep walking forever, Rock," she said. "The kids are exhausted and frightened. I'm about to have a nervous breakdown. We need a car. And I just don't see us getting one. Not one that works."

"There's no rhyme or reason," James explained. "If there was an electromagnetic pulse, which I'm pretty certain there was, it's all theory as to which electronic or motorized devices will fail."

"It's not theory now," she replied. "This"—she stretched her arms wide in frustration—"is not theory, Rock!"

"I understand." He tried to calm her, keep her from making too much noise. "We'll find a car. I'll find a car."

"What about that Subaru?" she pressed. "It was working? Is there a Subaru dealership around here?"

"It's not because it was a Subaru," he said. "At least I don't think that's the reason it was working. Plus," he said, "that Subaru was being driven by police officers. They probably had it in a garage and—" James's face lit up with an idea.

"What?" Now it was Leigh's turn to ask the question.

"The Faraday effect." He snapped his fingers.

"Faraday?" she asked. "Wasn't he a guy on the TV show *Lost*?"

"Yes." James nodded. "But that's not who I'm talking about. Faraday was a nineteenth-century physicist. He worked with light. He was the first to observe the rotation of the plane of—"

"Dumb it down, Rock." Leigh sighed. She plopped herself on the curb, took off her pack, and waved over the kids. They were all beat tired. Leigh handed them both a bottle of water and they sat next to her on the concrete, in the muck.

"Okay." James stood over his family, explaining his revelation. "There's this thing called a Faraday cage. We use it all the time to protect our electronics. It's basically a protective shell that prevents electromagnetic radiation from getting to whatever is inside the cage."

"So?" Leigh took a swig of water and gulped it down. She'd pulled her hair into a ponytail. "What's that have to do with our issues?"

"The EMP is electromagnetic radiation," James said, squatting at the curb to look his wife in the face. "While I can't predict what kinds of cars it'll kill, I know it can't effect any car inside a Faraday cage."

"Who keeps cars in Faraday cages?" asked Max.

"A lot of people," explained James. "A concrete garage with a solid rebar frame could work. A chain carport with a chain-link fence might work. They trap the energy and distribute it around the cage. A car inside of it would be unaffected."

"Where are we going to find one, Rock?" Leigh's voice hinted at hope, but was soaked in exhaustion and doubt.

"A car repair shop?" he guessed. "There's gotta be one close by."

"A gas station?" Max suggested. "One with a garage?"

James snapped his fingers and pointed at his son. "Yes! Perfect! There's bound to be several of them along the highway before we reach the interstate. That's not far from here."

"I feel like we're in search of the wizard," said Leigh, "but we're surrounded by flying monkeys."

"I don't like the flying monkeys," said Sloane.

"Neither do I," agreed James. "But we'll be okay. Remember, the monkeys never really hurt Dorothy."

"She had ruby slippers, though," reasoned the eight-year-old. "She just had to click her heels to get home."

"True," said James, "but if your brother's right and we find a car in a garage, it might as well be like ruby slippers. And we'll be home before you know it."

James didn't remind his daughter that the entirety of Dorothy's adventure was a dream and what they were living was Technicolor reality.

CHAPTER 12

EVENT +7:42 Hours
South Portland, Maine

The gray Subaru pulled alongside the Rockwells as they marched along Broadway. They'd just crossed over Main Street, a cemetery was to their right and Dairy Queen across the street to the left.

"Sir." The passenger-side window buzzed open as the Subaru slowed to match the family's pace. "I'm gonna need you to stop for us."

The South Portland police officer was young, maybe in his mid-twenties, James thought. He looked over at Leigh, who shrugged and stopped walking. The kids stopped too. James waved at the officer and put his hands on his hips, awaiting further instruction.

The officer and his partner, who was driving the Subaru, hopped out of the car and walked over to James. They both suffered from dark circles under their eyes and stubble on their chins. It was obvious they'd been up as long as the Rockwells.

"Could I please see some identification?" asked the driver. "Do you have any on you?"

"Did we do something wrong?" asked James. "We're just walking."

"I understand that, sir." The officer inched closer to James, his right hand resting on the top of his service weapon. "But given the circumstances, I'll need to see your ID."

"What are the circumstances?" asked Leigh. "What happened?"

"ID?" asked the younger officer, holding out his hand.

James and Leigh looked at each other and then removed their packs, tossing them onto the sidewalk. Inside the front pocket of both backpacks, they kept waterproof bags with their driver's licenses, a credit card, and some cash.

They both handed over their licenses to the younger officer. He glanced at them and then handed them to his partner.

"Maryland, huh?" said the driver. "How'd you end up here?"

"Vacation," offered James.

"Some vacation." The younger officer chuckled. Neither of the Rockwells found it humorous.

"So, Mr. and Mrs. Rockwell," said the driver, handing back the licenses to James, "the Department of Homeland Security has declared a national state of emergency."

"Why?" James asked, handing his wife her license. "You still haven't told us what happened here? Did it happen elsewhere too?" He looked at the driver's name badge. It read HARKER.

"We don't have a lot of details," said Officer Harker. "We're just doing what we're told to do."

"What is *that*, then, Officer Harker?" James was growing suspicious. These officers didn't stop them to serve and protect.

"Do you have a weapon?" Harker said, his hand tightening around his weapon. "If so, I'm gonna need to take that from you."

"Yes," James said, thinking better than to reach for his waistband. "I have a small handgun in my waist. But it's—"

The younger officer pulled his weapon and leveled it at James. "Please put your hands above your head."

"Whoa!" James backed up, raising his hands above his head, revealing the small nine millimeter handgun tucked into his waist. "What's this? I have a permit for it. It's legal."

"I'm sorry, Mr. Rockwell." Harker approached slowly. "But given the circumstances, I have to relieve you of the weapon." He reached for the gun and took it.

"That's not legal," James argued. "It's my second amendment

right to carry that weapon. I have a permit for it."

"Not in Maine you don't," said the younger officer, his gun still trained on James.

"I'm sure there's a reciprocal agreement," James said, his hands still above his head.

"Not with Maryland, I'm afraid," said Harker. "We have agreements with eight states for a concealed handgun. Maryland is not one of them. But it wouldn't matter. The state of emergency trumps that."

"It trumps the Bill of Rights?" James was agitated, on the verge of an outburst. "Nothing trumps the Bill of Rights!"

"Calm down, Rock." Leigh put her hand on his back and rubbed it. "We'll be fine."

"This is illegal," he repeated. "They can't do this." He looked over at the Subaru, noticing a window sticker for the local United Methodist Church.

"Sir," said Harker, "I need you to calm down."

"Did you steal that car?" James snapped. "Like you just stole my gun?"

"Calm down, Rock." Leigh moved her hand to her husband's shoulder and squeezed. "It's not worth it."

"We aren't stealing anything, sir," said Harker, exchanging glances with his younger partner. "We are keeping order as is our job. As for the vehicles, we need as many as we can get. Most of our patrol cars are dead from the EMP after the blast."

"You never told us what happened," interjected Leigh, trying to diffuse the tension.

"We don't know exactly, ma'am," answered Harker. "We know there was a detonation of some kind and a subsequent wind blast, followed by that surge of water from the bay."

"The tsunami," said James. "Can I put my hands down?"

"Yes, sir," said Harker. "And you can lower your weapon, Jenkins," he instructed his partner.

"How far does the damage go?" asked Leigh. "I mean, how are we supposed to get home?"

"I can't help you with that, ma'am," said Harker. "We're happy to escort you to a location of your choosing nearby, but other—"

"No, thank you!" James interrupted. "Are we free to go?"

Harker looked over and Jenkins and shrugged. "Yes, but you might want to get off the streets. It's not safe." The officers returned to the car, its engine still running, and drove west on Broadway past the cemetery and toward the interstate.

"Rock," Leigh said to her husband as they watched the taillights of the Subaru disappear in the distance. "You can't challenge authority like that. What would we do if they'd arrested you or shot you?"

"You're right." James coughed and bent over at the waist to clear the phlegm from his throat. "But that was illegal what they just did. They've left us defenseless." James looked up across Broadway, past the Dairy Queen, onto Main Street. He squinted to make sure his eyes weren't fooling him. A smile spread across his face.

"Let's go," he told his wife. "I'll help you with your pack."

CHAPTER 13

EVENT +8:20 Hours
South Portland, Maine

The Ocean Street Auto Repair shop was closed, but there was a light on inside the shop. That boded well, James figured as his family crossed the parking lot to the gray concrete building, its exterior stamped to look like bricks.

Underneath the red-lettered sign, *Ocean Street Auto*, was a blue and yellow NAPA sign reading "Have your electrical system check today!" James chuckled as he approached the metal-framed glass bay doors. He banged on one of them and cupped his hands around his face as he pressed his nose to the glass. There were two cars and an SUV inside.

"Do you think anybody is here?" asked Max, imitating his father and peering inside the garage.

"I don't know," answered James, "but the lights are on."

"So," asked Leigh, her arm around Sloane, "are we stealing a car now?"

James turned around and glared at his wife. "Really?!"

"We can't steal a car," she argued. "That makes us no better than those men on the boat."

She still hadn't told James what they'd said to her on the water, why they tried to overtake the kayak. There would be plenty of time for that. There would be time to talk about her husband's deadly aim and the way in which he killed three men in front of their children.

Leigh couldn't reconcile any of it. As badly as she wanted to be home, wanted to wake up from this hell, she didn't want her family losing its sense of right and wrong.

"What would you have me do, Leigh?" James said through clenched teeth. "You want to wait for a fairy godmother to wave a wand and give us a golden chariot? Because that's not happening."

"I don't want us stealing anything," she reiterated. "I don't think that's right. I don't—"

"Hello?" a voice asked through the glass. "Can I help you?"

James turned back to see a gray-haired man in a blue mechanic's jumpsuit. He was tall and thin, grease streaked on his cheeks. He was wringing his hands with a dirty shop rag.

"Yes, sir," James asked. "Do you have a car that works?"

The man surveyed the family on the other side of the glass, chuckled, and raised a finger. "Hang on a second," he said and walked toward the back of the garage. He pushed a button on the rear wall and a bay door opened mechanically.

"C'mon in." The man welcomed the Rockwells with a wave. "The kids can have a seat over there." He pointed to a long vinyl-padded bench at the far side of the shop.

"Thank you," said Leigh. "Very kind of you."

"It's no bother," said the man. His name, written in cursive on his chest, read Barney. "You look like nice folks who could use a rest for a beat."

"Yes," said James, unloading his pack onto the black-stained concrete floor before helping Leigh with hers, "thank you."

"I'm Barney." He offered a hand to James, shook it hard, and then gently took Leigh's hand. "Pleasure to meet you."

"I'm Leigh," she replied. "This is my husband, James, and those are our children, Max and Sloane."

"So you need a car, do you?" Barney's voice was thick with the stereotypical Mainer's accent. Car sounded like *cah*. You sounded like *yuh*.

"Ours was washed out," explained James. "We're on vacation and need to get home."

"Everybody needs to get home." Barney nodded. "I can appreciate the pickle. Quite a mess we have here, ayuh. I figured you were from away and not here."

"I notice you have electricity," said James. "How's that?"

"I have a gas-powered generator out back." Barney nodded toward the rear of the shop.

"Are any of these cars yours?" James was back on task.

"Ayuh," said Barney. "Two of them. They're not the finest kind of car, but they'll do in a pinch. You're in a pinch, I'm guessing."

"We're all in a pinch," said Leigh. "Do you know what happened?"

"Not for sure." Barney stuffed his hands in his coverall pockets. "I was up early, per usual and saw the bright lights apiece down the coast. Then the lights died. I hear the water came pretty close to here too."

"It did," offered Leigh. She turned to see her children lying down on the bench. Both of them had their eyes closed.

"Couldn't tell you what happened"—Barney shrugged—"but I do know the cops are a bit antsy. They come looking for my cars. I told them they were deader than a steamer. They left."

"Are they dead?" James pressed.

"No." Barney shook his head. "They're good. Which one tickles your fancy?"

"The Ford." James nodded toward the SUV. "How much?"

"That one's got a full tank of gas." Barney scratched his chin. "She's old but in good shape, ayuh. I'd normally ask fifteen hundred. But I know you got some kids you need to get home. How's a thousand?"

James nodded and countered, "I've only five hundred in cash. I need to keep a little of it. You don't take credit cards, do you?" He knew it was a stupid question as soon as it left it lips.

"I wish I could"—Barney sighed—"but there's no way to do that. The system isn't working. And to be honest, the only reason I'd sell is 'cause I need some cash. Gotta walk down to Shaw's and get a prescription filled. Maybe buy a little milk for my coffee. You're doing me a favor with cash."

"Can you do three hundred?" James asked.

"Not on the Ford"—Barney shook his head—"but on that there Nissan I could. She's got maybe a half tank of gas. Runs good. The transmission slips a scrid. Get down on your Prayer Handle and ask her to keep moving, she'll be fine."

"How far will a half tank get me?" asked James, kneeling down to pull the cash from his bag.

"I don't know," said Barney. "Not as far as you think, probably. I hear you need to stay off the main roads. Take the long way home."

"Where'd you hear that?" asked Leigh.

"The cops," said Barney, taking the three hundred dollars from James. "They said it's bad out there and getting worse fast. They're thinking martial law is the way to go."

"Yeah," James said, "we're figuring that out. Thanks for the heads-up."

"Not a problem," said Barney. "I'll get you the keys and a map."

CHAPTER 14

EVENT +11:30 Hours
Waterboro, Maine

"Are you sure this is the best way to go?" Leigh was driving, James was navigating. It wasn't that Leigh couldn't read a map, but she didn't like to do it.

"I'm just trying to avoid the interstate," said James, "so I'm taking us west before we head south."

"This is *really* far west, Rock," she complained. "Don't you think we're better off finding a southern route now. We've been driving for more than three hours and we've gone maybe twenty miles."

"It's not my fault the roads are blocked or impassable," said James, rustling the map. "And I want to go slowly enough to be able to see and avoid any police checkpoints."

"I get it," she said, slapping his thigh. "I'm just tired, that's all. You wanna drive?"

"Sure," he offered. "Let's get into Waterboro. There's a school on the map. Maybe we can find a bathroom or something for the kids. Then we'll switch out there."

"Okay," Leigh said, her eyes back on the road, "I'm good with that."

Waterboro was a small town on the southern edge of narrow Lake Arrowhead at Little Ossipee Pond. It was hilly and heavily forested, an idyllic New England village under any other circumstances.

Just south and east of Waterboro was East Waterboro. It sat at the intersection of highway 202 and highway 4. Leigh approached the T intersection and slowed to a stop.

"Which way do I go?" she asked her husband, whose face was buried in the map.

"Straight," he said, looking up. "Head straight north on five. That'll take us to the school."

Leigh pressed the accelerator on the Nissan, which hesitated before switching into gear. The family didn't see the silver BMW SUV approaching quickly up highway 4 as they passed through the intersection. But Leigh caught it in her rearview mirror as it sped quickly behind them, narrowing the distance.

"This isn't good," she said. "There's somebody speeding behind us. It's like they're chasing us."

James turned around in his seat to look out the back window. Both kids were buckled and sleeping. They'd barely woken up when they loaded them into the back of the '96 Altima. They'd dozed on and off for most of the ride.

He looked past his children and out the window. The BMW was tailgating them. It was less than a car length behind them. James could tell there was a driver and a passenger in the front. He couldn't tell if anyone was in the back. The driver flashed his lights. He flashed them again.

"He wants me to pull over." Leigh's eyes were darting between the road and rearview. "What should I do?" She passed over a small stream and zoomed past a restaurant off to the left. It looked like an oversized, polished chrome train car. She considered pulling into the parking lot.

"Don't pull over." James coughed. His wheezing wasn't going away. "Keep going. These guys are not good."

The BMW sped up and pulled alongside the Rockwells. The driver was on the wrong side of the road. His passenger was motioning to Leigh, telling her to pull over. He had a beer can in his hand and took a long swig. The driver flashed a gun, a semiautomatic pistol. He waved it at Leigh and laughed.

"What do I do, Rock?" she asked, trying to avoid eye contact with the passenger.

"Keep going." James popped open the glove box, looking for anything that might help their situation. Nothing. Then he remembered his pack. It was strapped into the rear middle seat, separating the kids. He unbuckled his belt and reached between the front seats to grab his pack.

"What are you doing?" Leigh asked.

"Just drive," James answered, unzipping the pack and rifling through it.

Leigh slammed on her brakes without warning, tossing James backward into the dash. "Oh! Sorry!" she cried, grabbing his arm. "I'm trying to avoid these guys."

The BMW kept moving, only hitting its brake lights after passing the intersection at which Leigh turned left. She found herself at another intersection and turned left again onto what looked like a loop.

"I'm fine." James coughed. "Just give me a heads-up next time." He climbed back into his seat and reached back into the pack.

Leigh swung the Nissan around the curve in front of Massabesic Junior High School. She accelerated out of the curve, the car struggling to shift gears.

"The BMW's back," she said, seeing the SUV take the left turn to the junior high too quickly, sliding off the road before the driver recovered. "And I think he's pissed."

"He's about to be a lot more pissed," James said, buckling himself back into his seat, a package of matches and a pair of flares in his lap.

"What is that, Rock?" Leigh's eyes were wide with judgment. "What are you going to do?"

"Keep us safe, Leigh," he answered.

Leigh took another left and then a right, heading north on Old Alfred Road. The BMW was on her tail again and sped up. The driver flashed his lights and then rammed into the Nissan's fiberglass bumper. Leigh worked to keep the car from fishtailing, pushing the car into another gear. It didn't respond and sputtered, the engine whining as the RPMs climbed toward the red numbers on the dial.

The BMW shifted into the left lane and matched speeds with the Altima. The passenger was wagging his finger and shaking his head, scolding Leigh for not pulling over. He rolled down his window and started yelling something unintelligible at the Rockwells.

"Is he saying he's with a militia?" Leigh asked James. "Or the military?"

"He's not with the military," said James, opening the flare packaging with his teeth. "No way. They're thugs."

"Mommy?" Sloane was groggy but awake. "What's happening?"

"Dad?" Max was up too. "What are you doing?"

The BMW swerved right, hitting the Nissan. Sloane screamed. "Mommy!"

"That's it," James said. "Roll down the window. And when I tell you to hit the brakes, do it! Okay?"

"Okay." Leigh nodded, rolling down the window.

"Pull over!" screamed the passenger in the BMW. "That's an order. We're in charge of this area. You're in our area. Pull over now!"

James flicked a match against the flint on the side of the box, igniting it and touching it to the wick at the end of the flare. It sparked and crackled as James leaned over his wife and tossed the lit flare through the open window of the BMW right onto the screaming man's lap. The driver swerved.

"Now!" James said. "Brake now!"

Leigh slammed on the brakes, the tires screeching their resistance as they burned to a stop against the pavement. She slipped the car in reverse and turned around to head south, away from the BMW.

As she made the turn, James watched the action. The BMW was stopped fifty yards ahead of them. The passenger door was open and the screaming man was out of the SUV. There was a red glare throbbing from the luxury interior before the driver tossed the flare out his window and into the weeds next to the road.

They were across the street from the Waterboro Fire Department. James saw a couple of guys wander from the station's driveway and onto the street.

Leigh shifted back into drive and sped back the way they came. James turned to look out the rear window in time to see the screaming man pop two bullets into the firefighters. The flash of the semiautomatic was unmistakable, even if he couldn't hear the shots. The men dropped to the street like untethered puppets. James turned around without telling Leigh what he'd just seen and robotically reattached his seatbelt.

"We're good," James wheezed. "Just head south until you hit West Road. Then take a right."

Sloane was crying still, despite Max's efforts to comfort her. He looked at his father with the fear of a child whose innocence is on the verge of unexpected obliteration.

"Sloane baby," said Leigh, palming the sweat from her forehead, "we're okay. The bad men are gone. We're fine."

"We're not fine, Mom," Max shouted, gulping back tears. "Nothing is fine!"

"Max—" James started.

"Dad!" Max snipped. "It's not fine. Sloane knows it, I know it. We're kids, but we're not stupid."

"Nobody's calling you stupid," James corrected.

"You almost died twice today!" Max couldn't contain the tears streaming down his cheeks. His lips were quivering as he spoke the truth. "Mom and I almost got killed by crazy boaters, then you shot them. You shot them, Dad!"

"I know—"

"Now, some crazy guys want to drive us off the road and shoot Mom, so you throw a firecracker at them!" Max's chest was heaving as he unloaded. Sloane was sniffling, but her brother's outburst seemed to have calmed her.

"Max—"

"Dad!" he cried. "The whole world is upside down. I'm twelve years old and the world is ruined."

James looked over at his wife. Her eyes were on the road, but they were dripping with tears. She was silently commiserating with her son, agreeing with his dark and likely accurate assessment.

More than anything, James Rockwell wanted to hug his family. He wanted to console them, assure them there was light at the end of the tunnel. They'd make it home. They'd be okay. Life would return to normal as it had six years ago, in the weeks and months after the flu epidemic subsided and the spring thawed the icy winter.

But he couldn't hug them. He couldn't promise them salvation. He'd always told them the truth. The truth was he didn't know if they'd ever make it home.

He didn't know if they'd survive the night.

CHAPTER 15

EVENT +12:30 Hours
Waterboro, Maine

Massabesic High School was a pair of single-story buildings off of West Road. A small campus by most standards, it was the local public high school. Part of RSU 57, it was home to eleven hundred students. The ninth graders had their own building, the east building, and the sophomores, juniors, and seniors were schooled in the west building.

Despite Leigh's protests that they hadn't put enough distance between themselves and the BMW, James thought it a good place to regroup, find a bathroom, and maybe even take a nap.

The parking lot was empty. The maintenance crews clearly hadn't done their fall cleanup. Weeds ran through the cracks of the asphalt of the lot and rose and choked out the flower beds in front of the west building's main entrance.

"I don't think we should park in the lot," Leigh suggested as she pulled to a stop in front of the marquis by the front door. It read SUMMER TIME IS HERE! SEE YOU IN THE FALL!

"Good idea," James agreed. "No need for us to announce our presence here." James surveyed the campus. "How about over there?" He pointed to a road running behind the main building, parallel to West Road.

Leigh pressed the gas pedal and drove to the far end of the school before turning right. The road was as much a narrow parking lot extension as it was a throughway to the other end of the campus. To their left was a grass field and a baseball diamond. Beyond the diamond was a dense thicket of trees. Leigh was about to make the right turn and head back toward West Road when James put his hand on her arm.

"Right there." He pointed to her left at a pair of small portable buildings. "Park in between the trailers. We'll be hidden there."

Leigh swung the wheel to the left and put the Nissan in park. She shut off the ignition and leaned back in her seat, closing her eyes.

James put his hand on her leg and squeezed. "You okay?" he asked.

"Probably not the best question, Rock," she said without opening her eyes. "I'm barely holding on." She squeezed her eyes more tightly shut, pressing out what few tears she had left to shed. She swallowed hard before whispering, "I don't know if I can do this."

James knew what she meant. It had been maybe a half day since things went haywire. How could they last a full twenty-four hours at this rate, let alone a week or a month?

They had no idea what they were up against. How extensive was the damage from the bomb? Was there more than one bomb? Why was civilization deteriorating so quickly into chaos?

They didn't have the answers, nor were they likely to get them by wallowing in doubt and self-pity. They'd done plenty of both in the last six years. Now was not the time.

"C'mon." He slapped her leg, choosing to ignore her doubts rather than feed into them. "Let's find a place to chill."

Leigh's eyes popped open and she looked at her husband. She wiped her eyes with the backs of her index fingers and unlatched her seatbelt. Without questioning his lack of empathy, she nodded. "Okay." She exhaled. "Let's chill."

Carefully, the Rockwells crossed the short distance from the portables to the back of the high school's west building. James and Leigh lugged their packs. The kids walked quickly between their parents, hustling to the obscurity of the overhang along the back of the building.

James tried a pair of locked doors. Leigh tugged on another set. No luck.

"Dad." Max was beneath a window, about ten yards from his parents. "I think this window is open."

James walked over to his son and looked up. It was a half window about six feet off the ground. It was cracked.

"Let me lift you up, Max," he said. "Tell me what you see." James bent down onto one knee and Max climbed onto his dad's shoulders. With Leigh's help, James stood and Max could see into the window.

"It's dark in there," he said, peering through the glass. "There's no light. But I think it's a classroom."

"Can you lift the window all of the way open?" James asked his son.

"Yep." Max reached his finger through the gap and pulled up, opening the unlocked window. "It's open."

"Good," James said. "Now, I want you to climb through and hop down. Then find your way to the doors we just checked and open one of them."

"What about the alarm?" Leigh asked.

"It's probably not working," James guessed. "The power's out. There's no generator running."

"Be careful." Leigh grabbed her son's foot and shook it. "I love you."

"Love you, Mom." Max blinked back tears and then climbed from his dad' shoulders to the window, swinging himself through and landing on the inside of the classroom with a thud.

"I'm good!" he called from the inside. "I'll go let you in."

James took Sloane by the hand and led Leigh back to the set of doors closest to the open window. No sooner had they stopped in front of them than one of them swung wide open. Max was standing just inside the building, a huge grin on his face.

"C'mon in," he said proudly, waving his family into the school. His father rubbed his head and walked past him.

With the door closed behind them, it was dark in the building aside from the dim light shining through narrow exterior windows and the red glow from the battery-powered EXIT signs lining the long hallway.

"First things first," said James, "we need a bathroom. A toilet. A sink. Those will do wonders for all of us. Then a snack and a quick nap before we hit the road again."

"There's a boys' bathroom up ahead," offered Max. He walked ahead, seemingly eager to lead his family. James knew, after his son's emotional outburst in the car, Max wanted to feel in control of something. In the red-hued darkness, they found the boys' restroom. It was adjacent to the girls'.

"I think we'll use the girls' room," Leigh suggested. "We'll meet you back in the hall in a few minutes."

James agreed, "Just yell if you need help." He pushed his way into the restroom, holding the door for his son before kicking down the metal stop attached to the foot of the door.

He blinked his eyes to adjust to the relative darkness of the room before finding a bank of white porcelain sinks along one side of the space. He leaned on the edge of the sink and spun the hot and cold taps.

They sputtered at first but then sprang to life, forcing a steady stream of clean water into the bowl. James cupped his hands together under the faucet and then splashed his face. It was surprisingly cold and took his breath away at first. He coughed against the chill in his weakened lungs and then took another handful. Slowly, he brought his hands to his face, dipping his nose and cheeks in the water.

James stood and ran his wet hands through his hair, dragging his fingers along his scalp. He closed his eyes and inhaled as deeply as possible before staring at himself in the warped, reflective metal that passed for a mirror. He almost didn't recognize himself, and it wasn't because of the facial distortion.

His bloodshot eyes were sunk deep into the puffy, swollen sockets. His skin was sallow, not its normal olive complexion. He felt feverish. Whether it was from the cut on his leg teeming with bacteria or the fluid in his lungs, he didn't know. It didn't matter.

He reached down into his pack and pulled out another dose of amoxicillin and a pair of Tylenol extra strength tablets. The tap still running, he popped the pills in his mouth and bent down to suck a mouthful of water from the faucet.

James loosened his pants and dropped them around his ankles. The wound needed cleaning and a new wrap. His son was in a stall across from him. Now was as good a time as any to check the damage.

He carefully pulled the wide bandage from the back of his leg, taking hair with it. Underneath was a salve- and blood-soaked gauze that he peeled away with his eyes closed. James dropped the gauze and bandage into a trashcan next to the sink and turned to look at the wound.

It was a good two inches long and, from the width of it, appeared to be deep. The edges of the cut were jagged and swollen red. Even in the dim light of the restroom, James could tell it needed stitches. Otherwise, he'd surely get a debilitating infection he couldn't afford.

"Max," he called to his son, "you about finished in there?"

"Yeah," his son replied, grunting as he spoke. "Why?"

"I need your help."

Max finished up and emerged from the stall to find his father leaning over a sink, his pants around his ankles, and a nasty, weeping wound on the back of his leg. He gulped, exhaled, and asked his father what he needed.

"I need you to hold a light while I sew up my leg," James told him, looking over his shoulder. "Can you do that?"

"Ummm—"

"You can close your eyes," James told him, "so you don't have to watch. But I need to stitch this up."

"What about Mom?" Max asked, sounding every bit a twelve-year-old.

"She can't do it." James shook his head. "I don't want to ask her again. This is you and me. Okay? I know you can help. I believe in you, Max."

James knew he was asking a lot of his rising seventh grader. But he had no choice. His son had seen him put four bullets in three people and then toss one of the bodies into the bay. What was a little more blood?

Max agreed and helped his father pull the needed items from the pack: a sewing kit, gauze, a tube of bacitracin ointment, a small vial of iodine, an adhesive wrap, a small penlight, and a handheld mirror.

James sat down against the tiled wall at the far end of the sinks, bracing his leg against the edge of a stall partition. Max knelt in front of him, the penlight shining on the wound, exposing the seriousness of it.

James uncapped the vial of iodine and squeezed it onto the back of his leg. The sting forced his teeth into his cheek, biting down on the inside flesh of his mouth. He clenched his fists and took controlled breaths in and out as if he were in labor.

Max winced at the sight of his father in pain. He had trouble holding the light still, but did the best he could as his father took a threaded needle and poked it through the back of his thigh.

"Okay, Max," James said with a raspy voice, "hold up the mirror. I need to see what I'm doing."

Reminding himself that everything was backwards, James slowly laced the wound like a pillow seam. He gently tugged on the thread with each stitch, careful not to pull the knotted end through the wound. The pain was so acute from the wound and the iodine, he couldn't feel the prick of the needle or the tug of the thread. It was an easier operation than he'd anticipated.

Once he'd sewn it tight, Max handed him the open tube of bacitracin. James squeezed gobs of it along the wound and covered it with clean gauze. Then he wrapped the adhesive bandage around his thigh. Max adjusted the mirror so his dad could admire his handiwork.

"That looks pretty good, Dad," Max offered. "It was totally disgusting to watch. But you did a good job."

"Couldn't have done it without you, Max," James said. He was sweating profusely and wiped his forehead with the bottom of his T-shirt. "You were a man just now."

Max, whose complexion had lost its color watching his father sew his own leg back together, blushed with pride. He helped his father to his feet and together they repacked the survival kit. Leigh was calling them from the hallway.

"You guys okay?" she asked, peeking her head into the open doorway.

"Yeah." James heaved the pack on one shoulder and walked toward his wife. "We're good."

"You don't look good," she said, putting her hand flat on James's forehead as he approached. "You're sweating. Do you have a fever?"

"I don't know," James said. "But I'm fine. Max helped me fix up my leg. It won't be a problem."

Leigh shot Max a look. Her son shrugged and smiled weakly.

"Let's find somewhere to lie down." James changed the subject. "We need to eat something and get some sleep. This could be our last chance for a while. We all need a breather."

CHAPTER 16

EVENT +14:00 Hours
Waterboro, Maine

"Promise me something." Leigh was resting her head on her husband's chest. She could hear the rattle in his lungs.

"Anything," James whispered. He was lying on a thick rubber gymnastic mat in the corner of the high school gymnasium. His wife's body was pressed up against his. The children were feet away, sound asleep.

The gym was the best place to sleep, they'd concluded. The foam mats were the closest thing to beds they could find. Hanging on the walls above them were green and purple banners celebrating the school's athletic championships: Football in 2000; Boys Swimming 2008–09; Wrestling 1975, 1998, 2007, 2008; Boys Cross-Country 2012. James could envision the pep rallies in the gym as those banners were hung. He could see the excited students, proud coaches and parents cheering and relishing the accomplishments. He could almost hear the rhythmic chants of the cheerleaders, the refrain of the school fight song echoing against the rafters. James had a strong suspicion nobody would be hanging banners this year.

"Promise me we'll make it home," she asked.

"I promise," he said, pulling his arm around her back, stroking her hair. He knew it was an unreasonable request, but he had no choice in his answer. He had to project strength and resolve.

"I wish we were there now," she said, her eyes closed, "on the hammock out back, listening to the crickets chirp. Watching the fireflies dance around."

"I'd like that," he said. "Kids asleep. Some smooth jazz playing in the background."

"Smooth jazz?" She laughed. "Since when do we listen to smooth jazz?"

"It could be gangster rap if you'd rather." He chuckled. "Or that twangy country music you love."

"You're hilarious." She rubbed his chest with her hand. "You know I'm more of a polka groupie."

"Lawrence Welk?" He chuckled.

"Who's that?" She feigned ignorance. "I was thinking someone like John Tesh."

"He's new age," James corrected.

"I meant Kenny G," she quipped. "You know, smooth jazz."

It was the first time they'd laughed all day.

"We'll make it back, Leigh," he said, the seriousness returning to his voice. "I'll get us home."

"I know you will," she said.

They lay there silently for a few minutes, listening to their children breathe. Max tried to match Max's pattern with his own breath but couldn't. His son inhaled too quickly. Sloane snored like a drunken sailor. The volume of her nasal roar was impressive.

"Can I ask you a question?" Leigh interrupted the chorus.

"Sure."

"How did you do it?"

"Do what?"

"Kill those men on the boat?"

"What do you mean?" James whispered. "I shot them."

"No," Leigh replied. "I mean, how did you pull the trigger? You reacted so quickly. And the look on your face…"

"What?"

"You were possessed."

"I don't know," James answered. He hadn't thought about it. He hadn't had time to think about it. Since the bright red light woke him up at five o'clock in the morning, he'd been battling one catastrophe after another. "Did I scare you?"

"A little," she said. "I didn't know you had that kind of violent side."

"I didn't either," he admitted. "My instincts just took over. I was protecting you and the kids. That's all that registered."

"And the flare," she added.

"I don't know what made me think of it," James said. "It just came to me. I didn't have a gun. The flare popped into my head. I reacted. That was it."

"Oh."

"I'm sorry if I frightened you"—James rubbed his wife's back—"but I'd do it again."

"You might have to," Leigh whispered. "I'm okay with that. But it freaks me out a little."

James didn't respond. He wasn't sure what to say to her. Instead, he closed his eyes and listened to the sound of his children breathing. Eventually he drifted off to sleep. It was an uneasy, ragged sleep. But it was sleep, nonetheless, and he knew it was a commodity more valuable than gold if he was going to follow through on his promise and get his family home.

CHAPTER 17

EVENT +22:00 Hours
Waterboro, Maine

James was caught between sleep and consciousness. He could feel himself trying to move his legs, his arms. He tried talking. He couldn't do it. His REM cycle wasn't finished. He was paralyzed and beginning to panic. Thinking he was underwater and sinking deeper into a swirling abyss, his breathing quickened, his heart rate accelerated.

From the surface, his wife was calling him, her voice muted by the water. He could see her shimmering image grow dimmer as he sank. He was powerless. Until he wasn't.

"Rock!" Leigh was kneeling beside her husband, shaking him awake by the shoulders. He was sweating and murmuring in his sleep. He was wheezing, his breaths shallow and unnerving. "Rock, wake up!"

He shuddered and his eyes opened. Coughing, he blinked away the disorientation. Puffing his cheeks, he exhaled again and cleared his throat. He could feel his T-shirt sticking to his back, the hair matted against the nape of his neck. His fever was breaking.

"Are you okay?" Leigh wiped his brow, her face directly above her husband's. "You're soaking wet."

"I'm fine." James coughed before sitting up on his elbows. "Just a bad dream."

"We've been asleep for a while, I think," Leigh said. "The kids are awake now, whispering to each other. I think the sun's going to be up in a couple of hours, if not sooner."

"Why do you say that?" James asked. "It's completely dark. It could be any time of night."

"I went to a window in one of the classrooms," she explained. "The moon is setting. I looked in that camping almanac you bought. It was in my pack. It has moonset at three thirty in the morning. So it must be right around there. Sunrise is at five thirty."

"We don't want to head out until the sun is up." James leaned up and pulled his knees to his chest. He could feel the stitches in his leg resist. "I don't think it's safe to be moving in the dark."

"I agree." Leigh nodded. "How far do you think we can get today? Will we even make it out of Maine?"

"There's no telling." James didn't know what to expect. He could only imagine things were getting worse by the hour. "Do you remember how much gas we had left in the Nissan?"

Leigh pursed her lips. "No," she said. "I didn't check it. Why?" Her eyes narrowed with concern.

"We didn't have a full tank when we bought the car," he reasoned. "We burned a lot of fuel driving around roadblocks and major roads. Then there was the BMW."

"The BMW…" she echoed.

"I need to check the tank before we leave," James said, pushing himself to his feet. "We can't get stuck out there without gas."

"Let me get the keys out of my pack." Leigh scooted over a couple of feet and unzipped her pack. She pulled out the keys and dangled them in front of her husband. "Bring these back!" She smiled, her teeth being almost all that was visible in the darkness.

James kissed her on the forehead and then turned to walk out of the gym. His footsteps echoed against the varnished hardwood, occasionally squeaking as he pivoted to find a line to the exit.

On the way out, James found a classroom and pulled an eraser from the ledge of a chalkboard. He used the eraser as a doorstop when he exited the double doors they'd used to enter the west building hours earlier.

He quietly hustled across the narrow parking lot to the twin portables and unlocked the Nissan. He slipped into the driver's seat and turned the ignition one click, activating the gauges without turning over the engine.

At first he thought it hadn't worked. The fuel gauge didn't move. He tried it again. Still nothing. But then he noticed the orange low fuel light on the opposite side of the driver's display.

They were almost empty.

Not good.

James pulled the keys from the ignition and used them to pop the trunk. He hadn't bothered to check the trunk when they'd loaded into the Altima to leave South Portland. They'd been in too much of a hurry. Thankfully, in the surprisingly large space, he found jumper cables, a full-sized spare tire, and a pair of five-gallon, plastic gas cans.

He pulled the gas cans from the trunk and quietly closed it. James sighed, suppressing a cough, and looked around. The moon wasn't much help with visibility. It had slipped beneath the horizon, well below the trees that surrounded him on all sides but one. To his south was the baseball field.

James pulled the penlight from his pocket and, taking the gas cans with him, walked south. He crossed the baseball field, a football practice field, a field hockey field, and then a soccer field. There was a lot of open grass to cover before he reached what he thought, at first, might be salvation: a parking lot full of school buses.

It wasn't until he read the fine print at the gas tanks that he knew his walk was just beginning. They were diesel buses. The Nissan Altima was regular unleaded.

Somewhere, somehow, he'd need to find someone willing to part with gasoline. If he couldn't, his family was stuck here.

CHAPTER 18

EVENT +24:03 Hours
Waterboro, Maine

Leigh took the news remarkably well. Max, not so much.

When James told them he'd need to walk to find gasoline for the car before they could leave, Leigh seemed almost relieved to have a couple more hours of relative safety. And while she wasn't thrilled about her husband wandering the Thunderdome alone, she understood the necessity of it. There were no options.

Max, on the other hand, wanted to go with his father. He wanted to help. He didn't want to be separated from the man he idolized. He stood at the back door, holding the eraser in his hand, dejected as James walked away from the west building to find fossil fuel salvation.

James had assured him he'd be okay, he wouldn't be gone long, and that he needed Max to take care of the girls. His son had reluctantly agreed, knowing perhaps he had no choice.

James couldn't turn around to look at his son as he began his trek. If he had, he might not have had the strength to leave. Instead, he slung his pack onto his back, carried a gas can in each hand and marched off. Now, two hours later, he hoped he'd found the right place.

He'd walked east from the high school and then turned north onto Main Street. After a half hour, with the sun on the verge of rising, he turned west and found an electrical easement. It was a wide, grassy path surrounded by thick woods on either side. James thought it was the safest way to travel, the best way to avoid any unwelcome entanglements. It was oddly quiet, and James noticed the conspicuous absence of transformer hum.

That hum, any student of electricity of physics would know, was a product of magnetostriction, a phenomenon which causes a piece of magnetic steel to expand and contract as its magnetization is amplified and reduced. Alternating voltage and current in high-tension power lines produces that eerie, ubiquitous hum.

Without power there was no hum. Instead there was only the slight rustle of the trees to break up the monotonous beat of James's Merrells trudging through the high grass. He adjusted his grips on the gas cans and looked at the sky.

The clouds were returning. They looked dark and swollen. It wasn't long, he'd figured, before it would start raining. He'd sensed the humidity in his lungs as he breathed. So it was a godsend, he'd reasoned, when he found the "Blast From The Past" Diner, a large gas generator rumbling in the parking lot.

James pushed his way through the open polished chrome door and found himself in the 1950s. There was a jukebox in one corner, the floor was checkboard, and the service counter was straight off Route 66.

"Can I help you?" asked the stubby brunette behind the counter. Her eyes spotted the gas can in his hand and she was instantly unsure of the stranger in her restaurant. James could hear the suspicion in her husky voice. "You're up early."

"Hi." He smiled and kept his distance, choosing not to belly up to the bar. "My name is James Rockwell, and I'm a tourist."

"No kidding," said a tall, thin man in an unseasonably warm plaid wool shirt leaning on the far end of the counter. He was stirring a spoon in a steaming cup. A pot of coffee sat in front of him as he spun back and forth on the red vinyl barstool. Other than the short-order cook clanging in the kitchen, James figured they were the only two in the building.

The brunette chuckled but kept her gaze on James. She didn't return his first volley.

"My family and I are trying to get home to Maryland," he said, shifting the pack on his shoulders. "We're out of gas. I'm hoping someone here might be able to help me out."

"I don't know," she said, raking her teeth across her bottom lip. "That wouldn't be up to me. You'd have to talk to Frank." She sounded like a cross between Kathleen Turner, Suzanne Pleshette, and James Earl Jones.

"Frank would be the man," offered tall and thin from his seat. "She's right."

James sucked in a breath of patience and smiled. "Is Frank *here*?"

"Yep," said the brunette. "He's here."

"Ayuh," tall and thin echoed. "He's here. Where else would he be?"

"Could I please speak with Frank?" James shifted his weight off of his injured thigh. He must have winced, because the brunette's brow furrowed.

"You hurt?" she asked, leaning forward onto the counter, dropping her green order pad onto the bar.

James coughed and nodded. "Yes," he admitted. "We were on Peaks Island and I got caught in the water. Something cut the back of my leg. It's okay. But it hurts from the long walk over here."

"You didn't walk from Peaks Island," said the brunette. She was both the waitress and master of the obvious.

"No way you could have walked from Peaks," said tall and thin, pulling the coffee cup to his mouth and slurping a mouthful.

"I didn't walk from Peaks Island," agreed James. "I walked from a couple miles away." He didn't want to tell them where his family was holed up. He was growing increasingly wary of the *Wayward Pines* vibe he was getting from the two. "Could I please talk to Frank?"

"Frank!" the brunette called to the kitchen. The clanging stopped and the cook emerged. He was wearing a grease-stained white apron around his neck and a Boston Bruins ball cap on his head. His Coke-bottle glasses were fogged.

"Ayuh?" said the cook. "What do you want? I got steamers on back there."

"This man here needs help," said the brunette.

"He needs help," echoed tall and thin. He was back to stirring his coffee, swiveling in his seat.

The cook took off his glasses and wiped them on the apron. He squinted at James without saying anything.

"I'm James Rockwell." James put down the gas cans, stepped to the counter, and offered his hand to the cook.

"I'm Frank," said the cook, taking James's hand and shaking it firmly. "What help do you need?"

"I could use some regular unleaded," James said, keeping his eyes on Frank but sensing the glares from Succubus and Incubus. "My Nissan's about out of gas. I'm from Maryland and I'm trying to get my family home."

Frank pursed his lips and moved them to one side of his face before pushing his glasses up on his nose. "I might be able to help you, but it can't be free."

"Can't be free," said tall and thin.

"I'd be happy to pay," said James eagerly. Maybe too eagerly. "How much? I've got some cash on me."

Frank looked the stranger up and down and nodded. "I could use the cash," he admitted, "but that'll only get me so far."

"Only so far." Tall and thin was a parrot.

"I understand," said James. "I'm looking for ten gallons."

"I figured," said Frank, looking past James to the two red plastic cans on the floor. "What's in that pack of yours?"

"Survival gear, mostly," said James, pulling it from his shoulders and plopping it on the counter.

"Weapons?" asked Frank. "We could use some weapons. People aren't always benevolent when the world collapses."

"Has the *world* collapsed?" asked James, unzipping the pack.

"I heard it's China," said Frank. "They dropped the bomb."

"A nuclear bomb," offered tall and thin.

"Could be aliens too," said the brunette, sounding a little like E.T. "You know, riding in on the Perseids."

"Where are you hearing this?" asked James, fishing out a six-inch folded knife from the bag and sliding it across the countertop.

"I heard rumors of some attack on my shortwave before it stopped working," said Frank. "People talking about some Chinese launch. Then the chatter stopped. The radio was dead. I tried to get it working for hours. Nothing."

"Nothing." Tall and thin pulled the spoon from the cup.

"Then a couple of kids in a fancy BMW pulled up last night," said Frank. "They were punks. Left without paying. Said they had authority and were helping set up a new government. They were part of a militia. They knew anarchy was coming. They blamed the Chinese too. And the Russians."

"The Russians too." Tall and thin spun in his chair.

"I still think it's aliens," offered the brunette.

"The kids," James asked, "they were in a silver BMW?"

"Yep," said Frank. "Two of them. One had a gun tucked in the front of his jeans. Had on black motorcycle boots. Said they'd be back. It's kinda why I need more weapons. They took my shotgun. All I got is a nine millimeter back there. And I'm out of ammo."

"You can have the knife here." James suddenly felt rushed. "And I have a box of ammo too. It's nine millimeter. I don't have the gun anymore, so the box is yours. It's almost full." He pulled the box from the bag and placed it next to the knife.

Frank looked at the offering and nodded. "Give me those and a hundred bucks," he said. "Then we have a deal."

James nodded. "Deal."

CHAPTER 19

Event +24:47 Hours
Waterboro, Maine

He knew it was too good to be true.

James was finishing the fill on the second gas can when he heard the squeal of tires. He was behind the diner in its rear parking lot, tapping a portable gas tank. Frank had bid him goodbye and left him there.

"It ain't like you could take more than ten gallons," he'd figured and pushed the door to the kitchen. "Good luck to you, and watch your back."

James had thanked him and worked to fill the tanks as quickly as possible. He didn't want to risk running into the BMW or its occupants. He was too slow.

He'd turned off the pump and was replacing the cap on the can when the punks wheeled into the parking lot. James's gut told him to leave, to get out of there as fast as he could.

His family was counting on him.

And he might have left had it not been for his having left his pack inside the restaurant. He needed that pack, the medicine and supplies it contained. He couldn't risk leaving it behind, effectively cutting his family's rations in half.

Cursing himself for his stupidity, James grabbed both of the gas cans, heavy and full of five gallons each, and backed his way into the kitchen. The griddle on the far right side was hissing and spitting. Clams popped and snapped on the gaslit heat. James put down one of the cans and inched his way, crouching low, toward the door leading to the dining room.

"That's not what I asked, Frankie," said one of the punks. "If I wanted to know what was on the menu, I'd have asked what was on the menu."

James surveilled the kitchen for something he could use, if needed. He saw a butcher knife stuck to a magnetized strip above the industrial stove. There was a pot of water boiling on a burner. Some dishes were stacked next to the cooktop. There was an apron hanging on a hook next to the door. Frank's ball cap was sitting on a butcher block island next to his Smith & Wesson.

"We want to know if you've seen a Nissan driving around," said the other punk.

"Shut up, Bruce!" said the first punk. "I ask the questions. It's my dad who put me in charge!"

"Sorry, Drake," said Bruce. "Just trying to—"

"You speak when I tell you!" Drake snapped. "Got it?"

"Got it," said Bruce.

"Now." Drake cleared his throat. "Frank. It's Frank, right?"

"Ayuh," the old man answered.

"Have you seen a man and a woman in a Nissan?" Drake asked. "It was gray or white and probably had some damage to the paint on the driver's side."

"I haven't seen anything," Frank answered. "Nobody's been in here but Lyle over there, Gertrude here, and me. Of course, you fellas stopped by yesterday."

"Right." Drake dragged out the word. He was doubtful. He mumbled something James couldn't hear.

So James leaned forward against the butcher block, trying to better hear the conversation. But he knocked into a large ladle, clanging it to the linoleum floor.

"What's that?" Drake asked. "Who's back there?"

"Oh, oh," Frank stuttered. "I did hire on a short-order cook. He's back there working on some food."

"Get him out here!" ordered Drake. "Hey!" he called back to James. "Get out here, cook!"

James grabbed the Bruins cap and pulled it low on his head. Then he grabbed the apron at the door and dropped it around his neck before pushing his way into the dining area. His backpack was on the floor behind the counter. Frank must have moved it.

"Can I help you?" James asked, keeping his eyes down. "You guys need something to eat? I was just—"

"Who are you?" Drake pulled his handgun from the front of his jeans and leveled it at James.

James immediately raised his hands in surrender. "Hey, brother," he said softly, "no need for that. I'm just a cook." He recognized Drake as the BMW's driver. The punk next to him, Bruce, was the passenger.

"What's your name?" Drake leaned forward, resting his elbows on the counter. He was still aiming the weapon at James's chest.

"Jimmy," said James.

"Jimmy what?"

"Jimmy James." It was the best he could do without forethought and a gun pointed at him.

"That's a stupid name!" said Bruce. "Were your parents stupid?"

James looked at Frank and then over at Gertrude, the waitress. They averted eye contact and, instead, kept their gazes at the floor.

"I guess maybe they were." James nodded. "I'm not that smart either, tell you the truth. Can't keep a job, can't keep a woman—"

"You have a ring on your finger," observed Drake. "Why's that if you can't keep a woman?" His lips wormed their way into a sneer.

"Dead wife," said James, pulling his hand down to look at the ring. "Can't let go."

"Maybe that's why you can't keep a woman!" Bruce laughed.

"How'd she die?" Drake wasn't ending the interrogation. "When did she die?"

"Car accident," James said without thinking about it. "Six years ago," he spit out, "during the pandemic."

Drake lowered the gun, apparently satisfied James was who he said he was. His eyes narrowed and he nodded. "What do you have to eat back there?"

"Clams," said James. "They're probably about to burn if I don't get back there. You want some?"

Drake nodded, tucking the gun in his pants. "You got a cold one too?"

"There should be some in the cooler," Frank said. "Budweiser."

James slipped back into the kitchen and hurriedly made two plates of clams. He found some chips in an open bag and dumped a handful onto both plates. He backed his way out of the kitchen and into the dining room.

"Here you go." He slid the plates to the punks. They'd taken seats at the bar.

"Where's the beer?" asked Drake.

"Getting it now." James bowed, adjusted the cap on his head, and returned to the kitchen. He found the cooler and pulled out two six packs of Budweiser by the end of the plastic yokes holding them together. He hoped providing them with more than they expected would momentarily ingratiate him to the punks.

"Here's the beer," said James, banging the six packs onto the counter. "A sixer for both of you." James saw their eyes light up. Then he noticed Frank's grimace.

"Wicked awesome!" said Bruce. "Love it, Jimmy James."

Drake, fork in hand and his mouth full of clams, nodded his appreciation and then returned to his plate. James used the distraction to grab his pack and drag it into the kitchen without either punk saying anything.

"I'll be right back," Frank said to his guests and followed James through the kitchen door. "You're the guy they're looking for," he whispered, standing just inches from James at the butcher block.

James nodded and took off the hat, handing it to Frank. He pulled the apron over his head and hung it next to the door.

"What did you do?" Frank asked, looking at the door as he spoke. "Why are they after you?"

"Long story, Frank." James slung the pack onto his back. "I gotta go."

"Okay," said Frank.

"Hey," Drake called from the dining room. "Grab me another six pack, Frank! We'll be hanging out at Hannigan's, looking for that Nissan. I'm gonna need something to keep me busy."

"Sure thing!" Frank called back before offering his hand to James. "You be careful, Jimmy James." A smile crept across the old man's face, his eyes alight behind the thick lenses of his eyeglasses.

"It's good to know there are kind people out there, Frank," said James. "I was beginning to lose hope."

"Don't lose hope," said Frank. "Right now, it's all we got."

CHAPTER 20

EVENT +28:09 Hours
Waterboro, Maine

"We're ready to go," said Leigh. "Everybody's gone to the bathroom one last time. We're fed. We're rested. We're fueled up?"

"We're fueled up," said James, closing the Nissan's trunk. "I'll drive the first shift. Okay?"

Leigh sidled up to her husband, putting her hands on his chest. "Are you sure you're up to it? You walked for four or five hours, carrying those heavy cans for half of it."

"I'm fine," James lied. He felt weak and shaky. Occasionally a chill would run through his body. But he wanted to drive. He wanted to feel some sense of control.

The kids plopped into the backseats of the Nissan and Leigh agreed to let her husband take the wheel. They had a long trip ahead of them.

James knew the punks, Bruce and Drake, would be at Hannigan's. While he didn't know where, or what, exactly it was, he assumed it was in town. So rather than risk a drive south through Waterboro, he chose to head farther west.

"Why are you driving west?" Leigh questioned him, about fifteen minutes into the drive. "Don't we need to head south?"

"How do you know I'm driving west?" James hadn't told her about the diner encounter with the punks.

"I have a map." She looked at him as if his parents had named him Jimmy James.

"It's better to stay off the main roads, remember?" He coughed as he explained.

"Okay." Her eyes narrowed. "But there were plenty of ways to head south without going this far west. What's up?"

"I'm avoiding the BMW," he admitted, keeping his eyes on the road.

"What?" She shifted in her seat, turning toward James and tugging on the shoulder strap of her seatbelt. "What do you mean?"

"I mean I saw those guys when I was getting the gas," James said.

"And?" Leigh's voice rose an octave.

"What do you mean you saw those guys?" Max bounced forward, sticking his head between the two front seats. "Dad? Seriously?"

"They showed up at the diner looking for us." James exhaled as he told them the truth. "Actually, they were looking for the Nissan."

"Did they see you?" Leigh folded her arms across her chest. "Did they recognize you? They couldn't have recognized you."

"They didn't recognize me," James said, "but they did talk to me."

"And?" Leigh said, slapping her husband's leg. "Sheesh, Rock, you're not giving us anything. What happened?"

James relayed the details of his close call at the diner, how he'd pretended to be a cook and fed the two punks a meal. He also explained they were part of some militia in charge of "protecting" the area.

"What does that mean?" asked Leigh. "What does militia mean? I thought the police were in charge. They're taking everyone's cars and guns. Why aren't the police in charge? How could some militia have any power?"

"I don't know," said James, slowing the Nissan to avoid a large branch in the road. "I just know what they said. One of them said his dad was the leader of the militia and they were put in charge of that area."

"So, how big is the militia?" asked Leigh.

"What is a militia?" asked Max.

"A militia is a group of armed citizens," answered James. "I don't know how big this group is or what they're trying to accomplish. But typically, a militia acts like it's an army. It can be good or bad."

"How is it good?" asked Max.

"The founders of our country were in a militia," said James. "They weren't a real army at first. When they challenged the British, they were basically a militia."

"Do we have to worry about them?" Leigh asked.

"I don't know," James answered. "That's why I'm trying my best to avoid them."

Chapter 21

EVENT +29:35 Hours
Acton, Maine

The Nissan's windshield wipers did little to swipe the downpour of raindrops from James's vision. The storm, building for much of the past day, had finally unloaded itself on the Rockwells.

They'd traveled just twenty-two miles in an hour and a half. James was seated as far forward as possible so as to see through the deluge. On the narrow back roads, in the rain, he couldn't see much more than ten feet in front of the car. That's why he didn't see the three men, dressed in fatigues, standing guard at a small bridge.

One of them stood in the middle of the road, a semiautomatic rifle slung across his chest. He was holding out his hand, instructing them to stop.

"This isn't good," Leigh murmured, grabbing her husband's thigh. "What do we do?"

"Play along," said James, coughing and clearing his throat. "That's all we can do right now."

"Mommy?" Sloane whimpered. "What's happening?'

"Everything's okay, baby," said Leigh. She turned and looked at Max. He shook his head, apparently aware of the danger ahead of them.

One of the men strode to James's window and knocked. James rolled down the window, rain spraying into the car.

"State your business." The man had a handheld radio.

"Just trying to get home," said James. "We're from Maryland. We were on—"

"You can't cross here," said the man. A second armed man approached the window. He aimed his rifle at James.

"We're just trying to get home, sir. We—"

"Nothing gets across in either direction," barked the radioman. "Those are my orders."

"Whose orders?" James asked. "Homeland Security?"

The gunman laughed. The radioman answered, "No. We're with the Maine Liberty Militia."

"Okay." James looked over at Leigh before turning his attention back to the thugs. The rain was lessening, but still soaking the inside of the car. "Who can give us permission to head south, then?"

"That's not happening," said the gunman.

"What's going on here?" The man who'd stopped the Rockwells moved from the front of the car to the window. Now all three of the men were huddled around the open window. "Is there a problem?"

"There's no problem." James raised his hands off of the wheel. "We just want to go south, toward our home in Maryland. "How can we make that happen?"

"We're not letting anyone across, sir," said the radioman. "I explained that to him." He turned to the third man.

"We don't want a repeat of 2013," said the third man. "When the pandemic happened, there was a lot of looting, a lot of violence. We're preventing that from happening."

"We're not looting anyone," James argued. "We're a family trying to get home."

"Look," said the radioman, "you have two options. One is to turn around and head back the way you came. The other is to surrender your car. We'll take you to Sanford or Springvale and then it's up to you how you proceed from there."

"Yeah." James laughed. "I'm not giving up my car."

"We're not giving up our car," said Leigh, leaning toward the open window.

"Then you'll have to—" The radioman was interrupted by someone on the radio. "Hang on, please."

The radioman stepped away from the car and turned his back. He held the radio to his ear, spoke into it, and listened again. Then he turned, glanced at James, and waved to both of his compatriots.

"What are they doing?" asked Leigh, her voice quavering.

"I don't know," James said.

The radioman started to walk toward the car and then pivoted and stepped around behind it. The rear window was fogged and James couldn't see what the man was doing.

He returned and looked at James again before running his finger along the side of the Nissan. He called the other two back to the car.

"We got a communiqué about a Nissan causing some trouble in Waterboro yesterday," he said. "White or gray in color, likely damage along the driver's side. Were you in Waterboro?"

"We—" Before James could answer, the radioman pulled open the back door and aimed his rifle at Sloane.

"Get out of the car!" said the radioman. "Now!"

"Wait!" James said. "Hang on!"

The other two gunmen descended on James, unlatching his seatbelt and yanking him from the car. He was forced to his knees as the men pulled the rest of his family from their seats.

"You messed with the wrong people," sneered the radioman. "It'll be a mistake you don't live to regret."

CHAPTER 22

EVENT +30:59 Hours
Acton, Maine

James looked over at his wife, his children. He swallowed hard.

"Pick up the pace, *Rock*," said the executioner. "Keep moving."

A breeze blew across James's face. It was damp and cool, a sign of the approaching fall. He could hear it whispering its way through the trees ahead of him.

Do something! They were telling him. *Save your family.*

He shook his head as he trudged forward, certain the blow to his head had him hearing things. It was that or the lack of sleep.

You can't let them die here.

They were twenty-five yards from the beckoning woods, crossing the pavement of a parking lot entrance, when James wondered if his eyes were playing tricks on him too.

Facedown in the trampled weeds marking the entrance to the woods were five bodies. Two big, three small. He couldn't make out whether they were men or women, boys or girls, but that was irrelevant.

James knew, hallucinations or not, they wouldn't be the first family to die here. They wouldn't be the last either, unless he acted quickly…unless he killed first. It was a notion to which the high school physics teacher from Maryland had grown alarmingly accustomed in the last thirty-six hours.

But he was running out of time.

And then he wasn't.

James didn't know the direction from which the shots came. But he heard them zip through the air.

Two pops, a rifle barking twice in succession followed by the sound of the executioner hitting the pavement with a squeal and a grunt.

Another shot.

James turned to see blood spraying from the older thug's neck. He collapsed, grabbing at his neck as he fell.

"Run!" James didn't know who was shooting. And he wasn't going to stop to find out. He shoved Leigh in the back as she screamed for the children to race to the woods. They sprinted, the four of them, past a dozen bodies, until they were a good fifty yards into the trees. James tripped over a stump, falling into the thick, rain-soaked undergrowth.

"What happened?" Leigh knelt at her husband's side, helping him sit up. "What was that?"

"I don't know," said James. "An angel, maybe." In the distance, back toward the church, they could hear the crack of gunfire. It sounded like a war.

"What do we do?" Leigh asked. "Our car, our packs…"

"I don't know," James said. "There were a bunch of cars in that parking lot. I bet we could take one of them. I bet they still have keys in them."

"We can't take someone else's car," Leigh protested. "What if—"

"Those people are dead, Leigh." James pushed himself to his feet. "They're not going to need their cars."

Leigh looked back at the path they'd run into the woods, toward the bodies she'd sprinted past. "You're right," she conceded.

"I'm going back to get a car," James said. "You wait just past the edge of the trees. Stay hidden until I pull up in whatever I can get. Then get in and we'll get out of here."

"You can't go now!" Leigh pointed toward the church. "There's a gun battle going on over there."

"I can't wait." James took his wife by her shoulders. "We don't know who's winning and who's losing. That gunfight is the perfect distraction."

Leigh nodded. "C'mon, kids." She waved to her children and held both by the hand as they trudged back toward the church parking lot. "Keep your eyes closed," she instructed, not wanting them to see the bodies they were about to pass. "I'll lead you."

Neither child protested, both of them too much in shock to argue. They followed their mother, eyes closed, toward the sound of gunfire. They squeezed their mother's hands as tightly as was possible.

James marched a few feet ahead of them, focused on the task at hand. He ignored the pain in his thigh, the tightness in his chest. He wiped the rain from his brow and emerged from the trees.

"Wait here!" he called back to his family and then turned back to the parking lot. He stopped at the bodies of the thug and executioner, grabbing the handgun and one of the rifles.

Crouched low, he crossed the lot toward the cars. Ahead of him, at the church, he saw a Jeep slam on its brakes, its taillights illuminating streaks of rain in their red glow.

James couldn't tell how many people were attacking the church, but that's how it appeared. It was like a Seal Team 6 operation, James imagined. He wondered who, or what, was held captive inside the church.

Crossing the lot, he counted eight or nine cars. He tried the doors for a white minivan, a Mercedes crossover, and a Volvo station wagon. All of them were locked.

He moved to another row of vehicles, hoping for better luck. One of them was a Ford F-150 truck. It had four doors, and as James approached, he could see camping gear, gas tanks, and a large white Yeti cooler in its bed.

James kept low as he rounded the truck to the driver's side door. It was locked. He tried the rear door on the same side.

Bingo!

It was unlocked and James climbed into the rear of the truck's cabin. He turned his body and quietly shut the door before worming his way into the driver's seat. He reached for the ignition and found a key already inserted. He cranked it and the truck's engine responded, grumbling to an idle.

There was three-quarters of a tank, which was good. James knew that would carry them out of Maine, at least, and maybe through Massachusetts before they'd need more fuel.

Maybe things were better farther south, he hoped as he put the truck into gear and pressed the accelerator. He swung the truck around, past another row of cars and toward the woods. He pulled up, slammed the truck into park and hopped out on the pavement.

"Let's go!" James called to his family. He yanked open the rear door, herding his kids into the backseat. "Get in the driver's seat!" he yelled to Leigh, and she scurried past him into the truck. James dropped the rifle into the truck's bed, hiding it underneath a plastic blue tarp and securing it with a pair of bungees attached to the Yeti.

He ran around the back of the truck and climbed into the front passenger's seat. As he hopped inside, he looked out toward the church. Through the rain and fog, he could see the muzzle flashes from the firefight. He prayed for the person who'd saved his life, who'd rescued his family.

"Thank you," he mouthed toward the church as Leigh gunned the truck away from the church.

"I don't think that bridge is going to be a problem now," said Leigh. "I think we should head south."

"Go for it," James said. "Let's go home."

PART 2

REFUGE

CHAPTER 23

EVENT -5 Years, 9 Months, 1 Day, 16 Hours
Hagerstown, Maryland

James Rockwell couldn't shake the thought, nor could he reconcile it.

The coffin was too small. Coffins should not be so small.

I can't do this, he thought, his sweating palm flat against the casket's red mahogany lid. *A parent shouldn't bury his child.*

His daughter was eleven years old. She'd always be eleven years old. Time, for her, had stopped.

He moved his hand from the lid, toward her body, stroking her cheek with the back of his fingers.

She looked peaceful. Asleep. Not dead.

Even as a tween, she already carried the grace of her mother, Leigh. She was beautiful and sweet and kind.

James brushed her bangs away from her forehead and choked back the thick knot in his throat. He was dry of tears.

In the past week, he'd buried his parents and his mother-in-law. Now he was interring his eldest child.

It was the lot for so many families in the aftermath of what could best be described as a global plague. *The Jakarta Pandemic*, they called it.

A flu so virulent, so contagious, it killed countless people around the world. Combined with a nasty winter storm that knocked out power across much of the Mid-Atlantic and New England, panic doubled the chaos.

His daughter Nora was always small for her age. She'd struggled from birth. Her lungs were undeveloped, her heart had a hole, and her muscles were weak.

But she was a fighter and had overcome so much. Her younger siblings, Max and Sloane, were healthier. They were strong and their immune systems healthy.

Despite everyone in the family taking a preventative dose of TerraFlu, Nora got sick during the second week of the epidemic. It started with a cough and slight fever. Ten days later, she died in her parents' bed. By that time, three of her four grandparents had fallen ill and died. James's parents were in Philadelphia as was his wife's mother. They'd not taken any medication, unable to score the drug before supplies ran out.

Their bodies were cremated before James or Leigh could find a way north to Philadelphia. The health department sent them an email. That was as much of a eulogy as they were afforded.

So many had died, James was fortunate to be friends with the owner of the local funeral home. Otherwise, Nora would have shared the same fate or been dumped into one of FEMA's mass graves.

Instead, he was fortunate, neighbors said, to be able to say goodbye. He was blessed, others had told him, to have a service and a funeral.

He didn't feel blessed or fortunate.

He felt empty.

"Do you want the casket open or closed?" A man approached James from the rear of the chapel. "It's up to you."

James turned to see his friend, Bob Stumps, the funeral director. Bob was forty-five years old, but he looked sixty-five, much of the aging happening in the preceding weeks. He was dressed in a black suit, white shirt, and black tie. His spit-shined shoes squeaked as he walked.

"I think closed," James said, turning back to his daughter. "I don't think her mother wants to see her."

"Is the makeup okay?" asked Bob. "It's always a tricky balance with a child."

Child. The word stabbed at James. *Child.*

"The makeup is fine, Bob," he said. "You did a wonderful job, thank you." What else could he say?

"Is there anyone else who'd like to see her before we begin the service?" Bob put his hand on James's shoulder. "If not, I'll close the casket and prepare to welcome the attendees."

"There won't be many people here," James admitted. "The flu still has everyone nervous. Even if the worst has passed. Nobody wants to be in large groups."

"I assumed as much," said Bob. "We haven't had a service with more than a dozen people since this happened."

"I just need a minute, okay?" James asked his friend.

Bob nodded and walked past the casket and through a door at the front of the chapel.

James leaned over to kiss his daughter on her forehead. He held her hand and whispered in her ear.

"I am so sorry I didn't protect you," he whispered. "I am so sorry I couldn't save you. I love you, Noodle."

CHAPTER 24

EVENT +72:01 Hours
West of Back Mountain, Pennsylvania

Leigh Rockwell was speeding. Her husband was delirious with fever and having trouble breathing. He was wrapped in a blanket, shivering in the seat next to her.

It was a full three days since their lives were turned upside down: witnessing an atomic blast, surviving the resulting tsunami, kayaking their way off of an island, fighting off marauders and would-be militias. Leigh could hardly believe it was only three days as she recounted the events in her head.

Her husband, James, nearly drowned on the island. He'd cut his leg badly. She didn't know whether the fever was a result of the cut or the onset of pneumonia from nearly drowning.

He clearly had fluid in his lungs. There was an infection somewhere, causing his fever to spike.

James needed help. He was dying.

Leigh took the turn on Route 118 too fast and the Ford F-150 fishtailed. She overcompensated and regained control of the truck as she headed west and south. They'd been avoiding major interstates and large cities, no small task along the East Coast. Now they were getting closer to their home in Maryland. But Leigh knew they wouldn't make it without finding a doctor and medicine for her husband.

In rural Pennsylvania, there wasn't much more than mining and fracking. She'd passed one man camp near a natural gas site, but the trailers were empty. No people, no medicine.

So she drove almost aimlessly, hoping she'd find something. Now, as the sun began to rise, she saw a possibility.

At the intersection of Routes 118 and 29 was Pikes Creek Veterinary Hospital. There was a truck in the parking lot and lights glowing from the inside. Leigh hit the parking lot at forty-five miles per hour and screeched to a stop next to the truck.

"Kids," she called to twelve-year-old Max and eight-year-old Sloane in the backseat. "Hop out. Max, help me with Dad. Sloane, get the door."

With her son's help, Leigh slung her husband's arm over her shoulder. They half-guided, half-carried James into the clinic. A man greeted them as soon as they crossed the threshold.

"What's wrong?" asked the man, taking James's weight from Leigh and leading him to a chair. "What's happening?"

Leigh was out of breath, but tried to speak as calmly as she could. "My husband has an infection. I think it might be pneumonia. He's not doing well. I need your help. Can you help?"

The man, wide-eyed, nodded but said nothing. He knelt in front of James and felt his pulse at his neck. It was weak and James was hot to the touch. He could hear James wheezing with each attempted breath.

The man, still kneeling, looked up at Leigh. "I'm a veterinarian, you know," he offered. "Your husband really should see a physician. You're right; he's very ill."

"There are no physicians," Leigh explained. "There are no hospitals taking patients. You're it. Please, isn't there something you can do?"

The man ran his hand through his thick black hair and nodded. "Okay," he said, "let's get him into one of my examining rooms."

Together, they carried James through a pair of swinging doors and into a large room in the back of the building. "I use this for larger animals," the veterinarian explained. "Let's lay him here." He nodded towards a large, low-slung table intended for pigs and goats.

James was mumbling unintelligibly. His eyes were alternately open and squeezed shut. His body went limp on the table, one leg dangling to the floor.

"When is the last time he ate or drank anything?" the veterinarian asked Leigh. He was busy at a cabinet, piecing together an intravenous bag. He pinched James's thumb and checked his nailbed.

"I don't know," said Leigh. "Maybe yesterday?"

"Is Daddy going to die?" asked Sloane. She was clutching a small stuffed bear.

"You might want to take them out into the waiting room," said the vet. "There's a computer out there. No Internet connection, of course, but they can play solitaire."

Leigh nodded and led the children out of the room. "I'll be back," she told the vet.

The vet couldn't find a viable vein in James's arm, even after using a tourniquet. Undeterred, he took the syringe and slipped it into James's foot. He attached it to a lead, which started pumping a mixture of saline and electrolytes into James's dehydrated body just as Leigh returned.

"I'm getting him hydrated," explained the vet. "I'm going to run a second line with an antibiotic. It's amoxicillin. It's a broad-spectrum treatment for pets. It'll work fine on your husband and should help with the infection."

"What about his breathing?" Leigh sat in the only chair in the room. Her hands were covering her mouth as she spoke. Her eyes were sunken, the lids swollen from lack of sleep. "Can you do anything for that?"

The vet crossed his arms and rubbed his chin with one hand. "I've got prednisone. It's a steroid. It could help open his breathing. But I don't think it's good to give him that as an injection. It'll stay too localized. I've got some pills he can take once he's lucid."

"Thank you," Leigh said, blinking back tears. "Thank you so much."

"You're welcome," said the vet, offering his hand to Leigh. "I'm Dr. Driggers. You can call me Steve."

"I'm Leigh Rockwell." She took his hand and shook it firmly, looking him in the eyes. "My husband is James. My children are Max and Sloane."

Steve Driggers nodded and smiled. "I'll take care of him," he assured her. "It's just lucky I was here. I don't know how much farther he'd have made it."

"I know." Leigh dropped her head, her hair falling around her face as she stared at her feet. "We're in so much trouble."

"How so?" Steve asked.

"We're trying to get home," she explained without looking up. "James is sick. My kids are terrified. We have food and gas, but not enough to make it to Maryland. It's just—"

"These are difficult days," empathized Steve, "for everyone."

"Oh, I know!" Leigh suddenly felt flush, embarrassed by her myopia. "I don't mean to diminish what everyone else is suffering. We're just one family of so many who are out of sorts. I'm sorry if I sounded…"

"No apologies needed," Steve said, moving to check the flow of liquid into James's foot. He could see the color returning to his patient's face and limbs. "These are confusing times. Four days ago the world was normal. Now, who knows?"

"Have you heard anything about what happened?" Leigh asked, realizing Steve might have some valuable information. "Was it a bomb?"

"It's still too early for anyone to know anything for certain," he said. "With the lack of television or radio transmissions, with the Internet spotty and cell service nonexistent, much of what we hear is rumor and speculation."

"What have you heard?" Leigh leaned back in the chair, pulling her hair from her face.

"We know some sort of bomb was detonated," he answered, his

back to her as he looked at James's eyes and ears. "Everyone seems to think it was the Chinese."

"We heard that rumor," Leigh said.

"I don't know." He shook his head. "It could be something else. But that's just campfire speculation. We talk about it at the farm."

"You and your wife?" Leigh asked, wondering why the vet would be here if he had family at home.

"My wife"—he turned and smiled—"my thirteen-year-old son, Connor, and some of our likeminded friends. We're surviving this together."

"It's good to have that support system," Leigh said. She rubbed her eyes with her thumb and forefingers. "It's good to be home, I imagine."

"It is." Steve turned and put his hands on his hips. He pursed his lips and sighed, drawing Leigh's attention. "Look, the truth is, your husband is going to need time to recuperate. The steroids and antibiotics aren't going to make him well enough to travel for another forty-eight hours, if not longer."

"Oh," Leigh said, shrinking in the chair and immediately considering her next move. "I understand. We couldn't expect any more than what you've already done. I'm so grateful."

"You misunderstand me." Steve shook his head. "I can't in good conscience let you leave with him like this. I'm offering you and your family a place to stay for the next few days."

Leigh stood and stepped to Steve, throwing her arms around him. "Thank you so much!"

Steve patted Leigh on the shoulders and then held her at arm's distance. "It's what any good person would do," he said, taking a step back.

"This is so nice," she said. "I'm sorry if I made you uncomfortable. I just…"

"I get it." He nodded. "No problem. Once this bag empties, I'm going to replace the line with the antibiotics. That'll take a couple of hours to drip."

"Okay." Leigh looked over at her husband. He was looking better.

"I'm going to run home and give everyone advance notice of your arrival," he explained. "Then I'll come back here. We'll assess James's condition and get all four of you to our place. Deal?"

"Deal."

CHAPTER 25

EVENT +75:13 Hours
Sweet Valley, Pennsylvania

Steve Driggers' home was more like a compound. His six acres were surrounded on all sides by electrified, razor-wire-topped cattle fencing. There was just one wide, automatic entry gate off Route 4024. It was guarded by a security camera and key panel entry.

Inside the fence there was a long asphalt drive to the center of the pie-shaped lot, which ended at a circular roundabout providing access to three large buildings.

At the center was a five-thousand-square-foot, two-story house. It was built with five bedrooms, a small basement, and a natural-gas generator powerful enough to run the home at its normal electrical usage.

To the right of the circular drive was a long four-car garage. Inside were two pickup trucks and two all-terrain vehicles. To the left of the drive, set back next to the house, was a one-bedroom, single-story cottage. It had its own gas generator and full kitchen.

A crushed granite walking path wound between the house and cottage, leading to a swimming pool and a large barn. The barn was equipped with its own generator, cedar-lined dry storage, and twin freezers. At the far southwestern corner of the property, backing up to Pennsylvania state game land, was a large tree house.

There were seven cameras on the six acres, each of them wide-angle and full color with infrared night vision. Each building also had its own series of cameras. The security system was wired underground to the barn, controlled remotely via computer, and recorded on a pair of five terabyte hard drives.

Since the event, when his gas generators rumbled to life and his alarm system triggered a power loss alert, Steve Driggers had left his compound twice. The first was to gather the two other families who would hunker down with his until they figured out a long-term survival plan.

The second was to raid his veterinary clinic of as many first aid supplies as he could carry in his truck. Despite his years of planning, he neglected to stock enough ointments and antibiotics. The basics used on animals could apply to humans in a pinch. His wife, Kosia, wanted him to wait.

"There's plenty of time for this," she'd told him. "We're fine for the next couple of weeks."

"The world won't be fine in a couple of weeks," Steve had suggested ominously. "The longer this drags on, the worse it gets. Better for me to make my trips now amidst the confusion of these early hours."

Kosia relented and Steve left the compound. He drove the short distance to the clinic as the sun was peeking through the thick late-summer foliage of keystone trees. He kicked on the generator and opened up his business. He was taking inventory when the Rockwells burst through the door.

Now they were in his home. Kosia, skeptical but understanding of her husband's desire to help, helped Leigh herd the children upstairs to their room.

"There are two beds in your room," Kosia explained, leading three of the Rockwells down a long, open hallway. "There's a bathroom en suite, so you'll have plenty of privacy."

"You're too kind," Leigh told her hostess as they stopped outside one of the rooms. "I can't thank you enough."

"Oh"—Kosia laughed and flipped the light switch in the Rockwells' room—"we have plenty of room. We planned on taking in strays at some point. I'm glad we could help you."

"Strays?" Max asked as he bounded through the doorway into the room. He wasn't one for tact.

"I'm sorry." Kosia laughed again and covered her mouth, her cheeks reddening. "I didn't mean it that way. Given that Steve is a vet, we just…"

"It's okay." Leigh put her hand on Kosia's arm. "It was funny. And, in truth, we are strays."

Kosia's lips spread into a genuine smile. "There are plenty of linens and towels in the closet. We'll be eating lunch in a couple of hours. I'll let you know."

"And James?" Leigh asked. "Where is he for now?"

"Steve has him in the cottage next to the house," Kosia answered, stepping back into the hallway. "It's better he's separated in a quiet place until he's healthier. But you can go there whenever you want. The door's unlocked." Kosia pulled the door closed and left the Rockwells alone.

Max and Sloane already claimed a spot to sleep, climbing on top of a frilly white duvet. Leigh looked at the clock on the armoire opposite the beds. It was the same type of clock as they'd had in the rental house on Peaks Island. It was a little more than three days since they ran from that quiet cottage, since they barely escaped with their lives.

Her eyes glazed at the red numbers on the clock. It seemed so much longer ago than three short days.

CHAPTER 26

EVENT +75:13 Hours
Nanticoke, Pennsylvania

Vincent Gore stared at a near-empty, sweating refrigerator. His stomach grumbled as did he.

"Where's the wings?" Vincent called to his girlfriend, Lana. She was in the lone bedroom of their small home.

"I ate 'em yesterday, *Vince*," she called back, putting special emphasis on his name. Lana was reading a year old *Ok! Magazine* she'd swiped from the nail salon. "There should be some bologna in there! Eat that."

Of course she ate them.

Vincent leaned on the refrigerator door, staring at the contents of the fridge. There was a package of bologna with a few slices left. There were two beers and a wine cooler. In the produce drawer, there was an unopened block of cheddar cheese and three oranges.

"You want anything?" he yelled back to Lana. She didn't respond. "Lana!" he called again.

"No, *Vincent*," she said, "I don't want anything." He'd grown to hate the way she said his name as much as he imagined she hated saying it.

In three days without power, he had worked hard to save what little food they had. It didn't really work and now they were down to scraps and a couple of soup cans.

Vincent rocked the door back and forth and slammed it shut. It didn't matter whether he kept it open or closed, the icebox was barely above room temperature.

He stomped from the kitchen, through the living room, past the bathroom, small home office, and into the bedroom. The windows were open, the vinyl blinds rolled all the way to the top. Lana was on the bed in a Grateful Dead T-Shirt and cutoff jean shorts, her black ink "Only God Can Judge Me" tattoo visible above the low cut of the shirt. Her fried-yellow hair was pulled into a ponytail on the top of her head, revealing the row of six earrings running up her right ear. The bottoms of her feet were black with dirt.

"We're gonna starve," he said as though he was talking about the weather. "We got almost nothing left."

Lana looked up from her magazine. "What do you want me to do about it?" She ran a finger along the edge of the magazine. Her nail polish was black. Kim Kardashian was on the cover.

Vincent gritted his teeth and silently seethed.

He didn't expect her to do anything.

That was the problem. It had been for months.

"I'm gonna go check with the boys," he said through his tightened jaw and turned to leave.

He didn't want to fight anymore. He didn't want to be told how terrible a businessman he was, how lousy he was in bed, or how he couldn't live up to her previous eight live-in boyfriends.

"You do that," she snapped, her eyes back on the pages of the magazine. "See if they got any brighter ideas about how to get food. You know the water stopped working this morning?"

He hadn't noticed.

"I tried to flush"—she ran her pierced tongue over her top lip—"and the tank didn't fill back up. Went to wash my hands. Nothing came out of the faucet."

"Nothing I can do about that," he explained, looking over his shoulder.

"Nothing you can do about anything," she mumbled.

He ignored her and marched back down the hall to his home

office. It was a small second bedroom he'd converted to serve as the headquarters for his electrical wiring business, Gore & Associates.

He thought the "& Associates" added a touch of class to his four-man operation. They were all high school buddies who never left town. Vince was the smartest of them and he'd learned a trade. Instead of flipping burgers or running the back of a garbage truck, he'd gone to night school and become an electrician.

After working for a couple of larger companies in Wilkes-Barre and Scranton, Vincent thought it better to be on his own. He partnered with his friends, taught them some of what he knew, and staked his claim. He was hopeful and hung his shingle in November 2013, the month the pandemic hit.

The banks wanted their loans back faster than he could pay them. Thankfully, with a little bit of cash his flu-stricken father had bequeathed him, he was able to stay afloat.

Even after most everything was back to normal, though, business was sporadic. He'd get a few subcontracting jobs here and there. He landed a couple of big projects, did some side work for friends. All in all it was enough to almost pay the bills, but it left little else. Since he'd met Lana, things had spiraled downward financially.

Now, in the middle of whatever crisis had befallen Northeastern Pennsylvania, he was dumfounded. Vincent reached into a small lockbox in the office closet and pulled out a Glock nine millimeter. He checked the cartridge and then stuffed it in his waistband. He wasn't about to venture anywhere without protection.

There were bad people out there.

CHAPTER 27

EVENT +75:30 Hours
Sweet Valley, Pennsylvania

James Rockwell sucked in a deep breath before coughing it back. He was feeling better. The dizziness and headache were gone. The chills had subsided.

"You look so much better, Rock," Leigh said sweetly. She was sitting next to his bed, both of her hands wrapped around one of his. "The color is back in your face. Your eyes look a little brighter."

"I feel better," he said, the phlegm thick in his throat. "Not one hundred percent. But better."

"I was so worried about you," she said, rubbing his hand.

"Sorry to worry you." James looked at the line running from his foot to a liquid-filled plastic bag hanging from the bedpost behind him.

"That's another round of antibiotics," Leigh explained. "The doctor gave you one bag at the clinic. He's giving you another one here. He thinks two bags will do it. Then you can start taking the steroid."

"What doctor?" James had only a fuzzy recollection of the last several hours. He remembered watching the windshield wipers squeal back and forth after the rain had stopped, lacking the strength to tell Leigh to turn them off. He recalled a man lifting him onto some sort of table and the odor of antiseptic mixed with wet dog. And then he was here.

"Steve Driggers," answered Leigh. "We're at his home"—she chuckled—"which is actually more like a retreat."

"Why aren't we at his clinic?" James looked past his wife to the photographs hanging on the walls. He recognized them. One was Ronald Reagan on horseback in California. Another was George W. Bush chopping wood at Prairie Chapel Ranch in Crawford, Texas. Still another was former Congressman Ron Paul at a rally in New Hampshire. "Aren't there other patients? Why are we here?"

"He doesn't have any other patients, Rock," explained Leigh. "He's actually a veterinarian. His clinic is a pet hospital. That's where I took you."

James tried clearing his throat and coughed. "Really?!" He was pleasantly surprised at his wife's resourcefulness. "That's hilarious!" He tried laughing, but wasn't good at it.

"He's been so kind, Rock," she said, letting go of his hand and brushing his forehead. "He probably saved your life."

"You saved my life." James grabbed her hand and kissed it. "You amaze me."

Leigh blushed and leaned in to kiss her husband's lips at the moment there was a knock at the door.

"I don't mean to intrude." Steve Driggers poked his head into the cottage through the crack in the door.

"No intrusion," said Leigh. "He seems to be doing so much better."

"Just wanted to check back with our patient." Steve approached the Rockwells, his hands in his pockets. "It's so odd to treat someone who can tell me how he's feeling."

James chuckled. "Thanks, Dr. Driggers, for helping us out. I don't know how we can repay you." He reached across his body to try to shake Steve's hand.

"It's our pleasure." He shook James's hand. "Thankfully we're able to help." Steve checked the line. "Almost finished. It's probably time to start taking the steroids."

"That's good, right?" Leigh asked.

"It is," said Steve, pulling a small bottle from his pocket. "These should help open up your airways. Breathing should become easier within twenty-four hours."

"Leigh tells me you have a compound here." James was trying to change the subject. He didn't want to talk about his health anymore. "Quite a setup."

"Yes." Steve nodded. "We built the place after the 2013 pandemic. We weren't as prepared as we should have been. I vowed it wouldn't happen again. So Kosia and I built this place. We call it Camp Driggers. Our friends call it Fort Knox."

"Fort Knox?" James popped open the bottle of prednisone and shook a pill into his hand. "How so?"

"Well," Steve explained, sitting on the edge of the bed opposite Leigh, "we have six acres here. The entire perimeter is fenced. We have a pretty advanced security system. The entire property is on its own well, so we don't have to worry about government-supplied water. We put in natural gas generators to run the place as if the electrical grid were intact. We have a small vegetable garden out by the tree house."

"It does sound like Fort Knox." James took a bottled water from Leigh and swallowed the pill. "Pays to be a vet." He toasted the doctor. "Which by the way," James added, "we'd like to pay you for your help. We don't want to be a burden."

"Don't be silly," Steve said. "We were fortunate to own a lot of gold before the pandemic. As you know, it ballooned to more than twelve thousand dollars per ounce afterward."

"I wish we'd been smart enough to own some," said James. "I heard a lot of people did really well financially."

"We were fortunate," admitted Steve. "It allowed us to be as prepared as possible this time." He stood from the bed. "I'm going to get back to the main house and help Kosia prepare our lunch. I'll make sure we save a plate for you, if you're up to it, James."

"Thanks," he replied. "By the way"—he turned to Leigh—"where are the kids?"

"They're at the tree house," she said, "playing with the Driggerses' son, Connor."

"Good," he said, closing his eyes. "They need to feel like kids for a minute." James took a deep breath, wondering if it all seemed too good to be true.

CHAPTER 28

EVENT +75:50
Nanticoke, Pennsylvania

"I dunno, Vince." Bruno Williams took a final slurp from his last can of Coca-Cola. He crumpled it up and tossed it into the dirt. "I think we're all screwed."

"There's gotta be a way to turn things around, right?" Vincent Gore was sitting on the porch that fronted Bruno's rental house. "I mean, we're gonna die otherwise."

"At least when I was in lockup"—Bruno sighed—"they gave me three meals a day. Maybe we oughta break into jail." He laughed, exposing the gap in his mouth where three teeth should have been.

"Right," said Vince, closing his eyes to think, "break into jail."

"Hey brotha'." A thickly muscled body with a small head attached to it trudged up the pine-needle path to Bruno's house. "You wanted all of us here?"

"Hi, Dunk!" said Vince to his childhood friend Leonard Dunkleman. Everyone called him Dunk. "Yeah, we gotta talk through some things. What about Gooz? Where is he?"

"He's on his way." Dunk rubbed his bicep with his hand, flexing as he did it.

"I'm here." Chuck Guzman was a few steps behind Dunk. He was Gooz to everyone who knew him, which included most of the patrol officers with the Nanticoke Police Department.

Gooz and Dunk greeted Vincent and Bruno with one-armed hugs and slaps on the back. They exchanged stories about what they'd been doing to survive the last three days, when Vincent got serious.

"We can't go on like this," he suggested. "The grocery stores are empty and closed, the convenience stores are useless. None of us have enough gas in our cars to make it as far as Back Mountain. Forget about trying to get to Scranton or Pittsburgh. Even Wilkes-Barre is being run by syndicates."

"I heard Pittsburgh is out of control," said Gooz. "I mean, like the army is taking control. There are bodies floating in the Allegheny. I mean, that's what my cousin told me."

"All the big cities are bad," added Dunk. "I got people who tried to get to Boston. They said it's like Fallujah, all warlike and such."

"So we're stuck here," said Vincent. "Which means we need to make something happen."

"Like what?" asked Dunk. "Somebody gonna suddenly hire you to run wires?"

"There isn't any power, you idiot," sniped Bruno. "How thick *is* your neck?"

"Seriously, Bruno?" Dunk flexed. "You wanna go there?"

"Actually"—Vincent raised his hands, speaking loudly enough to drown out the bubbling disagreement amongst his friends—"that gives me an idea."

"What?" Bruno asked.

"See, I gave him an idea." Dunk frogged Bruno in the arm.

"Shut up!" Gooz tried to quiet them so he could hear Vincent's idea.

"I did a job a few years back for a rich dude." Vincent's stare was beyond his friends. He was speaking quickly. "I ran wires for his security system."

"So?" asked Bruno, rubbing the sore spot on his arm.

"He lived over in Sweet Valley, right off of 4024," Vincent recalled. "He had like three or four buildings. It was at least four, maybe five acres. Super nice. Right near one of the game preserves."

"He fenced off the whole place." Vincent was talking with his hands. "The guy had these huge freezers, a ton of storage. It was in a barn."

His friends were quiet, listening to Vincent intently.

"I remember the super on the job telling me that the guy was building a survivalist compound," he said. "He built the place with his wife in case there was another flu outbreak, he'd be prepared. I think he was a veterinarian."

"That clinic up off 29?" asked Bruno. "I took my cat there once."

"Maybe," answered Vincent. "I don't remember."

"How does that help us?" Gooz asked. "This vet with a bunch of refrigerators?"

"I wired the security system," explained Vincent. "I know how it works. I can get us in. We can get what we need and get out. They'll never miss a few cans of beans and some jugs of water."

"Dude," said Bruno, shaking his head, "I dunno. I don't want to end up back in jail. I was just kidding about the free food."

"We won't get caught." Vincent smiled. "It'll be easy. In and out. Who's with me?"

CHAPTER 29

EVENT +78:05
Sweet Valley, Pennsylvania

"Is everyone okay with quinoa and boiled chicken?" Kosia Driggers worked her way around the large farm table at the center of her dining room. At each of the twelve plates, she spooned a steaming mound of the goosefoot grain. Her husband followed with shredded pieces of chicken.

Those gathered at the table all nodded or spoke their approval. No one was in a position to forsake a meal of any quality.

Along with the Driggerses and Leigh and her children were the Kelly family and the Starlings. Mike and Michelle Kelly were longtime friends of the Driggerses. They both worked at a bank in Scranton. Their children, Mitch and Molly, were high school age. The Starlings, Felix and Denise, were an older couple without children. Felix was a realtor. Denise was a part-time nanny.

"What's quinoa?" whispered Sloane, her hand cupped around her mouth and her mother's ear.

"It's like rice," answered Leigh. "You'll like it."

"Shall we say grace?" asked Kosia, taking her seat next to Steve at the head of the table. They held hands, as did their guests, and Steve blessed the food. He prayed for health and guidance and safety.

Amen!

"Have you heard the latest?" asked Felix Starling, pointing his fork at Steve.

"What's that?" Steve sipped from a glass of iced tea.

"It's a false flag," Felix said. "It's not the Chinese at all."

"How do you figure that?" asked Mike.

"The government has been trying to erode our freedoms for years," explained Felix as he chewed on a piece of chicken. "Take the Patriot Act after 9/11, the martial law imposed after Katrina and Sandy, not to mention the way police shut down Boston after the marathon bombings."

"What does that have to do with this?" pressed Mike. "You're saying all of those horrible events were concocted by the government? The government can't stir up a hurricane, Felix."

"I'm not saying those events were all false flags," Felix clarified. "I'm saying they proved to the government what people would be willing to accept, the loss of freedoms to which they'd agree."

"So how is this a false flag, then?" asked Mike. He was leaning forward in his seat, his elbows on the table.

"What's a false flag?" asked Mike's son, Mitch.

"It's when a government attacks its own people," explained Steve, his eyes on Mike, "and then blames someone else. The government then uses that attack to remove the civil liberties of its citizens."

"Why would they do that?" asked Mitch, his eyes darting between his father and Felix. "I don't understand that." He grabbed his tea and took a nervous gulp.

"To take away our freedom," Felix said. "The government can't take our liberty, but if they create a situation in which we ask them to take it from us, then it does so without argument."

"So you think this attack," Leigh interjected, "wasn't the Chinese? That's all we kept hearing on our way south. Everybody thinks it's the Chinese."

"That quickly?" Felix laughed. "How could anybody know it was the Chinese so quickly? That's almost as ludicrous as the FBI or CIA identifying the 9/11 hijackers within hours of the attacks, despite their inability to piece together what they were doing for months?"

"That's enough, honey." Felix's wife, Denise, put her hand on his arm. "We don't need to do this."

"I'm just saying"—Felix was undeterred—"this 'event' is just the beginning. And I'm thankful to be here in this doomsday compound you were smart enough to build." Felix dug into a piece of chicken with his fork and shoveled it into his mouth.

"That's a roundabout way to get to 'Thank you!'" said Mike under his breath but loud enough for Felix to hear him.

"Look." Steve put down his fork and knife. "It's good that we have these debates. It's healthy. We're all conservatives here. We all believe in the Bill of Rights. We all know there are times when those rights seem perilously endangered—"

"That's all I'm saying," quipped Felix.

"Now is probably not the time to be throwing darts at our own government," said Steve. "Where are you hearing these rumors, anyhow?"

"That shortwave radio you had buried in the barn," answered Felix. "I got it working. There's occasional chatter. Most of it seems to be Canadian."

"So the Canadians are speculating our government did this to us?" Mike almost stood from his seat.

"Maybe we should stay off the radio for a couple of days," suggested Steve.

"I think that's a good idea," Felix's wife, Denise, agreed.

"Okay." Felix shook his head and moved the quinoa around on the plate. "I was just trying to make conversation. I didn't mean to upset anyone."

"More chicken anyone?" Kosia exhaled and pushed back her chair. "Refills on the tea?"

CHAPTER 30

EVENT +80:17 Hours
Sweet Valley, Pennsylvania

"So how are you gonna do it?" Gooz was belly down in the grass, perched on his elbows. "You gonna hop the fence?"

"No," said Vincent, "the fence is electrified."

The two were running reconnaissance, hidden in a ditch across Route 4024, in front of a wide wrought-iron metal gate. Vincent's SUV was parked several blocks away.

Dunk and Bruno were at Bruno's house, looking for flashlight batteries and trash bags.

"So then what?" asked Gooz, shifting on his elbows. The wet grass was making them itch.

"There's a control box right by the key panel." Vincent handed his binoculars to Gooz. "Look to the left of the gate. See it? It looks like a junction box."

"I see it." Gooz nodded, his eyes pressed to the lenses. "It's beneath the camera."

"Yeah," Vincent said. "That's it. I can run a bypass wire in that box. The system will think it's still powered, but it's not. That'll turn off the electrical supply to the fence."

"Then what?" Gooz lowered the binoculars and looked at Vincent.

"I'll be at the box," said Vincent. "You, Dunk, and Bruno will be on the other side of the property. There's open land behind it. It's close to the barn. I'll signal you when the fence is off and you three jump it."

"How are you going to signal us?"

"We'll have walkie-talkies." Vincent looked back across the road at the gate. Atop the gate was a large arch decorated with the name *Camp Driggers*. "I have four of them. At least three still have a charge."

"And we go to the barn," assumed Gooz. "We break in, grab what we can, and get out."

"Almost," said Vincent. "There's an alarm."

Gooz looked through the binoculars again. "What if an alarm goes off?"

"I'll take care of that," said Vincent. "Each of the buildings is powered separately when the grid fails. They've got gas generators running independently at the houses and the barn."

"What does that mean?" Gooz rubbed his chin.

"I'll jump the fence in the front." Vincent rolled onto his side to face Gooz. "Then I'll bolt to the generator at the barn. I'll shut it off and the security to the barn will shut down for about thirty seconds before a battery backup resets the alarm. We don't have to worry about an immediate cellular backup, because cell service is dead."

"So we've got thirty seconds to get in and out?" Gooz shook his head. "We can't do that."

"No." Vincent shook his head. "You've got thirty seconds to get in. The system reboots, but you're already inside, past the alarms. Then I'll restart the generator and turn it off again. That'll give you another thirty seconds to get out."

"Won't the cameras see us?" Gooz challenged. "And won't the generator make a lot of noise?"

"The cameras are irrelevant." Vincent shook his head. "Even if they get any decent images, the police aren't going to be interested. They've got too much other stuff going on."

"Good point." Gooz pushed himself back onto his knees. "So what time we gonna do this?"

"I'm thinking four o'clock in the morning," Vincent said. "Everyone should be asleep. By the time they wake up, if they do, we'll be long gone."

"With bags full of food!" Gooz smiled.

"Yep!" said Vincent. "Bags full of food."

CHAPTER 31

EVENT +81:01 Hours
Nanticoke, Pennsylvania

Lana rolled off of her lover and reached for a cigarette. There was only one left in the pack.

"You got a lighter?" she asked, trailing her finger down his bare chest. "I think my stupid-ass boyfriend took the matches."

"When's Vincent gonna be back?" asked the lover, his breathing accelerated from the six minutes of fun he'd just enjoyed with another man's woman. "I don't want to have to beat him for taking your matches."

Lana grabbed his thick bicep, squeezing it with a throaty giggle. "I wouldn't mind if you did."

"Why are you with him?" he asked. "You could leave him."

"Right," she said. "Where am I gonna go? You won't leave your wife. I don't have a job since the club closed down. He's all I got. You got a lighter?"

"Yeah," he grunted, sitting up in Vincent's bed. "Sorry. Let me get it."

"Thank you." She slapped his bare backside as he moved from the bed to his pile of clothing on the floor. The cigarette was hanging from her lip.

"You got any food?" he asked. "I'm hungry."

"No." The cigarette bounced as she spoke. "Some bologna

maybe. That's it."

He rummaged through his pockets and found a silver-plated lighter with his name etched in it. "Here you go." He tossed it to Lana, who was sitting up in the bed. "Guess I'll have to feed myself later."

"Reggie," she said, thumbing her fingers across the calligraphy on the lighter. "So cute that you have a personalized lighter." She giggled and cupped the lighter to the cigarette, flicking it alight. She took a deep drag and then blew out the smoke.

"You're so sexy," Reggie said, jumping back into the bed, dragging her body to his by her legs. "Have I told you that?"

"Stop!" She giggled. "I'm gonna set something on fire with this smoke." She pushed him away. "How long are you in town?"

"I don't know." He shook his head, feigning rejection. "I've got some stuff working in Wilkes-Barre. This whole 'apocalypse' deal is good for business."

"How so?" She sucked on the cigarette and flicked the ashes into a tray by the bed before offering it to Reggie.

"I know people," he said coyly, taking the cigarette. "They need things. And in an uncertain environment, such as it is, I provide things to people I know."

"Black market stuff?" she asked, reaching for the smoke.

"Maybe." He laughed. "I like to refer to it as a gray market, or maybe underground market."

"What kind of stuff?" she pressed, pulling the sheet up over her bare torso.

"You ask too many questions," he said, his tone less playful.

"Ooooooh, sorry!!" She waved her hands, her eyes wide with false fright. "Don't want to ask too many questions."

"Not funny, Lana." He rolled away from her. "Business is business. It's better if I don't talk too much."

Lana looked at the tattoo on his upper right shoulder. It was an odd design, somewhat like a lowercase 'h' or an upside down '4' and was poorly inked. She'd noticed it before but never thought to ask about it.

"Tell me about your ink," she said, running her black fingernails down his spine. She was trying to change the subject before he got angry.

"Got it when I was doing five in Albion for agg assault," he said without turning around. "It's a Chinese symbol. Means strength."

"How do you get a tattoo in prison?" She tapped out the cigarette in the tray and slid over closer to Reggie. He still had his back to her.

"I don't know." He shrugged. "There's a tattoo man. You pay him with whatever and he gives you what you want."

"What's the ink made from?" Lana pulled the sheet from her body and pushed herself onto her knees. She inched her way to Reggie and pressed her chest against his back before moving her lips to the tattoo.

"It's like boot polish and baby oil," he explained. "The tattoo man mixes it up, scrapes it, heats it, and then inks you up."

"You can get anything you want in prison?" she asked, her mouth paused above the ink.

"Just about," he answered. "Ink, meth, pot, cell phones, chalk. Anything you can't get at the A&P you can find on the gray market." He chuckled.

"Everything but a woman," she purred.

"True." He reached his hand around to the back of Lana's head, grabbing a handful of hair. "Enough talk."

"I agree." She spun around on his lap to face him on the edge of the bed. "Vincent will be home soon."

"Let's do this, then," he growled. "I got people to see."

CHAPTER 32

EVENT +82:00 Hours
Sweet Valley, Pennsylvania

"I heard the lunch conversation was interesting." James was baiting his host, Steve. The vet was checking James's vitals, assuring the medicine was doing what it was supposed to do.

"Take a deep breath." Steve swam past the hook and pressed his stethoscope against James's back. "Another."

James sucked in as much as he could before he coughed. A stabbing pain accompanied each hack. James winced.

"That's better," Steve said. "You've still got fluid in there, which isn't surprising, but I can tell your airways are opening up a bit."

"How long until I'm back to normal?" James asked.

"It depends," Steve answered. "Pneumonia after a near drowning isn't common, but it can happen under the right circumstances. Given the type of water you ingested, fouled with oil and gas and junk from the island, you're more susceptible. It's good the water was cold, however. That retards bacterial growth."

"Okay." James nodded, lying back against the pillow-cushioned headboard. "I'll take it easy for now. Not that I'm upset about the break from near-death experiences."

"Your wife told us about your adventures during lunch." Steve laughed. "It's amazing you're all here in one piece."

"So speaking of lunch…" James was dangling the line again.

"Yes." Steve sighed. "We had our moments at lunch today. Felix, well-intentioned as he may be, ruffled some feathers with his talk of false flags."

"You think that's possible?" James asked.

"No." Steve shook his head. "It wouldn't make sense for our own government to drop a nuclear weapon off of our own coastline."

"I don't think it was nuclear," said James.

"Really?" Steve sat up, cocking his head like one of his Labrador patients. "Why do you say that?"

"I thought for a while it was nuclear," explained James. "I saw the blast from Peaks Island. It certainly appeared nuclear."

"Which would explain the loss of power, cell phones, Internet, and other infrastructure," said Steve.

"Yes." James pushed himself up against the pillow. His back was sore. His thigh was sweating underneath the wrap protecting his stitches. "That's the electromagnetic pulse effect, which is not dissimilar from a massive solar storm."

"Like George Clooney's crew in *Ocean's Eleven*," Steve added, "when they shut down the power grid in Vegas."

"Exactly." James's face lit up from the pop culture reference. "Or when Keanu Reeves used one in *The Matrix* to fend off a robotic squid."

"Didn't see that one." Steve shook his head. "But I get the point."

"Well"—James nodded—"if it was the result of a nuclear blast, there would be other resulting issues. We headed west and south after the explosion, toward the blast. There was no rain until the next day. Typically, as was the case in Hiroshima, the heat and airborne debris from the explosion causes rain."

"Rain?" Steve cocked his head again.

"It's called black rain," James explained, "because of its oily appearance."

"Oh."

"That didn't happen in this case," James repeated. "Also, the dynamic pressure from the blast wasn't as violent as a nuclear blast might have caused. And lastly, the altitude of the detonation was too low."

"Why is that?" Steve questioned. "I thought nuclear bombs were detonated in the air."

"They are," James confirmed. "But there is an ideal height for maximum damage. That height is the cubed root of the yield in kilotons multiplied by the ideal height."

"You lost me." Steve shook his head, laughing at the complexity of it.

"The formula doesn't really matter," said James. "I was really just thinking aloud. But the most telling aspect to me is that the blast occurred over water."

"How so?"

"If you wanted to detonate a nuclear bomb, wouldn't you do it over land?" James shrugged. "An EMP, theoretically, could be off the coast and still do an immense amount of damage. The blast from an EMP is tangential. Detonate more than one…"

"You know there's chatter there was more than one explosion," Steve revealed.

"I didn't," James admitted. "But it makes sense. A single blast south of Maine wouldn't kill the power throughout New England and into Pennsylvania."

"I guess that bolsters your theory," Steve said. "Which is good, right? I mean, no radiation and no fallout."

"True," James admitted. "But an EMP, whoever detonated it, would throw us back to the Stone Age. It could take years, if not decades to repair the damage to our power grid alone."

"Not to mention cellular towers," added Steve.

"Computers"—James nodded—"transistorized telephone equipment, the list goes on and on."

"How do you know all of this?" Steve stood from the bed and stretched.

"I'm a physics teacher." James coughed.

"That makes sense, then." Steve laughed. "I guess none of this is funny, really."

"It's pretty bad, actually," James confirmed, but he was still thinking about the blast, the outages, and the tsunami. As he'd just verbalized his theory to Steve, something wasn't adding up. There was an element he was missing. Could a high-altitude EMP cause a tsunami?

"Well"—Steve sighed—"you're welcome to stay here as long as you like. Especially since it could be a while before things get back to normal."

"I do appreciate it," said James. "But if it's just the same, I'd like to get home. As soon as you give me the discharge papers, we're outta here."

"I understand." Steve walked toward the door. "Just remember, this is as safe a place as you'll find anywhere."

CHAPTER 33

EVENT +84:35 Hours
Nanticoke, Pennsylvania

"The bologna's gone?" Vincent yelled from the refrigerator. "You ate the last of it?" He thought he knew the answer without asking, but he had to press his point. "How selfish are you?"

Lana was sitting on the leather sofa in the living room, picking at a tear in the seat cushion next to her. She was out of cigarettes. Vincent stomped into the room, his fists clenched as tight as his jaw.

Lana looked up at him and rolled her eyes. "Yes. I ate it. I was hungry. Shoot me." She turned her attention to the rip, twirling her nail down into the foam.

"Don't tempt me," he said. "I don't know why I keep you around, Lana. You're miserable."

"I don't know why I stay," she countered. "Oh, yeah, it's 'cause you're the least worst guy I know."

"That makes no sense!" he yelled. "You make no sense!"

"Whatever, *Vincent*," she sniped.

Vincent huffed off to the bedroom to change. He shoved his way through the door, pulling the Glock from his waistband to toss it on the bed, when he did a double take.

She made the bed?!

The duvet was pulled up and tucked in at the sides. The three pillows were sitting neatly against the brass headboard. Even the *Home Sweet Home* cross-stitch pillow was in its place.

When was the last time she made the bed?

Vincent thought it odd, but then wondered if he'd been too hard on her just now. They were both hungry. She was just as entitled to the food as he was. He spun on his heel and trudged back to the living room.

"I'm sorry," he said, folding his arms across his chest.

"For what?" Lana's eyes shot up from the hole in the sofa to look at her boyfriend.

"I shouldn't have yelled at you for the bologna," he admitted. "This is your house too. Plus, I should say thank you."

"For what?" Lana craned her neck like a chicken.

"You made the bed." Vincent smiled. "I appreciate it. I mean, I know things are tough and I say you don't do stuff to help. So you made the bed. You helped. Thank you."

"You're welcome," she said. "And I forgive you. Now sit with me. I'm bored." She patted the empty seat on the sofa.

"I can't," he said, sitting on the rectangular oak coffee table in front of the sofa. He was facing Lana. "I got some stuff to do with the guys tonight."

"Great," she huffed and stuck her finger back into the tear. "Leave me for the boys."

"No," Vincent explained, "this *is* great. I'll be back in the morning with a big surprise for you."

"Oh really." Lana's right eyebrow arched higher than the left. "What?"

"Can't tell you." He slapped her thigh and leaned over to kiss her forehead. "But you'll be happy."

Vincent returned to the bedroom with more bounce in his step. He opened up a chest of drawers and pulled out a black Megadeth concert T-Shirt. He held it up to his chest. It would do. Now he needed to find a black beanie and his darkest pair of pants.

"I'm going all Seal Team Six." He laughed to himself. "Like Special-Ops and stuff."

He checked the pocket watch his father gave him. It was almost 6:15. He had an hour until he needed to be back at Bruno's place.

The plan was going to work. He was sure of it.

CHAPTER 34

EVENT +85:55 Hours
Sweet Valley, Pennsylvania

Max Rockwell was hiding from his sister. He'd climbed the tree house at the southwest corner of Camp Driggers. There was less than a half hour of sunlight left in the day and Leigh had already given the five-minute warning. Playtime was almost up.

Max sat in the tree house with his knees pulled to his chest, relishing his sister's inability to find him as much as the diversion of hide and seek. He looked up at the broad, green sycamore leaves over his head and took a deep breath.

He wondered how many more moments he'd have like this: alone with his thoughts, no immediate worries about food, shelter, or pain. Max knew his family wouldn't stay in this relative utopia forever, but he was glad to stay as long as his parents were willing.

"Psst." It was Connor, the Driggerses' son. "You up here, Max?" He was climbing up the wooden ladder.

"Yeah." Max leaned forward to look over his knees and saw Connor poke his head through the opening. "Where is she?"

"She's wandering over by the cottage." Connor pulled himself into the tree house. "Molly Kelly is trying to help her find you, but your sister keeps ignoring her ideas."

"That's Sloane." Max smirked. "A mind of her own."

"What's with the stuffed bear?" asked Connor. "She carries it everywhere. My mom said she wanted an extra seat for it at lunch." He snickered.

"That's a long story," said Max.

"I've got time," said Connor. "It's not like there's a Pirates game on TV."

"Its name is Noodle," explained Max. "And it's a big deal to her because our older sister gave it to Sloane when she was born."

"Older sister?" asked Connor, crossing his legs in front of him, leaning back on his palms. "I thought it was just the four of you. Is she in college or something?"

"No," answered Max, his eyes finding their way to the dusty wood plank floor of the tree house. "She's dead."

"What?" Connor sat straight. "Hey, I'm sorry. I didn't—"

"No, no." Max waved him off. "Don't worry about it. You didn't know. It happened a while ago."

The boys exchanged silence for a moment before Connor pressed, "What was her name?"

"Nora."

"Can I ask how she died?"

"The flu," Max said. "She was a little younger than I am now. It was during the flu outbreak. So, like, six years ago."

"What happened?"

"She was always kinda sick," Max revealed. "I mean, not in bed all of the time, but she went to the doctor a lot. My parents said she was born early and then had different medical problems."

"Oh."

"When the flu first started spreading," Max remembered, "my parents pulled us out of school before everybody else. They didn't want us getting it and passing it around, you know? Plus, Sloane was only a baby. She was two years old."

"Yeah." Connor nodded.

"We were all at home," said Max, "and my mom was friends with a nurse who got us these sample packages of medicine. I remember they were these huge pills and we had to take them for a week."

"I remember taking those," said Connor. "Those things were like horse pills. That's what my dad called them."

"My parents thought we were going to be fine," added Max, "but Nora caught it anyway. She got really sick. Nobody could help her." His gaze drifted off past the walls of the tree house. He could see his sister's weakened body struggling against the fever that racked her weakened body.

She seemed so small, so tiny in that bed, he remembered. She was his *older* sister, but she didn't look it. Nora was a shell of herself. And her hand…it was so cold when he held it.

"Sorry to bring it up." Connor snapped Max back to the present.

"It's okay." Max shrugged. "It was a long time ago."

"I didn't know anybody who died from the flu back then," Connor admitted. "I knew a couple of kids whose grandparents died. One kid's mom got it and died. That was it."

"Did you live here?" asked Max, eager to change the focus.

"No," said Connor. "We lived in Scranton. It was crazy there during the flu outbreak. I don't really remember too much. But my parents say it was super dangerous in any city. People went nuts."

"What do you mean?"

"People panicked," Connor explained. "They broke into people's houses and businesses and stole stuff. My dad's office got looted."

"Is that why you moved here?" asked Max. "To the country?"

"Yeah." Connor nodded. "My parents wanted us to be safer. My dad told us we'd never be unprepared again."

"That's why you have the generators and the fences?" Max turned and looked toward the western edge of the property. He could see the fence in the fading light, outlined against the stretch of grass and trees beyond it.

"And the cameras," Connor added. "And the guns."

"Guns?" Max whipped his head back to Connor. "What guns?"

"My dad has, like, a bunch of guns and other stuff in the garage," Connor said before pursing his lips. "Don't say anything. I wasn't supposed to tell anyone. "

"I won't," Max said, "but why'd he buy so many guns?"

"He said he doesn't trust people." Connor shrugged. "He said that when things get bad, people get worse."

Max thought back to the men in the boat, the ones who tried to rip them from their kayaks to steal their backpacks. And more.

He winced against the memory of his dad plowing holes into the men with his handgun. He'd never forget the blank, empty stare of the one with the blood spewing from his neck as he lost his grip on Max's kayak and slipped beneath the surface of the water, leaking a red mushroom cloud behind as his body sank.

"You okay?" Connor tapped Max on his knee, bringing him back to the tree house.

"Yeah." Max shook his head. "I was just thinking."

"Max!!" a squeaky voice called from directly underneath the tree house. "I found you!"

The boys looked down the opening to see Sloane and Molly looking up at them. Sloane held up Noodle and waved a nappy paw for him.

"Hey, guys," Molly called, "your moms want you back inside. It's getting dark and dinner's almost ready."

"Okay!" the boys said in unison.

"Remember," said Connor as they began their descent, "don't talk about the guns."

CHAPTER 35

EVENT +88:00 Hours
Wilkes-Barre, Pennsylvania

Reggie was late. He was bouncing his knee up and down as he pulled his truck into a parking spot next to the tennis courts at Coal Street Park. Being late was not good.

Two men approached him as soon as he slipped the truck into park. The larger of the two rapped on the window and Reggie rolled it down. Reggie was mean. These men were meaner.

"Malcolm—" Reggie started, but stopped when the man held his finger to his lips.

"Shhh!" The man, Malcolm Kepler, closed his eyes when he spoke. "You're fifteen minutes late. I don't like that."

"It took me longer to get back than—" Reggie was still trying to make a case.

"I don't care," Kepler interrupted. His calm, even tone was more frightening than if he were to yell in anger. "There are no excuses here. Either you are capable of doing what's asked of you or we will find someone who is."

Reggie nodded, masking his desire to stab Kepler in the neck. He knew better than to speak again, despite his dislike for the man. He couldn't fight the hierarchy of things. It had been that way since prison. He knew the man's power.

Malcolm Kepler would have him killed if he had to "find someone else". He'd seen him do it in prison and on the street. With a shiv, with a paperclip and pencil, and with his thickly calloused bare hands.

Kepler, wiry and athletic, was the unchallenged leader of a small gang called the United Brothers, a skinhead splinter group of the more organized and much larger Keystone United.

Before the event, they ran untaxed cigarettes, liquor, and a growing amount of methamphetamines. Their "territory" ran from Scranton and Wilkes-Barre to Williamsport. Since the event, they'd quickly seized upon the need for food, water, and medicine. They'd looted a half-dozen pharmacies and grocery stores in the three days since their area of influence went dark.

"I have another small shipment for you," Kepler offered, rubbing the stubble on his head, "if you believe you can handle it. On time."

Reggie nodded again.

"I need you to take it back across the river." Kepler leaned in, pressing his hands against the open windowsill. "The Market Street Bridge is closed to all traffic. Local cops are checking identification. You don't need that hassle."

The other man, Kepler's bodyguard and former cellmate, stepped forward and whispered something in his ear. The cellmate was holding a G28 semiautomatic gas-operated rifle across his prison-built chest.

Reggie recognized the weapon from his days as a pawn shop manager. He'd become a quasi-expert on weapons, guitars, and Rolex watches.

"Berger here says to head south to Mocanaqua and take the crossing there," Kepler suggested. "There's nobody there yet. So that's your best route. Got it so far?"

"I got it," said Reggie. "Though I just came across the—"

"Cross at Mocanaqua," Kepler insisted.

"Okay." Reggie raised his hands from the wheel, surrendering the discussion.

"Then head to Ricketts Glen State Park," Kepler said. "There'll be a friend waiting for your delivery. You'll offload. He'll give you the requisite payment. All is good. You come back and meet me here in ten hours."

"Okay."

"Not ten hours and fifteen minutes." Kepler pointed his finger at Reggie. "Ten hours exactly."

Reggie nodded and asked, "Where's the load?"

"Berger's gonna help you load it." Kepler rapped his hands on the door sill. "Get out."

Kepler backed away from the truck, and Reggie climbed out to help Berger the cellmate. They crossed the parking lot to a small Chevy SUV. Berger, still handling the Heckler & Koch rifle, popped open the tailgate with one hand. Then he placed the weapon in the back of the SUV.

"That's a pretty nice rifle." Reggie approached Berger at the back of the Chevy. "A little heavy compared to the MR762, but I like the green and brown finish. Very slick."

Berger turned his thick neck to look at Reggie. He said nothing and reached into the back of the SUV to pull out a box labeled *Suboxone.*

"Grab a box." Kepler was standing behind Reggie. "Take it to your truck."

"What is that stuff?" Reggie asked. "Suboxone?" He grabbed two boxes, felt the pills rattling around in their individual bottles, and turned to walk back to his truck.

"It's like methadone," said Kepler, "for smack addicts."

Reggie hauled the boxes to his truck and went back for more. In addition to the Suboxone, there were cases of pseudoephedrine and Dexedrine. He'd be driving a mobile pharmacy.

"Hit the road," Kepler ordered as Reggie slammed shut the rear tailgate on the truck. He and Berger pulled a large canvas tarp across the boxes and secured it with short bungee cords. "Don't stop. Don't talk to anybody. You good on fuel?"

Reggie hopped in the cab and cranked the ignition. "Yeah. I've got a half tank. That should be plenty."

"Your contact should hand you one hundred and twenty large," explained Kepler. "When you get back, I'll give you a cut and then load you up again."

"More drugs?" asked Reggie.

Kepler licked his upper lip and sniffed. He glared at Reggie for a moment before answering. "Probably food. By tomorrow, it'll be worth more than crack to a whore."

"Got it." Reggie pulled on his seatbelt and pulled out of the parking lot. He had a long night ahead of him. And lucky for him, his delivery took him right by Nanticoke and his side lady, Lana.

CHAPTER 36

EVENT +91:15 Hours
Nanticoke, Pennsylvania

Vincent Gore couldn't sit still. It was just after midnight and he was having second thoughts. He adjusted the nine millimeter in his waistband. His stomach groaned.

"Dude," said Dunk, "you need to chill. We got this."

"Seriously, Vince," added Bruno. "This is not going to be a problem. I mean, the worst thing that happens is the alarm goes off and we bolt. It's not the end of the world."

"It *is* the end of the world," countered Vincent. "That's exactly the deal here. This rich dude could be in a bunker mentality, you know?" He rapped his knuckles against the side of his head. "We could be walking into a hornet's nest."

"That's not gonna happen," said Dunk. "They'll be asleep. You said it. This is perfect timing."

"You're not being a puss about it, are you?" asked Gooz. He was sitting in a La-Z-Boy recliner, his eyes closed as he listened to the debate. "We looked at the place. We checked it out. We're all good. Why are you getting all freaked?"

"Do we need to do this?" Vince asked himself as much as the group. "Do we need to put ourselves at risk?"

"Yes!" they replied in unison. Gooz opened his eyes and leaned forward, rocking the La-Z-Boy as he did.

"We are out of food, Vince," he argued. "And if we wait another couple of days, we won't have the energy to do anything about it."

"I'm starving, dude," added Dunk. "I got, like, I don't know, two cans of green beans left. Something like that. We need this."

"I've had a headache for the last six hours," said Bruno. "I'm thirsty. I'm hungry. If we don't do this now, we're screwed."

"What about a grocery store?" Vince was racking his mildly dehydrated brain for an alternative.

"What grocery store?" chided Gooz. "We've been through this. Hitting that place is the best thing we can do. We grab what we can carry. It'll last us until the lights come back on."

"What if the lights don't come back on?" Vince played devil's advocate.

"Then we worry about that when we run out of our new stash," argued Gooz. "We can grab enough to last us for at least a week or two."

"You said these were big freezers, right?" asked Bruno. He was sitting on the hearth of an empty fireplace. "There should be plenty of food."

"Yeah." Vincent couldn't shake the bad feeling that had washed over him. He couldn't explain it, but his gut was more than empty. It was prescient. But he shook it off as nerves. "There should be plenty for all of us."

"So tell us again how this is going to go down." Dunk was sitting on a barstool in front of the counter of Bruno's galley kitchen. He swiveled in the chair, the ball bearings complaining under his weight.

"All right." Vincent sighed. "Here's the plan…" He then laid out the mission as he and Gooz had conceived it.

They'd take two vehicles. Vincent would drive himself to the front of the property and work his magic there.

The rest of the team would approach from the north, off of Route 118. They'd have to walk about a half mile to the back of the property, navigating the brush and trees populating State Game Lands Number 206. It was an expansive preserve with a small creek called Shingle Run running north and south close to Camp Driggers.

Dunk, Bruno, and Gooz would use the creek as their guide if they got disoriented. Bruno and Gooz would carry walkie-talkies and would communicate with Vincent when needed. They'd each have trash bags and pillow cases to carry the merchandise.

"The only potential hitch is the noise from the generator," explained Vincent. "When I crank it on and off, it could wake up the owners. If that happens, if there's any sign we're busted, you gotta run."

"Isn't the fence electrified?" asked Dunk, his attention half given to the flex of his triceps. He ran his hand along the bulge stretched along his arm.

"Yes," confirmed Vincent. "If we have to get out fast, and it's on, you'll have to cope. Gooz will have a pair of bolt cutters with him. He'll be able to cut through the razor wire along the top of the fence once I've shut off the power the first time."

He took another deep breath and sighed. He was smart enough to know better, but desperate enough to attempt the raid.

Vincent was out of options.

CHAPTER 37

EVENT +92:00 Hours
Sweet Valley, Pennsylvania

Steve Driggers' hands were in his front pockets as he walked the path between the main house and the cottage. He noticed the lights were off in the cottage and figured his patient must be asleep. Everybody in the main house had long ago called it a night.

Driggers didn't sleep much. He never had. He was what scientists called a "short sleeper" and was among those the Wall Street Journal had dubbed "the sleepless elite". He could function on five hours of sleep a night, sometimes less. Less than two percent of the population shared what researchers believed was a genetic mutation that allowed for his lessened need for sleep.

It served him well in college and veterinary school. He could stay up late studying, sleep a few hours, and feel refreshed and alert in the morning. It was a curse with which he was happy to live.

Every night, after his wife and son had gone to bed, he'd read a book or play *Call of Duty* on Connor's Xbox. He'd wander the property, enjoying the quiet and admiring the stars above.

Just four nights ago he'd caught a glimpse of the Perseid meteor shower. They were bright, brief streaks across the sky, fiery balls of dust and ice escaping the comet's pull just long enough to offer a brilliant show.

Now, he looked up and longed for those fireworks, wishing he could use his sleeplessness to figure out time travel. He'd take his family back to that Monday night. It was peaceful. Their world had a seemingly certain future.

Steve opened the barn door and walked into the large open space. To his left was the security closet. Above that closet, wired into the wall, were three thirty-two-inch LED televisions. Each of the televisions had a split-screen display for the security cameras dotting Camp Driggers.

Steve looked at the monitors and saw nothing unusual. He opened the cabinet to check the hard drives. They were humming quietly, alit with small green diodes flashing to indicate they were recording. He closed the cabinet and locked it shut.

To his right, on the wall opposite the entry door, were two large walk-in freezers. They were eight-foot galvanized steel cubes with latching, hinged doors. There were no shelves on the inside of the freezers, so the Driggerses installed PVC storage racks to accommodate their needs.

He considered pulling a beer from the freezer, but instead walked to the wall-length dry goods cabinet on the right side of the barn and pulled open the heavy, cedar-lined door. He flipped on the light and checked his stash.

Inside the twelve-by-three-foot space there was a trove of dry goods and nonperishable foods. The Driggerses spent weeks researching the best use of their space, and weeks more organizing it when they started stocking the cabinet's four tiered, wall-to-wall shelves.

On the top shelf, closest to the ceiling, were a series of five-gallon, food-grade bins. The bins were labeled with their contents; salt, brown sugar, white sugar, buckwheat, dry corn, kamut, durum wheat, spelt, barley, quinoa, and rye. All of the items, further packed in large gallon plastic bags, would last anywhere from eight to ten years.

There were extra bins of salt at the far end of the cabinet. The Driggerses planned on using the excess for bartering if it came to it.

On the second shelf from the top were the pastas and various kinds of flour. They too could last up to eight years. There were also airtight containers of pinto and kidney beans, lentils and garbanzos.

There were ten large vats of coconut oil, which had a longer shelf life than most oils. It would be good for two years. Large bottles of olive oil and jugs of vinegar sat next to the coconut oil. They wouldn't last as long.

On the lower two shelves were the foods with only two to five years of shelf life: canned tuna and chicken, canned vegetables and sauces, coffee, and peanut butter. There were a half-dozen unopened boxes of powdered milk and baking soda, and several jars of raw honey. The honey, Steve read, was good for wound healing as well as a sweet treat.

Along the floor under the shelves were countless rolls of toilet paper, paper towels, and cases of bottled water. There were stacks of homemade candles, carefully crafted by Kosia, in the event the supply of gas shut off. There were cans of lighter fluid, bags of charcoal, and boxes full of soap.

On a separate, smaller shelf, to the right of the entry door, Steve stored the emergency medicines, vitamins, bandages, peroxide, iodine, and cotton swabs.

Everything looked in order, except for the quinoa container. He'd not closed the lid all of the way when pulling out the bag from which Kosia had cooked the side dish for lunch and dinner. He stepped onto a small ladder and reached up to push the box closed. Satisfied it was sealed, he stepped down and walked over to the spot where they stored hard candy. He cranked open a mason jar full of butterscotch and popped a piece in his mouth.

He sucked on the sweet taste of brown sugar and butter, relishing the momentary distraction. Steve Driggers knew they were as prepared as they could be.

They'd spent the last six years taking steps to avoid the mistakes of 2013. They'd moved from their hometown, a thriving practice, and the friends they cherished to an outpost sixty miles away. Sure, it wasn't as if they'd relocated to the West Coast. But for a family so entrenched in Scranton, it was emotionally taxing to leave.

They'd uprooted Connor from his school and soccer teammates.

There was no neighborhood trick-or-treating on Halloween or block parties on July fourth. Instead they were loners, dependent on one another for support and entertainment. The pool and the tree house were poor substitutes for a close-knit cul-de-sac.

They wondered if they'd made the right choice, or if they were the fringe-thinking lunatics some of their "friends" had suggested. They were ready for the disaster that might never come. And then it did.

They were vindicated, Steve thought. They were right to do what they did, to make the sacrifices they made. Still, there were nagging questions he couldn't shake. Even if he'd been able to sleep, he'd have lain awake.

Did they save enough? Was their home secure? What did they forget to do?

He knew with every passing day their preparedness, or unforeseen lack of it, would be increasingly tested.

At what point, he wondered as he made his way back to the main house, would they fail?

CHAPTER 38

EVENT +95:00 Hours
Sweet Valley, Pennsylvania

Vincent looked up at the waning moon, half of it alit with sunlight, and prayed quietly to himself as he crossed Route 4024 in front of Camp Driggers. He wasn't a religious man and didn't really expect any celestial help, but thought it couldn't hurt. Never mind he was violating commandments eight and ten.

He gripped the walkie-talkie in one hand, a small bag of tools draped over his shoulder. Quietly, he knelt in front of the small metal junction box perched six inches above the ground on a conduit that ran up to the gate panel and adjacent camera. That conduit also carried the electrical wiring underground to other parts of the property.

Vincent placed his bag on the soft grass, unzipped it, and pulled out a small ratchet screwdriver. He twisted out a pair of flathead screws, pulled the faceplate from the box and laid them together on the grass.

He made quick work of the wiring, attaching a battery-cell bypass switch to fool the system into thinking it was still on.

The switch was typically used to replace irremovable dead lithium ion batteries in electronic circuits. It was rated to handle continuous current and was perfectly adaptable to Vincent's needs. Once he had the switch attached, he cut the wires supplying power to the fence. For the moment, the power stayed on. Then he hit the switch and held his breath.

No alarms.

Vincent took the ratchet screwdriver, with its plastic handle, and held it against the fence wire closest to him.

Nothing.

He put his tools back into his bag and keyed the walkie-talkie.

***

"Gotcha," Dunk whispered into the walkie-talkie. "Over."

He and his two conspirators were at the northwestern corner of the property. They'd had no problems following the creek bed to the edge of Camp Driggers. Gooz was out of shape and sweating profusely. Bruno was complaining about blisters on his heels. But they made it. And now the fence was off.

"Take the cutters and snap that razor wire along the top," Dunk ordered Bruno. "We'll pull it away once you cut it."

Bruno did as instructed and within a minute all three of them had hopped the fence and were no more than fifteen yards from the rear of the barn.

"There's a camera above us," said Gooz, wiping his forehead with the back of his sleeve. "So don't turn around to give it a shot of your faces."

Bruno resisted the strong urge to spin and look up. But he knew if he did, Gooz might turn him into a pillar of salt. He placed the bolt cutter up against a small pine tree and adjusted the heel on his shoe.

"Let's go," said Gooz, waving the other two to follow him. Crouched low, their bags in hand, the men moved with purpose to the barn, moving to the side opposite the generator.

"Shouldn't we be where the generator is?" whispered Dunk. "So we can hear it shut off?"

Gooz shook his head. "Vince is gonna tell us when it's off. Plus I can hear it from here anyhow." He waved the men to inch their way to the southwestern corner of the barn, ready to enter once the generator was off.

***

Vincent followed the eastern edge of the driveway to the parking circle in front of the main house. There were lights on upstairs, but from what Vincent could see, they appeared to be in the hallway. All of the front-facing downstairs windows were dark.

He sprinted between the garage and the house, careful to lower his head as he approached a camera set high on the soffit of the house. Once on the right side of the house, there were no cameras. It was dark. He moved deliberately to the rear of the house, toward the low rumble and hiss of the generator.

As he reached the generator, he ran his hand along it, feeling the power run up his arm and into his chest. He quickly familiarized himself with the make and model and then darted past the pool to the generator on the eastern side of the barn. It was dark enough that he couldn't see his compatriots as he passed the front of the building.

He knelt beside the generator and placed his hands on it. He knew there were a couple of ways he could shut it down temporarily. He could remove the fuse built into the controller, or he could hit the circuit breakers at the transfer switch. Either way would work.

He looked at the wall to the left of the generator and saw the automatic transfer switch was unlocked. That was the way to go. He popped it open and flipped the breaker. The generator rumbled, spat, and hissed its way to silence.

He keyed his walkie-talkie a second time.

***

"It's off," Dunk said. "Let's go."

The men wormed their way to the front of the barn and pulled the handle, swinging the door inward. A moment later Vincent was behind them, closing the door.

"So far, so good," Vincent said. "Dunk, you and Bruno hit the freezers first. Gooz and I will do the pantry." The men agreed as the battery backup kicked on, repowering the generator.

The freezers beeped and their refrigeration units powered up.

Dunk and Bruno strode to the back of the barn and the pair of walk-in freezers. Neither of them could stop from smiling when they opened the doors and found the treasures inside.

"Gooz," Vincent reconsidered, "you go to the pantry. I wanna look at the security." He nodded to his left, in the direction of the wall monitors. Gooz opened the pantry door and stepped in to begin his work.

Vincent walked to the opposite wall and looked up at the monitors. The security cameras were infrared, as he'd suspected. But the images were relatively poor, inverse black-and-white stop-motion frames. Lana could be looking at the video, Vincent thought, and even if he stared straight into a lens, she wouldn't know it was him.

They were good.

He opened the cabinet beneath the screens and checked the recording device. It was humming along, counting the time on the hard drive, small green diodes blinking on the face of the DVR.

There was a control panel tucked into the wall. All of the security wiring for the property ran through that box. Vincent considered flipping the breaker, but decided against it. That could trigger a silent alarm in the house. They'd already risked it once by turning off the generator for thirty seconds. There was no point in taking another chance.

"Vince," Gooz called from the open pantry doorway. "Dude, get in here and grab your stuff. There's all kinds of food and supplies."

Vincent crossed the barn floor toward the pantry when a wave of nausea stopped him cold.

What have I done? He bent over at his knees and closed his eyes.

"What is it?" Gooz dropped his bag and walked over to Vincent. "You okay?"

"No." Vincent shook his head, unable to look at his friend. "We're screwed."

"What?" Gooz looked around the barn. "We're fine. What's the problem?"

"I wasn't supposed to come in here," Vincent said. "I was supposed to stay outside at the generator to shut off the alarm." He slowly lifted his head and met Gooz's eyes.

"You were, weren't you." Gooz took a deep breath. "We'll just have to run like hell."

Vincent didn't say anything. He cursed himself for being an idiot.

"You might as well grab some food, Vincent," Gooz told him. "We're fine until we open that door."

Vincent nodded and walked to the pantry. He blankly pulled cans and jars from the shelves, unaware of what he was taking. He couldn't focus. His mind wandered to all of the horrible possibilities unfolding in the next ten minutes.

"Vincent." Dunk snapped him from his haze. "Gooz told us what happened. It's cool. We'll get out of here."

Vincent turned and faked a smile. "Maybe." He tied the top of his pillowcase into a loose knot and walked past Dunk into the barn's open space. Bruno and Gooz were standing there, near the door, ready to go.

"What's the plan?" Gooz asked. "As soon as we open that door, the alarm goes off, right?"

"Probably," said Vincent.

"Then we need to run," said Gooz. "Right?'

"Yeah." Vincent nodded, trying to regain his focus. "I think you three go back the way you came. Hop the fence and get into the trees. Follow the creek back to your car and get to Bruno's place. Don't speed. You'll be fine."

"What about you?" asked Dunk. "What are you going to do? You could come with us?"

"No, I can't leave my truck parked across the road from the front entrance," he said.

"You could jump the fence with us and then walk the perimeter to get back to your truck," suggested Bruno.

"That'll take too long," said Vincent. "I just have to sprint straight for the front gate, jump the fence, and hope I drive off before anybody tags me. I'll go home, unload my stuff, and then head over to Bruno's. Cool?"

They all agreed that was the best plan and moved to the door. Vincent grabbed the door handle and pulled inward. "Here we go!"

CHAPTER 39

EVENT +95:05 Hours
Nanticoke, Pennsylvania

Reggie sat in the cab of his truck, counting the cash. All of it was there, one hundred twenty thousand dollars in cash. He looked at the clock on his dash. It was early.

The drop had been easy. No problems.

The meet was at a park bench. Three men were waiting for him when he got there. None of them said anything, though Reggie thought he recognized one of them from Albion. His swastika tattoo wasn't unique, but that it ran across the front of his neck in red and black glory was familiar.

He was frisked and cleared by the largest of them, a bald, mustachioed dude with gauges in both ears. He nodded to Nazi neck that Reggie was clean and then grabbed Reggie by the arm. Reggie was as big as him, but didn't resist. He was outnumbered. And they were armed.

Reggie sat on the bench, his arms folded in front of him, and watched the transfer.

Box by box, the trio unloaded the drugs. They declined Reggie's help when he offered.

Mustache or the third man would carry a box to their awaiting Mercedes GL450. They dropped it into the SUV and cut open the flaps. Nazi neck would then rifle through the boxes, checking the labels and the security caps, making sure they were legitimate and sealed. The process took less than an hour.

Nazi neck walked around to the front of the Mercedes and pulled an envelope from the glove box. He strode back to Reggie, the chains on his motorcycle boots jingling as he walked, and handed him the envelope.

"Count it," he said, his voice deeper than Reggie imagined it would be. "Should be one twenty." The swastika wobbled on his neck as he talked.

Reggie thumbed through the series of fifty- and one-hundred-dollar bills, counting it in his head. He worked through the envelope front to back and then back to front before confirming the amount.

"Tell Kepler we're good," Nazi neck grumbled and spun on his boot heel back to the Mercedes. The two other climbed into the SUV and they sped off, leaving Reggie sitting on the park bench in the quiet.

He sat there for a moment, listening to the cricket and frog symphony in the thick woods behind him. He looked in the envelope again.

It was a lot of money.

He shoved the thought from his mind before it could fully materialize. He'd get his cut and that would suffice. Plus, he reasoned, who knew if cash would have any value in another couple of weeks if the power didn't come back.

It took him less than an hour to get back to Nanticoke. He knew he shouldn't have stopped. Kepler warned him not to do it. But he couldn't help himself. The nectar was too sweet, the siren's song too powerful. Besides, he had more than four hours to kill before meeting Kepler in Wilkes-Barre. It shouldn't take him more than two hours to get there. That was more than enough time for what he had in mind.

He rapped his hands on the steering wheel and looked at the small home in front of him. It was dark and the driveway was empty. That meant Lana was home alone. He could use a little more of her before he ran back to his boss or his wife.

Reggie leaned over and opened the glove box. He pulled out a small bottle and shook out a blue pill. He popped it in his mouth and swallowed it dry. Laughing to himself, anticipating the fun he was about to have, he shoved the bottle back in the glove box and hopped out of the truck. Reggie bounded up to the front door. It was unlocked, so he pushed his way inside.

Familiar with the home's modest layout, he walked past the living room and kitchen and along the narrow hall that led to the bedroom. He stepped lightly, not wanting to wake his conquest. But the floor creaked as he passed the bathroom.

The creak was immediately followed by the sound of mattress springs crunching. "Who's there?" Lana whispered. "Vincent? That you?"

She was in the doorway, in a tank top and matching bottoms, before Reggie could answer. And before he could do anything about it, she was barreling her shoulder into his chest, knocking him backward.

"Who the—" she screamed as her arms flailed against the intruder. "Get the—"

"It's me," Reggie said, grabbing her wrists with both of his hands. He managed to gain his balance against the wall. "It's Reggie. Chill!"

He pressed her, arms above her head, against the wall on the opposite side of the hallway. She spat in his face before registering what he'd just said, her knee about to thrust upward when she heard him.

"Reggie?" She stopped struggling against him. "Seriously? Why wouldn't you—"

He pressed his mouth against hers, muting her complaints.

She relaxed against his body, returning the kiss with aggression.

This was their dance, oblivious to the world around them. Lost in their passion, they didn't consider the risks.

CHAPTER 40

EVENT +95:08 Hours
Sweet Valley, Pennsylvania

Steve Driggers heard the noise first. It sounded like the generator was struggling. He was in bed, his eyes open, listening to the sounds.

At first, he thought it was the generator for the main house. But the rumble was too distant.

The barn?

He checked the tablet next to his bed and punched open the security app, checking the cameras and their status. It was connected to a low-power transmitter on the property that acted as a private, narrow-band Wi-Fi signal. It was just strong enough to let the security system communicate with itself.

"What's wrong?" Kosia rolled over, touching her husband's back. "Is everything okay?"

"I don't know," he said, scrolling through to the right page. "I thought the generator surged." He tapped the screen again and then sat up to make sure he was reading it correctly.

"What do you mean?" Kosia sat up too, rubbing the sleep from her eyes. The tablet's bright screen made it difficult to focus.

"Somebody's here," he said. The security application indicated a temporary power loss. The system was running on a battery backup. But it was only one generator that failed. The others were running properly. They'd suffered no interruption. And from what the system was telling him, the perimeter fence was still electrified. "They're in the barn."

"Could it be one of our guests?" Kosia reasoned, seeing the red alert box at the top of the screen.

"No." Steve shook his head. "They know the alarm is set. Plus, none of them would have a reason to go into the barn. There's plenty of food in the main house, and James has what he needs in the guest cottage." He touched another button to check the series of cameras. They were working. He rewound the recordings past the white noise to six minutes earlier. He couldn't see anything in any of them until—

"See that?" He pointed to a camera aimed at the generator at the side of the main house. "Somebody just moved past the camera! Well, they did about six minutes ago."

"What do we do?" Kosia had her wits about her now. "Do we do anything?"

"Hang on." He switched to a camera at the northwestern corner of the property. Its lens was aimed at the generator powering the barn. He watched twenty seconds of stop motion before he saw the figure move into the frame behind the generator. "There he is again! He's at the barn generator." Steve held the tablet so Kosia could see it and together they watched the figure move to the wall of the barn. The glowing white image stood and opened the door to the automatic transfer switch. Then the screen turned black before the white noise replaced it for thirty seconds. When the image returned, there was nobody there.

"He's in the barn," he said. "No doubt. Someone is stealing from us."

"How would anybody know?" Kosia asked. "How would they know?"

"I don't know." Steve pulled the covers from his body and hopped from the bed. "But I'm not letting it happen."

"Steve," she said, "is that a good idea?"

"Probably not." He shrugged, pulling on a pair of shorts. He reached into a drawer next to the bed and pulled out a revolver. He checked the cylinder to make sure it was loaded. "Get Connor and get into the basement."

***

Max Rockwell knew somebody was outside the open bedroom window. Despite the constant hum of the generator, he could hear someone shuffling around.

Max gently pulled the thin sheet from his body and quietly tiptoed to the window. He looked straight down in time to see someone in black running toward the pool. He couldn't tell if it was a man or a woman. He wasn't even one hundred percent certain it was a person.

He stood there for a moment, his head outside the window, listening for anymore sounds. There was nothing at first, and he was about to go back to bed, convinced what he'd seen was an animal, when there was a rumble in the distance.

It was coming from the back of the property, near the barn. It sounded like a generator had stopped, the ubiquitous hum somewhat less loud.

He listened for another thirty seconds and heard the generator roar back to life. Something weird was happening, he thought to himself.

I better tell my dad.

Max slipped on some shorts, switched T-shirts, and then pulled on some shoes. He was moving toward the bedroom door when his mother's voice stopped him.

"Maxwell," she whispered, "what are you doing?"

Max turned, his hand hovering above the door handle, and sighed. He backed up and walked over to his mother. She was on her side, tucked under a blanket, facing the door.

"I gotta go get Dad," Max whispered, sidling up to his mom.

"Why?" Leigh propped herself up on an elbow. "It's the middle of the night, Max."

"I heard something outside," Max admitted. "I think somebody's here."

"So your instinct is to go running outside?" Leigh's eyes narrowed. "I don't think so."

"But what if they're stealing stuff?" Max pressed. "What if they break into Dad's cottage? Shouldn't we let him know?" Max pleaded with his eyes.

"Fine," she whispered, "but I'm coming with you. Wait for me." She shooed Max away from the bed so she could get up and throw on some clothes.

***

Steve walked down the stairs to the first floor, one hand wrapped around the revolver, the other on the bannister, guiding him down to the foyer.

He had the tablet tucked in his back, and when he got to the front door, he stopped to check it. He set the tablet down on a small table by the front door and then used a keypad on the wall to disable the alarm.

Steve thumbed the door open and slowly pulled inward. He stepped past the threshold onto the porch, leaving the door open.

He stood on the stoop. Quiet. Listening.

Hearing nothing, he stepped off the porch and turned right toward the path leading between the main house and the cottage. He moved quickly, the gun leveled at chest height. His eyes swept left and right as he pressed forward toward the barn.

He passed the cottage and moved to the open area adjacent to the pool. Feeling exposed, he hid behind the aged, thick trunk of a sycamore. He was facing east, toward the pool. He peeked around the trunk to his right; he could barely make out the front of the barn. The moon was unobstructed, but wasn't full enough to illuminate the yard.

Steve stood in the darkness, trying to slow his heartbeat with even breathing through his nose.

In. Out. In. Out.

It wasn't helping. He could feel his heart racing through the pulsing thump in his neck. He wondered if he'd made the right decision by leaving the safety of his house.

***

Kosia started to knock on the Rockwells' bedroom door when it swung open. The women and the sons on either side of the doorway were startled.

"Kosia." Leigh sucked in a breath. "Are you okay?"

"We're moving to the basement," she said. "Steve heard something outside. He thinks it's best if we're downstairs."

"I heard it too," blurted Max. "We were going to tell my dad."

Kosia looked at Max and then at Leigh. "You should join us in the basement. Get Sloane too. I can help you if you need it."

"No." Leigh shook her head. "I'll get her, thanks. What about the Kelly family and the Starlings?"

"They're already on their way downstairs," Kosia explained. "Everybody's going to the basement."

"Tell you what." Leigh reconsidered. "I'll take you up on your offer. Can you grab Sloane? If somebody is out there, I don't want James to be the only one in the dark. Max and I will get him. Then we'll meet you in the basement."

"I don't know," Kosia said. "Even the men are going in the basement. Steve is the only one—"

"Kosia." Leigh was polite but firm. "I appreciate that. But I'm not leaving my sick husband alone. Especially if your husband thought it important enough that everyone else hide in the basement."

***

James Rockwell blinked his eyes open and focused on the wainscoted ceiling high above him. He wasn't sure if the commotion he heard was real or in his dream. He lay in bed, listening for any sounds other than the rhythmic hum and burp of the generator.

Nothing.

He closed his eyes, trying to think himself back to sleep.

Since his conversation with Steve earlier in the day, he'd been preoccupied with the thought that whatever happened nearly four days earlier was more than met the proverbial eye. It was nagging at him in the way that he felt unsettled when forgetting his place in a conversation. There was something out of sorts. But he couldn't put his finger on it.

And then, as he stared at the ceiling, his mind drifted to his family's last night on Peaks Island. They'd stayed up late watching the Perseid meteor shower, mesmerized by the intermittent streaks of fire across the New England sky.

There's something to it.

James pressed his memory, squeezing his eyes to think of lessons past. He'd taken some astronomy courses in college. They were required for a degree in physics. Space and time weren't his area of expertise, but he had better than a yeoman's knowledge of astronomical theories.

He recalled a Venn diagram about comets and asteroids from a survey course. Meteors were gas and dust in the tails of comets. Sometimes they'd contain metals, especially iron, but they were typically little more than burning dirt.

Asteroids were typically larger. They were rock and metal; the surface wouldn't burn off during an atmospheric entry as it would for most small meteors.

Comets and asteroids, he knew from that simple diagram, shared some qualities. Both orbit the sun. Both are active parts of the solar system, likely leftover from its creation. Both are irregular in shape and too small to be considered planets. And both have crashed into Earth.

Could it be?

It was possible, he reasoned. An asteroid hitting the ocean would explain the tsunami. It would account for the chaos along the Eastern Seaboard.

It wouldn't, he thought, be responsible for the breadth of the power outage, however. That had all the signs of an electromagnetic pulse. And wouldn't they have known about an asteroid heading toward the planet? Didn't the government track such things?

He stared blankly at the ceiling, trying to clear his head.

It just doesn't make sense.

James closed his eyes again, letting out a deep breath. He needed to get back to sleep. He was drifting off when he heard someone yelling and the cottage door swung open with a bang.

***

Steve was half hidden behind the tree when he heard the barn door creak open. He was glad he'd neglected greasing it. He peeked around the trunk and saw four figures stumbling over each other to get out of the barn.

Almost immediately, the security alarm started blaring from the main house. It was wailing an alternating high and low pitch. Steve knew it would sound for thirty seconds before going silent.

The alarm caught the attention of the four burglars. Steve saw they were all carrying bags with them. From their size, they all appeared to be men. Steve thought about approaching them, but didn't. He couldn't tell, in the shadows, if they were armed.

Three of the men turned toward the back fence, running west away from the main house. The fourth, however, was running straight toward him. In an instant, he darted past Steve, running between the cottage and the house. The man, dressed in black, was lugging a pillowcase as he ran. Steve froze for a moment and then shook loose the fear.

"Hey!" he yelled at the man, who he saw look over his shoulder as he bolted toward the parking circle in front of the main house. "Stop! Stop! I'll shoot you if you don't stop!"

Steve unglued his feet and started chasing the thief. He had the gun at shoulder level and was ready to fire as he split the cottage and main house. Just as he centered his aim on the man's back, he saw two figures in his peripheral vision.

He almost bowled over Max, who was steps from the cottage with his mom. But he avoided him and kept running. He tripped on a thick oak root to the right of the circular drive, but managed to keep his balance. He was closing in on the burglar as they approached the main fence at Route 4024.

The electrical fence will stop him!

Steve slowed his run as he neared the fence. He stopped and aimed, ready to fire. He knew the fence would slow the man as he tried to grab it.

That didn't happen. Instead, the man grabbed the top of the fence, disregarding the razor wire, and like a steeplechase champion, scaled the fence, landing in the drainage culvert on the other side.

Steve lowered the weapon and darted for the fence. He got there as the man was crossing the road toward a truck. He knew the distance wasn't optimal for a revolver. His accuracy would suffer. But Steve took aim at the man's head and fired a single shot.

***

"Dad!" Max yelled at James as he threw open the cabin door. "Somebody's here! They broke in. Mr. Driggers has a gun!"

"Rock!" Leigh burst across the threshold. She and her son raced to James's bedside before he could sit up. Both of them were huffing, talking over one another. He couldn't make sense of it.

"Okay." He tried to calm them. "One at a time. I can't—"

Pow!

"Was that a gunshot?" asked Leigh, her eyes wide enough for James to see the whites, even in the dark.

"Yes." James pushed himself up, swinging his legs over the edge of the bed. "That was a gunshot."

"What are you doing?" asked Leigh. "You shouldn't be out of bed."

"There shouldn't be any gunshots," James countered, walking stiffly toward the open door. "You stay here."

"Right," said Max, "like I'm staying inside." The twelve-year-old disregarded his father's orders and followed him outside. Leigh trailed a step behind.

James looked southeast, toward the main gate. He couldn't see anything. It was too dark. He stepped off the stoop and walked toward the main house, using the path that led to the circular drive. Standing on the porch was Connor, the Driggerses' son, and Mitch, the Kellys' boy.

"Did you see anything?" James called to them when he was close enough not to yell.

"No," said Mitch. "We heard the yelling and then the gunshot. So we came out here to see what happened."

"I thought you were in the basement?" Leigh asked, stepping next to her husband.

"We didn't make it down there," explained Connor. "My mom and the Starlings are down there with Molly. We came back up to get water from the refrigerator. Mr. Starling was thirsty. The alarm went off. That's when we—"

"Connor?" It was Steve Driggers, walking up to the house. "Is that you? Why are you out here? Why is everybody out here?" He was walking with the gun at his side.

"What happened?" asked Connor.

"Are you okay?" James stepped toward the vet, his eyes on the gun. "I'm assuming you're the one who fired the shot."

"Yeah." Steve walked up the steps onto the porch. "It was me."

"What happened, Dad?" Connor repeated.

"I shot him."

CHAPTER 41

EVENT +95:10 Hours
State Game Lands #206, Pennsylvania

"Did you hear that?" Dunk was carrying his bag and Gooz's. He stopped and turned back, gesturing toward Camp Driggers.

"I heard it," said Gooz. "It sounded like a gunshot."

"Vincent wasn't carrying a gun," added Bruno. "So that's not good."

"No, it's not," said Dunk. "What do we do?"

"We keep going," ordered Gooz. "Nothing we can do for him right now. We gotta keep moving along this creek bed and get out of here. Once we get to the house, we recalculate."

"I don't know." Dunk shook his head, but resumed his march north toward Route 118. "If he got shot, we can't just leave him to die."

"I get that," said Gooz. "But we do him no good by getting shot too."

They walked in silence along the creek bed. It was dark, and they took small steps through the weeds, not wanting to trip and fall down the embankment and into the water.

"You think he's okay?" Dunk asked, the twin bags bouncing against his back.

"No telling," said Bruno. "I mean, I guess it's good that it was only one shot, right?"

"That doesn't mean anything," Gooz said, huffing as he slugged along. "We won't know what happened to Vince until we get back to the house. If he doesn't show up, something bad happened. If he does, we know he's cool."

"Is that the road up ahead?" Bruno pointed with his empty hand.

"I think so," said Dunk, still leading the group.

"You know," said Gooz, his words punctuated by his difficulty breathing, "if Vince is okay, this was a good deal. I mean, he was right. It was like a gold mine."

"It was," agreed Bruno. "I think I got some frozen fish and some chicken. There's, like, cans of beans. I even got a couple of beers from the freezer."

"That veterinarian must be rolling in it," added Gooz. "I mean, did you see all of that stuff? Ridiculous. Did you see the shelves full of burger patties?"

"I grabbed some." Bruno laughed. "And some of the buns too. I didn't get me any ketchup, though."

"Or mustard," Gooz suggested. "I gotta have mustard on a burger. The yellow kind. Not that fancy golden stuff."

"Are you kidding me?" Dunk stopped again. "Are you seriously joking about mustard when we don't know if Vincent is dead? We wouldn't have any of this if it weren't for him. You guys are—"

"You're right," Gooz cut him off. "My bad. Just trying to lighten the mood."

"Like I lightened your load by carrying your bag," said Dunk. "You better hope Vince is okay."

"I do," said Gooz. "Seriously."

***

Vincent heard the shot and then, almost instantly, felt a searing heat in his left shoulder. He'd just reached for the door of his truck when the bullet tore through him, burying itself near his clavicle. Despite the explosion of pain, he managed to open the door, get in the truck, and drive off. He expected more shots to follow, but they didn't.

Instead, he was driving, one-armed, on 4024, north toward Routes 118 and 29. There was no fast way to get back to Nanticoke and his house. He'd have to cope with the pain and the blood he felt sticking to his concert T-shirt. The burning quickly gave way to an intense ache, throbbing with each pulse. He took deep breaths and blew out the air forcefully to refocus his mind on something else, anything else.

He glanced at the seat next to him in the truck, the bag of food he somehow tossed into the cab after getting hit. It was on top of his nine-millimeter handgun. He'd accidentally left it in the truck.

Pressing on the accelerator, he thought back about what had just happened, how he'd escaped with his life. He hoped the guys were long gone and on their way home.

He'd run as soon as he heard the alarm sound. He knew it was coming. In the dark, he thought he saw somebody behind a tree as he sprinted past it. But he couldn't be sure until he heard the man yell at him to stop. Vincent looked over his shoulder. Even in the dark, he recognized the man as the owner. He knew it was the veterinarian as he turned to run faster. He almost ran into a kid and a woman too. He didn't recognize them.

Vincent thought he'd make it. He hopped the fence, landed on his feet, and jumped onto the pavement, closing the distance between him and the truck. He stopped for an instant at the door.

That was my mistake.

He knew he'd let down his guard just long enough for the owner to take aim. He heard the shot; it startled him. It didn't register until he felt the heat and the pain.

Vincent put his left knee on the wheel and felt the front of his left shoulder with his right hand. There was no blood, no exit wound. The bullet was still inside him, lodged somewhere in his arm or shoulder.

Where am I going to get help?

Vincent knew he couldn't go to a hospital. He couldn't risk answering questions from the doctors. And that's if any of the nearby hospitals or clinics were even open. He didn't know of anything that was open since the power went out.

He was breathing harder, sweat pouring into his eyes. He blinked past the sting, keeping his eyes on the road.

By the time he pulled into his driveway, he was nearly blind from the shock. His heart was pounding against his chest, his breathing was shallow. Vincent slammed the truck into park and grabbed the bag and the gun, not noticing the other pickup in the driveway.

Stumbling through the door, he called for his girlfriend, "Lana!" He didn't recognize his own voice. It sounded raspy and weak. He dropped the bag in the hallway outside of the kitchen and, using the wall to keep his balance, worked his way toward the bedroom. The gun was still in his hand.

"Lana!" he cried. "I need your help!" Vincent was light-headed, on the verge of collapse when he leaned into the bedroom, propping himself against the door frame. He could have sworn he heard two voices whispering as he sank to the floor. He was almost certain it was a man who came at him as he collapsed onto his stomach. But it was dark. Vincent was delirious. He couldn't be sure.

CHAPTER 42

EVENT +95:58 Hours
Sweet Valley, Pennsylvania

"Why didn't you shoot more than once?" Kosia Driggers paced back and forth, running her hand along the granite on the kitchen island. "Why didn't you kill him?"

All four families were in the kitchen. The husbands leaned against the bar. The children were seated around the table, as was Leigh Rockwell, Michelle Kelly, and Denise Starling.

"I don't know." Steve shook his head. "After I got him with the one shot, I just…froze."

"You should have killed him," suggested Kosia. "Now he could come back."

"There were three other people too," he argued. "They could come back regardless of whether or not I shot the guy."

"You're sure you hit him?" asked Felix Starling. He took another swig of water from a plastic bottle.

"Yes." Steve rolled his eyes. "Again, Felix, I know I hit him. He grabbed at his shoulder and then used one arm to get in the truck."

"But it was dark," said Felix, tipping the bottle at Steve. "You said it yourself."

"I know what I saw," said Steve.

"So what next?" asked Mike Kelly. "What do we do if they come back?"

"The sun will be up soon," said James. "We can assess what they took, what we can do to reinforce the security Steve already has in place."

"A lot of good it did," chirped Felix.

"Look." Kosia leaned on the island, her glare drilling a hole into Felix Starling. "If you don't like what we've got going here, *Felix*, you are free to find refuge elsewhere."

"That's not what I—" Felix backpedaled.

"It's exactly what you meant." Kosia pointed her finger. "This is my home. My home was assaulted tonight. My safety was threatened. My husband fired a gun to protect us—"

"It's fine." Steve moved around the island to his wife. He put his hands on her shoulders. "There's no point to this. He's every bit as shaken as we all are. I'm sure he's thankful to be here."

"Then he needs to act like it." Kosia looked past her husband's shoulder at Felix and then over to his wife, Denise. "No offense, Denise, but your husband needs to keep his mouth shut."

"I agree," Denise said, giving her husband a look that told the entire room he shouldn't speak anymore.

Felix took a nervous sip from the bottle and cleared his throat. He found a seat on a barstool and said nothing.

"Look," Steve said, putting his arm around his wife's shoulder but speaking to everyone, "we're at four days now. This is where we get testy. Our patience is tested. Our faith wavers. But we'll be fine. Just trust we'll weather every challenge the way we handled the initial outage."

"What can I do to help?" asked James. "I'm sick of lying in bed."

"Nothing," said Steve. "We'll manage with—"

"I'm an adult," said James. "My family is in danger too if those guys come back. I'm helping you do whatever needs doing to make this place as secure as possible."

"I'm buoyed by the fact they weren't armed," said Mike Kelly. "I would think they're probably kids or stupid adults who just came looking for food."

"Good point," said Steve, "but if they were desperate after three days, imagine what they'll do in another week or two. And if they tell anyone else about Steve's stash in that barn, we could face an entirely different animal."

That sent a shudder through the room. The men nodded. The women pursed their lips. The children looked to their parents for comfort.

They knew, without having to be told, there would be more people coming. Others would want what they had.

"Can we handle another kind of animal?" asked James, breaking the uncomfortable silence.

"Yes," Kosia answered. "Without a doubt."

CHAPTER 43

EVENT +96:30 Hours
Nanticoke, Pennsylvania

"Wake up!"

Vincent felt a stabbing pain in his shoulder. Someone was poking at his wound.

"Wake up!"

Vincent opened his eyes. There was the beginning of daylight bathing the room. He was on the floor in the doorway to his bedroom. A man had his knee pressed into the small of his back.

"Wake up!"

"I'm awake." Vincent coughed, his cheek buried in the carpet. He winced against another poke at his wound. "Who are you?" He cursed and tried to slap away the hand.

"Where'd you get this, Vincent?" Reggie held up the pillowcase, letting it hover just above Vincent's face. "You didn't tell me about this, Lana! You didn't tell me your man was out getting food."

"Who are you?" Vincent cried. "Lana? Who is this?" He opened his eyes wide, trying to find Lana.

"Talk to me." Reggie grabbed Vincent's chin and yanked it. "Where did you get the food, Vincent? Tell me where you got it and I get you some help."

Vincent was confused and in pain. "Who are you?" he whimpered. "Tell me who you are and I tell you where I got the food."

"His name is Reggie." Lana stepped into Vincent's line of sight. "He's a friend of mine."

Reggie laughed at that suggestion. "Friend? I wouldn't quite put it that way, baby. But I'm a little upset you didn't tell me what your boy *Vincent* here had working."

"I didn't know," cried Lana. "Leave him alone."

"I was eating bologna," Reggie spat. "I hate that crap. But it's all you told me there was to eat."

"I didn't know, Reggie," she pleaded. "I swear."

"I guess your mouth was too busy to tell me." Reggie laughed.

Vincent swallowed hard against the dry knot in his throat. "Great…" He closed his eyes and winced against the pain, biting into his lip.

"Where did you get it?" The question. Again. Followed by a thumb into the wound. "Answer me, *Vincent*!" He pulled Vincent's gun from the back of his waistband and pushed the barrel against Vincent's head. "Tell me!"

"Stop!" Lana tried to grab Reggie's arm, but he shoved her with his elbow.

"I'm counting to three, Vincent," he snarled. "One…two…"

"A place in Sweet Valley!" Vincent cried out. "A house on 4024 south of 118. Camp Driggers."

"Good job, Vincent." Reggie patted him on the chest and stood up, tucking the gun in his pants. "I'm telling my people about this," he said. "They'll be very grateful for the information."

"But—" Vincent tried to talk, but it came out as an unintelligible whisper.

"I gotta go," said Reggie. "I'll talk to you later."

"Aren't you gonna help Vincent?" asked Lana. "You said you were going to help him."

"Right," he said. "I'm not helping *Vincent*, baby. But I will be helping myself to this food. When we hit that place in Sweet Valley, I'll bring some back for you."

Vincent saw the man step over him and heard his boot steps down the hallway and out of the house. Lana stepped into view and then knelt beside him.

"I'm so sorry," she whispered, her voice cracking through tears. "I didn't mean for—"

"I get it." Vincent tried to wave her off with his good arm. "You were—"

"Don't talk," Lana said. "Save your strength. You've lost a lot of blood."

"Who was he talking about?" Vincent mumbled. "Who is he telling?"

"He's telling—" she started, but stopped when the front door slammed open.

"I thought better of it," said Reggie, storming back into the house, his boot steps banging on the floor as he stomped his way toward the bedroom. "I don't think I'll be back."

"NO!" Lana screamed as she watched Reggie pull Vincent's nine millimeter from behind his back.

He pulled the trigger twice. "You were good," he said to Lana as she fell back onto the floor, her head banging awkwardly against the foot of the bed she shared with two men. "But not that good."

Reggie dropped the gun onto Vincent's chest and spun on a boot heel. He had ninety minutes to get to Wilkes-Barre and tell Kepler what he'd found.

CHAPTER 44

EVENT +97:40 Hours
Sweet Valley, Pennsylvania

"It's not as bad as it could have been." Steve stood in the barn pantry, trying to assess what was missing.

"How's that?" asked James. "It looks like they took half of the stuff on the bottom two shelves."

"They didn't take anything off of the top shelf," Steve explained. "Those are the long-term needs. They last forever. Everything they stole is off of the bottom shelves. They've got short lives."

"Hey, Steve," Kosia called from outside of the pantry. "They took a lot of the meat."

"Again," Steve said to James before answering his wife, "short shelf lives." He turned and walked out of the pantry and into the open space in the middle of the barn. James followed.

Both freezer doors were propped open while Kosia and Leigh took stock of the missing frozen inventory. The men walked up to their wives and stuck their heads inside the walk-ins.

"It's not as horrible as it could have been," said Kosia to her husband. "Some chicken, some fish, burgers and buns."

"They took hamburger buns?" asked Steve, sounding surprised.

"Yes," she said. "But they left the shelled eggs and the wild game."

"They left the duck and the pheasant?" Steve checked the

shelving. "That's good."

"Why is that good," asked James, "as opposed to the burgers?"

"Wild game can last up to a year in the freezer," said Steve. "The fowl we have in there is good for another six months at least. Those burgers were good for maybe a few weeks."

"So they didn't know what they were doing," said James.

"If they had," said Kosia, "they would have been prepared in the first place."

"So"—Steve rubbed his hands together—"despite some losses, we're in good shape. We maybe lost a couple of weeks' worth of food, a month at the outside. But we're fine."

"I feel better." Kosia sighed. "Now we have to figure out how to stop from losing any more. Have you figured out how they got by the fence?"

"They used a battery switch," said James. "It fooled the system into thinking the electrical current was running when it wasn't. They bypassed it."

"It's fixed," said Steve. "Felix flipped the switch on the bypass and closed up the junction box at the entrance. The fence is on again."

"And the generators?" she asked.

"All good," said Steve. "Up and running. Gas flowing. No problems."

"That's a start," said Kosia. "Have you been to the garage yet?"

"That's next," said Steve. "I've got Mike and Mitch Kelly in there now, organizing everything."

"Everything?" Kosia's right eyebrow rose higher than her left.

"Not everything," he said. "I was waiting for that until I had all of the adults together."

"I'll be done here in a minute," said Kosia.

"Meet you there." Steve kissed his wife on the forehead and waved James to follow him out of the barn.

James felt good, considering. The back of his leg was sore and itchy from the stitches. His chest felt tight, but he wasn't coughing as much. And he could take a reasonably deep breath for the first time in three days.

He slipped his hands into his pockets as he followed James across the property to the garage. It was cool for a late summer morning, evidence the autumn was fast approaching.

"So what's in the garage?" he asked Steve as they walked between the house and cottage?

"Toys." Steve looked over his shoulder and smiled. "Things we'll need to keep us safe."

"More guns?" James asked, knowing the answer as he posed the question. "Big guns?"

"Yes." Steve slowed his pace and lowered his voice. "And yes."

"Good to know," James said.

They crossed the parking circle and stepped to the garage. The three bay doors were already open, revealing two large F-350 trucks and a pair of four-wheeled all-terrain vehicles. To the side of the motor pool was a long workbench. Michael and Mitch were busy manipulating a machine James hadn't seen before. It was bolted to the table with two plastic jars flipped upside down at the top. They each contained some granular material. In front of the containers was a large crank lever. Beneath the lever was a series of small red plastic tubes.

"How's it going?" Steve asked.

"Good," said Mitch. "We've got fifty shells reloaded so far. This gadget's pretty handy."

"What is it?" asked James. "Are those shotgun shells?"

"Yes," explained Steve. "It's called a reloader. You crank it here"—he pointed to a lever on the side of the machine—"and it automatically fills the empty hulls with wadding and a tungsten-and-iron-blended powder. They're twelve gauge."

"Where are the guns?" James asked.

"I'll show you." Steve walked toward the back of the garage. "Mitch, Mike, take a break and come look."

"I thought we were waiting for everybody to get here," mentioned James.

"Oh"—Steve laughed—"I'm not showing you everything."

He led them to a door at the back of the garage, pulled out a key, and unlocked it. He pressed a light switch and overhead fluorescents clinked and blinked to life.

What they revealed was like the secret stash of a special agent.

"Wow!" said Mitch. "It's like *Halo* and *Call of Duty* all wrapped into one!"

Along the wall was a series of five identical nickel-finished shotguns. Next to the shotguns were three semiautomatic rifles.

"Wow is right." James stepped to the wall to admire the weaponry.

"Those rifles are super light," explained Steve. "They're nine pounds with twenty-round magazines. They fire thirty-oh-eight. I've got Versa-Pods for them too. Those scopes are good. Night vision."

"You're skilled with these?" asked Mike. "I mean, you're a good shot?"

"Yes," said Steve. "I'm a good shot. That is, when I don't freeze." He lowered his eyes and bit his lip.

"How about your wife?" Mike asked. "Can she handle these?"

"Kosia is okay." Steve looked up at the wall. "But that's why I have the shotguns. They're easy pump action. They weigh about six pounds. And the magazine can hold five rounds. You don't have to be accurate."

"Who doesn't have to be accurate?" Kosia was leading the rest of their guests into the garage. They wove between the trucks and stood outside the gun locker.

"I was just explaining"—Steve cleared his throat—"that you don't have to be accurate with a shotgun. Just pump and fire. The spray will be enough to stop whoever is coming at you."

"So you were showing off the guns?" asked Kosia. She turned to the others who'd followed her. "We have shotguns and rifles to go around. No shortage of guns."

"But that's only part of it." Steve's eyes widened. "We were waiting to show you all the rest of it."

Kosia stepped to the side and Steve walked out of the gun locker. Next to the locker was a second door. Steve unlocked and opened a treasure chest of home defense.

CHAPTER 45

EVENT +97:53
Nanticoke, Pennsylvania

"We should have heard from Vincent by now." Dunk was spooning peas out of a can. He didn't care they were room temperature. He was hungry. "It's bad we haven't heard from him."

"I agree." Bruno was nursing a bottle of water.

"So what do we do?" asked Gooz. "Should we run by his house? Maybe he got stuck with Lana."

"Lana." Dunk moaned. "I can't stand that woman."

"He's whipped," said Bruno. "No other way to explain it." He took a sip from the bottle.

"We should head over there," Gooz decided. "Make sure everything's cool."

"What if he's not there?" Dunk asked, spooning the last pea into his mouth. "What do we do then?"

"We cross that bridge when we get there," answered Gooz.

The three piled into Gooz's truck and drove the short distance to Vincent's house. The roads were empty. None of the men said anything until Gooz pulled into the driveway.

"That's a good sign," said Dunk. "Vincent's truck is here."

"That is good!" echoed Bruno.

They hopped out of the truck and walked up the path to the front door. Dunk looked through the sidelight. It was dark inside, and the early morning sunlight wasn't enough to reveal much. He knocked on the door.

"Maybe they're asleep," Bruno suggested.

"Maybe." Dunk cupped his hands around his face and pressed it to the glass again. "I can't really see anything." He knocked again.

"Let's just go inside," suggested Gooz. "Try the door."

Dunk nodded and gripped the doorknob, spinning it. He pushed against the door and it swung open. "It's unlocked."

"Hey, Vince!" Gooz called as the men stepped into the foyer. "You here?"

Out of habit, Bruno turned to the right and walked into the kitchen. Dunk stepped left and into the living room.

Gooz walked forward, down the hallway toward the bedroom. He'd taken four steps when he saw them. Backlit by the light coming from a bedroom window, it was hard to make out what it was at first. Gooz thought it was a pile of clothing until he took another step. His mind couldn't rationalize what he was seeing. It was too horrible to process.

"Guys," he called, "I found him." It was all he could bring himself to say, blankly stepping to the bedroom doorway.

"Where is—" Dunk was speechless when he saw the blood leaching its way along the carpet. His eyes followed it past Gooz to the heap in the doorway.

"That's good, isn't—" Bruno peeked his head into the hallway from the kitchen. He couldn't see what lay at the end of the hallway. His friends were blocking it. "What's going on?" He stepped into the hall, craning his neck to look around Dunk.

Gooz was at the doorway, looking back at them. His face was sallow, his lips quivering. His hands were at his sides, balled into fists.

In the doorway, facedown on the floor, was Vincent. He had a gunshot to his left shoulder and another in the back of his head, behind his left ear. His eyes were open and fixed. His mouth was open. Just beyond his body, propped like a rag doll against the end of the bed, was Lana. Her legs were splayed open, arms limp at her sides. Her face was racked with pain and fear. The bullet hole in her chest was the centerpiece to a dark, circular stain spreading outward on her tank top.

"How the—" Gooz tried to contain himself, but he screamed and cursed at the top of his lungs. "This makes no sense," he growled.

"It makes sense," said Bruno. "His gun is on his back. I don't see the bag of food anywhere."

"So?" asked Dunk. "What are you saying?"

"I'm saying the veterinarian followed him here and killed him," theorized Bruno. "Then he took his food back."

"I think you're right," said Dunk. "It makes sense. Who else would leave the truck and kill both of them before taking off with the food. Nobody else knew what we were doing."

"We need to go back," Gooz said, kneeling down to pick up the gun.

"Back where?" Dunk asked.

"That camp." Gooz wiped his nose with the back of his hand. "We need payback."

"What are we gonna do, Gooz?" Bruno stuffed his hands into his pockets. "What's your plan?"

"We're gonna go kill every last one of those people," said Gooz. "Then we're gonna move in and make the camp our own."

"Seriously?" Dunk laughed nervously. "How are we going to do that?"

"Vincent's got some guns in his office." Gooz nodded toward the room halfway down the hall. "We'll take those. We'll go tonight. We'll surprise them again. They won't know what to do."

"I don't know—" Dunk hedged.

"You're in or you're out." Gooz stood and stepped aggressively to Dunk, stopping two inches from his face. "Which is it, Dunk? Make a decision now!"

"I'm in." Dunk backed up, raising his hands. "I'm in, okay?"

"They're gonna regret this," said Gooz. "They should have just let the food go. Now they're gonna lose everything."

CHAPTER 46

EVENT +98:07
Wilkes-Barre, Pennsylvania

"You're late," Malcolm Kepler snarled as he strode across the tennis court parking lot. He was holding a Glock sideways, pointing it at Reggie's face. "I told you not to be late."

Reggie was parked on the far side of the lot. He'd gotten out of his truck and started walking toward Kepler and his bodyguard, Berger. He was carrying a pillowcase.

"Seven minutes might as well be an hour, Reggie," Kepler said, his arm fully extended. "Why should I not kill you right now, just on principle?"

"I was busy, Malcolm," Reggie said. "And those bridges across the Susquehanna River are all messed up. I had to go—"

"I don't care why you were late," said Kepler. "I only care that you were. Tell me, again, why I shouldn't kill you right now."

"Two reasons." Reggie was smug, full of confidence. "One, I got your money." He pulled the envelope from his pocket and tossed it at Berger, who caught it with both hands against his chest. "It's all there."

"You were supposed to have the money," Kepler said, "seven minutes ago."

"I also have this." Reggie offered the pillowcase to Kepler. "Look inside."

Kepler hesitated before lowering the gun and tucking it in his waistband. His eyes narrowed and he took the pillowcase from Reggie. He looked inside and shrugged. "What's this?"

"Food. Medicine. Supplies."

"So?"

"You said food and medicine were like gold, right?" Reggie was disappointed he had to explain. It lessened the impact. "You said we're gonna start running this stuff. There's a ton to make off the necessities, right?"

"This isn't enough for a week." Kepler tossed the pillowcase on the pavement. "I can't make anything off of that."

"I know where it came from," Reggie revealed. "I can get months' worth of this, a barn full of it."

"Where?" Kepler folded his arms and tucked his hands under his pits.

"Sweet Valley," Reggie said. "Maybe two hours from here. There's some camp. They've got tons of that stuff."

"How'd you find it?" Kepler nodded at the pillowcase on the ground. "Anybody else know about it?"

"Guy who told me is dead."

Kepler nodded and licked his teeth. "How many people at this camp?"

"Can't be many," said Reggie. "It's a house. They call it a camp."

Kepler turned to Berger. "The money there?"

Berger nodded and handed over the envelope. Kepler counted out three thousand dollars and handed it to Reggie.

"We good, then?" Reggie asked, folding the bills and stuffing them in his pocket.

"We will be after we hit Sweet Valley," Kepler said. "I got seven or eight guys I can use, plus you, Berger, and me. That should be enough, right?"

Reggie nodded.

"They armed?" asked Kepler. "The people in the house?"

"I think so," said Reggie. "The dude who's dead had a bullet wound."

"So these people killed him?" Kepler raised an eyebrow.

"No." Reggie shook his head. "I did."

Kepler sniffed and rubbed the four-day scruff on his chin. He closed his eyes and took a deep breath. "We'll head out in a couple of hours." He craned his neck to the right, cracking it. "We'll hit the place at night. In and out. Anybody tries to stop us, we take care of it."

"All right." Reggie smirked. "I'm in."

"You don't have a choice." Kepler wagged his finger. "This goes wrong, you're there when it happens. And you pay for it. Understand?"

Reggie nodded. "I got it." He reached out to shake Kepler's hand. "But nothing's going to go wrong. This is a sure thing."

CHAPTER 47

EVENT +104:00 Hours
Sweet Valley, Pennsylvania

James buried the paint can in the dirt, just inside the main gate. With a lighter, he softened the bottom of one of Kosia's homemade candles and affixed it to the inside bottom of the can.

"How long will it stay lit?" he asked Steve, who was attempting a similar project just ten feet from him.

"We tested it," he answered, "and even with the lid closed and limited air, it burned for thirteen hours. That's one of the large candles."

James adjusted the clear plastic tubing inserted at the base of the can. The tubing ran from the can, along its side, and above ground. He then took a metal can filled with dry corn flour. He carefully poured the flour, filling the can halfway up the length of the candle.

"How many of these do we have?" James asked. "And where did you put them?"

"We have ten of them," Steve answered. "We'll put five of them here by the entrance. The other five will be at the entrances to the buildings. All of the tubing, and we probably have one thousand yards of it, will run to the air compressors we have set up in the garage. I'll be able to activate the power on those compressors remotely."

"How?" asked James. "There's no Wi-Fi."

"I've got a closed system on the property that operates like a low-power radio transmitter," he explained. "It's not good for web surfing, but it allows me to access the security app on my tablet. I can turn on and off certain power switches through the app."

"You thought of everything." James admired the ingenuity.

"Almost," Steve said. "There's always something one forgets."

"You know exactly where all of them are so we can relight them if needed, right?" James asked.

"Yep." Steve looked at his guest and smiled. "Got it on a grid. We're good."

James took a small container of ball bearings and poured them into the corn flour. He lit the candle and carefully affixed the lid to the can, making sure it was tight. He covered the lid, painted brown, with a light dusting of dirt.

"That's it for me," said James. "I've done three here."

"Good," said Steve. "Why don't you check on Felix?"

"Will do." James stood and dusted himself off. He walked toward the cottage. It was getting warmer, more humid, and James was feeling it. His lungs were better, but not healed. Steve told him that would take at least a week. He cleared the phlegm from his throat as he walked between the cottage and the main house. Felix was there, working with tangled fishing line and cursing under his breath.

"Can I help you, Felix?" asked James, putting his hands on his hips to catch his breath.

"This is overkill," he grumbled. "I'm the radical, paranoid nut job, but Steve has us acting like the Viet Cong."

"It's just a precaution," James said. "Better safe than sorry."

"They were common thieves," said Felix. "They weren't armed that we know of, and they bungled the job at that."

"They could be back," James cautioned.

"I suppose," said Felix, struggling with the line. "But this is just too much. We have guns. Why do we need tripwires or whatever the heck this is?"

"None of us are crack shots," reasoned James, kneeling to help Felix with two tangled lines. "So any way we can delay or confuse the intruders, the better off we are."

"I still think this is our government at work." Felix threaded a large dual-pronged fishing hook onto one of the lines. "They want us begging for their help, their control. I'm telling you that's what this is. Nobody wants to hear it. But it's the truth."

"Maybe so," agreed James. "We can't say it's not what happened, right? I mean, nobody knows for sure." He was placating Felix so they could get the job done.

"That's all I'm saying." Felix's eyes widened. "Don't tell my wife this, James, but I was listening to that radio again."

"I won't say anything." James picked a small hook from a box and threaded it onto a long clear filament.

"They were saying that right before the big explosion and the electromagnetic pulse shut us down, there were streaks across the sky." He spoke just above a whisper. "They've got witnesses up and down the East Coast who saw these fireballs. They were fast and didn't last long. But they were there."

"So what does that mean?" James wondered if it meant his guess about an asteroid was right after all. But he wasn't about to share the theory with Felix.

"It means the government timed it out," he said, his eyes wild with excitement. His hands moved in front of his face as if he were performing a magic trick. "They launched two different attacks at the same time. One of them was hidden. They used the EMP as a distraction."

"Why would they do that?" James asked, slipping another hook onto the line.

"Who knows?!" said Felix. "It's the government. They've got their reasons. Maybe that second explosion, the fireballs were burning chemtrails. You know, the stuff they put in the air to keep us docile and compliant?"

"Hadn't thought about that," said James. "It's certainly a theory." He worked a hook onto the thin clear line and slid it a few inches before tying a knot to keep it in place.

"What a tangled web we weave." Felix laughed as he knotted a hook into place. "I just wish people wouldn't think me a nut for not trusting my government."

"By people," James clarified, "you mean Mike Kelly?"

"Yeah." Felix nodded. "Don't get me wrong, he's a good man. He and Steve Driggers go back farther than I do. Truth be told, I'm only here because my wife is in a book club with Kosia Driggers. I'm the outsider."

"Uh." James raised his hand. "Hello? I think I'm the outsider. Not to steal your title, but we're the freeloaders here."

"True." Felix looked at James and smiled a toothy grin. "Can't deny that."

***

"We should have done this a while ago," said Kosia. She was pouring liquid silicone onto the first-floor windowsills. "By a while ago, I guess I mean three days ago."

Michelle Kelly and Leigh were following Kosia as she moved from sill to sill. Each of them carried bags of broken glass. As Kosia poured the silicone, one of the women would shake out shards of glass onto the sill.

"This is pretty extreme," Michelle said. "When that silicone dries, it's gonna be a pain to remove it."

"It's not as though we'd be sleeping with the windows open anyhow," Kosia answered. "How are you on glass?"

"I'm good," said Leigh. "Plenty of big pieces left."

"Me too," answered Michelle. "Nasty stuff."

"Steve looks at it as a deterrent." Kosia ran her latex-glove-covered finger across the edge of the wooden sill, stopping a drip. "I look at it as a last defense. If somebody gets this close to the house, they're not deterred."

"You think Denise is okay with the kids?" asked Michelle. "She's babysitting four of them, including my teenagers, who might as well be toddlers."

"Denise Starling did this for a living, remember?" said Kosia. "She could watch all of us with her hands tied behind her back. I think she's getting lunch ready too."

"I *am* getting hungry," said Michelle.

"Meals might be a little sparse the next couple of days," Kosia warned. "We need to make up for the loss of the dry goods and meat that were stolen."

"I need some silicone over here," said Michelle.

Kosia obliged. "Here's a dab of it. That good?"

"Yep." Michelle stuck a chunk of ragged glass onto the sill.

"Why did you do this?" asked Leigh.

"To cut anyone who tries to climb into the windows." Kosia turned and looked as if Leigh had asked what letter comes after *A* in the alphabet.

"No," clarified Leigh, "why did you move here, build this place, become a *prepper*?"

"You say prepper like it's a bad thing," Kosia said. Michelle followed with a judgmental stare.

"I don't mean it that way," Leigh explained. "It's just," she hedged, "we had a rough time during the pandemic. My husband wanted to be more prepared this time. He read a lot of books and watched countless YouTube videos. But…"

"But what?" Kosia stopped with the silicone and turned to face Leigh.

"We never took that big step," Leigh admitted. "We talked about it. We bought some supplies here and there. But we never did *this*." She spread her arms, gesturing at the size of Camp Driggers.

"I don't know." Kosia shook her head. "We just did it without thinking too much about it. We talked about what it would take financially. And once we ran the numbers, we knew we had no excuses. We had to do it."

"I'm glad you did," Michelle offered and then looked at Leigh. "We all are."

"Of course we are." Leigh stiffened. "I think you mistook my tone. I'm beyond grateful to be here. We're strangers. You opened your home to us. Don't mistake my curiosity for judgment. I think I wish we'd been more prepared."

"It wouldn't have mattered," said Kosia. "You weren't meant to plan like we did."

"Why is that?" asked Leigh, emptying some glass onto a sill, making sure not to spread too much.

"You were meant to be here"—Leigh smiled—"with us. Everything happens for a reason, Leigh. I believe that with all of my heart."

"Everything?" Michelle questioned, suddenly realizing she was the third wheel in the conversation.

"Everything," said Kosia. "Now let's go eat and relax. It'll be dark soon. Who knows what that'll bring."

CHAPTER 48

EVENT +109:54 Hours
Sweet Valley, Pennsylvania

The sun was low in the sky, casting long shadows across Route 4024 from the west. Gooz couldn't wait any longer. It was time to avenge Vincent's death.

"It's not dark yet," said Dunk. "Shouldn't we wait another fifteen minutes?"

"I agree," said Bruno. "If it's dark, they won't see us."

"Ten minutes," Gooz compromised. "No more than that."

The three were lying belly down in the culvert across the road from the main gate, in roughly the same spot where Gooz and Vincent had run reconnaissance the day before.

Gooz looked through the binoculars, only able to see the east-facing side of the garage and a truck parked in the traffic circle. He didn't see any people.

"You think we're smart to come in the front?" asked Dunk. "Would it be better to hop the fence like we did last night?"

"I think a frontal attack is better," said Gooz. "Like we planned, we jump that main gate and split up. The alarm will go off. Somebody will come running outside and we ambush him. Once that hero is down, we hit the house. We take out whoever else is inside."

"What if there are kids?" asked Bruno.

"What if?" Gooz shrugged callously.

"We're killing kids now?" Dunk said. "I don't—"

"I'll do it!" snapped Gooz. "This is for Vincent. They've got what's coming."

Dunk and Gooz exchanged glances but said nothing.

From their right they could hear the rumbling of loud engines gunning toward them. The men ducked behind the weeds and pressed themselves as flat as they could to the ground.

The sound amplified as three large trucks and a SUV approached from the northeast. They slowed as they neared Camp Driggers front gate but didn't stop. Instead they kept heading along Route 4024 to the southwest, speeding up once they passed the southernmost edge of the property.

"What was that?" asked Dunk as the rumble faded, blending with the sounds of crickets and frogs.

"I could only see the guys in one of the trucks," said Bruno. "They definitely were looking at the camp. No doubt."

"I saw that too," said Gooz. He started to push himself from the ground when the rumbling returned. It was getting louder again. "They're coming back!"

On cue, the trucks sped into view, powering over a small rise before stopping just before the main gate, idling in the middle of the road. The SUV trailing the trucks pulled onto the shoulder and parked in the weeds just fifty yards from Vincent's gang.

Gooz turned to his left, still on the ground, and watched a muscular man in a white, ribbed tank top, torn jeans, and motorcycle boots hop from the SUV and walk toward the truck leading the caravan. He disappeared behind the truck, but Gooz could see underneath it and could tell the man was stopped at the driver's side window. He couldn't hear what they were saying over the engine noise.

"What are they doing?" Dunk whispered.

Gooz shook his head as the trucks slipped into reverse, one by one, and backed up to the shoulder ahead of the SUV. The drivers shut off the engines and it was quiet again.

One by one, a parade of shaved-headed storm troopers jumped

from the trucks onto the road. They were all dressed similarly: T-shirts or muscle-baring tanks, jeans, black boots, and sleeves of tattoos on their arms or necks.

It was nearly dark, but their white shirts made them visible as they huddled together just twenty yards from Gooz, Bruno, and Dunk. The childhood friends, partners in crime, had a decision to make.

"They're gonna beat us to it," said Bruno. "They're here to rob the place."

"Who *are* they?" asked Dunk. "How do *they* know about it?"

"I don't know," said Gooz. "But I'm going to talk to them."

"Wait." Dunk grabbed Gooz's arm. "I don't know about that. There's, like, ten of them. There's three of us."

"I'm just going to talk to them," said Gooz. "See if we can work something out."

"We should just let this go," Bruno said, "wait, and see what happens."

Gooz shook his head and stood up, brushing himself off. He took a step toward the pavement when eight of the ten skinheads spun around and leveled semiautomatic rifles at him.

Gooz raised his hands above his head. "Whoa, brothers!" he said as he walked toward the group. "No need for that."

One of the two men not holding a rifle stepped toward Gooz. He was wiry and muscular like a runner. "Who are you?" he demanded as he marched.

"Hey." Gooz slowed and offered his hand. "I'm Gooz. And it looks like we share a similar interest."

"What interest is that?" Malcolm Kepler looked at Gooz's hand but didn't shake it.

"The camp right here." Gooz nodded toward the fence to his right. "That's why you're here, right?"

"Why I'm here has nothing to do with you." Kepler folded his arms across his chest, sticking his thumbs under his biceps to make them appear larger. "You should leave."

"I can't do that." Gooz smiled and shook his head. "I've got some personal business in there."

"I don't care what your business is," said Kepler. "I told you to leave." He uncrossed his arms and put one hand behind his back.

"I don't think you understand," Gooz explained, turning to point at the camp. "My—"

The bullet hit Gooz right behind his left ear. He never finished his explanation. Instead, his neck snapped to the side and he fell over like a tree. Kepler stepped over to Gooz's convulsing body and put another bullet in his temple.

He stared at Gooz for a moment, kneeling down beside his face to watch the life seep from his eyes. There was something about a dead man's eyes that fascinated Kepler. He could have stared into them for an hour if it had not been for the blood pooling under his boots or the noise he heard in the weeds about fifteen yards ahead of him.

"Who's there?" he called, standing to step over Gooz's body. "You best get up or you're gonna die in the dirt." Kepler looked back at his men and nodded for a couple of them to join him.

Berger and another thug, gripping their rifles with one hand, the stocks stuck into their armpits as they moved, marched to their leader. They caught up with him in time to see two men rising from the weeds, their trembling hands above their heads.

"We didn't see anything," called the more muscular of the two. "We'll just take off."

"That isn't happening," Kepler snarled. He stopped at the edge of the road, his arms at his sides. "Who are you?"

"I'm Dunk," said the muscular one. "This is Bruno."

"Why are you here?" Kepler raised his right arm, leveling his handgun at Dunk.

"Same reason you are," answered Dunk. "We just—"

The first bullet hit Dunk in the chest, the second in his forehead. He grunted once and crumpled into the weeds. Bruno's arms started shaking violently.

"You don't know why I'm here," Kepler said to Bruno, aiming at his chest. "Why are you here?"

"We're here to kill the owner and take his stash." Bruno's voice was as unsteady as his legs. "But you can take it."

"Thank you," Kepler sneered. "Where is the stash?"

"It's in a barn at the back left corner of the property. There's a main house and a smaller house in front of it. From the road here, you can see the garage. I don't think there's anything in the garage. But I don't know."

Kepler snorted and spit into the weeds. "Now, I want you to leave. And I want you to tell all of your friends what just happened here. My name is Kepler. We are the United Brothers. Got that?"

Bruno nodded, his elbows dropping to his sides.

"Repeat it," Kepler ordered.

"You're K-K-Kepler," Bruno stuttered. "And you are the United Brothers."

"Good boy." Kepler waved the gun to the left, toward the northeast. "Now get going."

Bruno ran toward his truck, but Kepler called after him. "Not the truck," he said. "Walk!"

Bruno bypassed the truck and kept running. He disappeared into the darkness.

"Why'd you let him live?" Berger stepped to his boss. "He's just gonna rat us out."

"That's the point." Kepler tucked the gun in his waistband and strode to the abandoned truck. "I want him telling people. You leave a survivor, someone to tell the tale of your brutality, and the legend grows. Kill everyone, and nobody has a clue what you're capable of doing."

They reached the truck and found a couple of shotguns in the bed. There was nothing else of value. Kepler left the guns in the truck.

"We'll take this when we leave," he said. "Now it's time to do our thing."

CHAPTER 49

EVENT +110:00 Hours
Sweet Valley, Pennsylvania

"Rock, did you hear gunshots?" Leigh asked James. They were sitting in bed in the main house, having decided it was safer to have everybody together.

"I did," James said. "Four of them. They were close."

"What does that mean?" asked Max. He was on the floor, performing a "puppet show" for Sloane. Noodle was the star.

"I don't know," James said. "It could be a hunter."

"Or those guys coming back?" Max suggested.

"I don't—"

"James? Leigh?" Steve was at their door, knocking loudly. "James?"

"Come on in," James said, and Steve swung open the door, bounding into the room.

"We have a problem." Steve was pale, his breathing interfering with his speech.

"What?" James got up from the bed and led Steve out into the hallway, closing the door behind them. "What's wrong?"

"There are eight to ten men outside of our gate." Steve's eyes were wide with fear. "Maybe there are a dozen of them." He was talking with his hands. "I can't tell. It's dark and the infrared on the cameras just gives me green blurry shapes."

"Tell me more." James tried to keep Steve calm. This was the first time he'd seen his host flustered.

"They're armed. Heavily." He huffed. "And I don't know what happened out there, but they already killed at least one person."

"The gunshots?"

"Yes." Steve pointed toward the front of the house. "I know they killed one. I could see the body drop on the camera to the right of the gate. There are two cameras, actually. They both captured it."

"You think they killed more?"

"Well"—Steve was searching for words—"they, uh, walked out of frame. Then, uh, there were, uh, two more gunshots. So I don't know. But one camera at the far northeast corner, next to the fence, caught one person running away."

"Is everyone here accounted for?" James asked. "Is everyone in the house?"

Steve nodded. "Everyone is heading to the basement. Do you think we activate the plan?"

"Yes." Calm swept over James as he talked, as he listened. His mind was clear. He was focused. It was the same sensation he'd felt on Peaks Island when he watched the red and purple glow bloom on the horizon. He knew what had to be done. He would make it happen.

"But with that many men?" Steve questioned. "Can we hold them off?"

"We don't have a choice," James said. His voice was even and soothing. "Our job is to protect our families and your resources. They will take both from us if we don't fight. Do you understand, Steve?"

Steve nodded, but his mind was somewhere else. Somewhere dark. He'd gone to the worst possible outcome and let it control him.

"Steve." James put his hands on Steve's shoulders. "Look at me. We can do this. Now go down to the basement. I'll get my family. We'll meet you there. And then we act."

"Okay." Steve sucked in a deep breath and exhaled. "Okay." He turned and walked down the long hall to the stairs.

James opened the bedroom door. His family was together on the bed. Sloane was in Leigh's lap. Max had his arm around his mother. They were looking for comfort James couldn't give them.

"We need to go to the basement," James said. "Everybody's down there. It will be safe there. We'll be okay, but we need to hurry."

"There's no hunter, Dad." Max pushed his body closer to his mom. "Is there?"

"No, son," James admitted. "There isn't."

CHAPTER 50

EVENT +110:15 Hours
Sweet Valley, Pennsylvania

Reggie checked the hook. It was securely looped through the winch line, which ran from the front of his truck through the left side of the main entry gate. His was one of two trucks equipped with an automatic winch on the front end. Both were ready to go.

"They're secure," Reggie told Kepler. "We can start."

Kepler turned to Berger and the other men standing in the middle of Route 4024. The men looked like mercenaries. Kepler nodded his approval.

They were armed with matching Sig Sauer SIG516 Patrol rifles. The gas-piston-operated killing machines were loaded with detachable thirty-round magazines. They were super light, at just over seven pounds, and packed a lethal punch. Kepler got a dozen of them in a trade for a kilo of glass-grade crystal meth a few months earlier. It was street value for wholesale trade. At the time, Berger questioned the fairness of it, thinking Kepler got taken. But as Kepler stood in the street, reviewing the troops, he knew he got the better end of the deal.

"Listen, brothers," Kepler growled, "this is gonna be fast. As soon as we rip off that gate, I want three of you headed for the main house. It'll be the biggest building."

"Where is it on the property?" asked one of the men. "How do we know?"

"We don't know the layout," said Kepler. "Doesn't matter. Look for a house. It'll have lights on inside, I'm sure. The barn is gonna be behind the house somewhere. Back left corner."

"How many to the barn?" asked Berger.

"Three to the garage, which is right up here." Kepler pointed with two fingers, then his arm swept to the left. "Then back there, in front of the barn somewhere, is a second, smaller house. I want three men there."

"And the barn?" Berger repeated.

"Nobody to the barn, yet," said Kepler. "We need to clear the property of threats. The barn will be last."

"Do we enter the house?" asked Reggie.

"Yes," said Kepler. "Reggie, you lead the team to the house. I'll lead the team to the small house. Berger, you take the garage. That leaves one extra man. I want you to float. Look for issues and eliminate them as you see fit." Kepler pointed to a short, muscular grunt named Frederick. "Fred. That's you."

The men mumbled their approval and Kepler twirled his hand in the air. "Let's do this. We meet at the barn."

Two men jumped into the cabs of the trucks, cranked the engines and slammed into reverse. Within fifteen seconds, the gate exploded off its hinges. Camp Driggers and the thirteen people inside the fence were exposed.

***

"You good?" James looked at Steve, assessing whether or not the vet would have the guts to follow through. "Do you want me to run the controls?"

"No." Steve shook his head and whispered, "I need you on the rifle. I'll handle the controls."

The men were in the tree house, quietly perched twenty feet above the ground. With night-vision scopes, they could see the men gathered on the street. They watched as the men attached a pair of winches to the front gate. They could almost hear the barking of the man in charge as he pointed and waved his hands.

James was lying on his belly, legs spread wide for stability. He held the stock of the semiautomatic rifle against his shoulder. His cheek was pressed toward his arm. He looked through the scope, pivoting his view using the Versa-Pod under the barrel.

"I haven't shot one of these before," he admitted to Steve. "But I think it's probably the same as a twenty-two, right?"

"Yeah." Steve was sitting on his knees, his attention shifted to the tablet controls. "A little more kick, though. That's thirty caliber. Make sure you have the stick pressed tight to your shoulder, or it'll kick and hurt you."

"I'll be good." James followed one of the men as he got into the cab of a winch-pulling truck. His view was momentarily obscured by a tree toward the front of the property.

"I hope so." Steve exhaled. "I hope so."

***

Mike Kelly watched the gate explode from his spot near the garage. He was seated on an ATV, ready to crank and go when he got the signal. His heart was thumping against his chest. His hands were sweating as he gripped the handlebar. A lot of their success would rely on his ability to start the engine unnoticed and cross the circular driveway as fast as possible.

If his timing was off by just a couple of seconds, he'd be useless, and it would expose the main house. He was determined not to let the men get to the house.

He took a deep breath and wiped his hands on his shirt, thinking about his wife, Michelle, and their children. Michelle was the consummate wife. She was supportive and forthright. Even when they argued, as married couples do, they did it out of love for their family. They would celebrate twenty years together in just a couple of months.

Mitch was a starting safety on the football team. He was popular with his peers, and he'd done so well on the math portion of the SAT, schools from both coasts were pursuing him as a junior. He wanted to go to the Naval Academy and serve his country. Mike believed Mitch had a good shot at an appointment.

Molly was on the freshman cheerleading squad. She'd practiced so hard all summer to make the team. It had taken her weeks, and a lot of sore muscles, to perfect an aerial cartwheel. She cried at dinner when she announced her new skill.

Now, Mike knew, the three of them were prisoners in a basement, praying he would do his job. He knew they were scared for themselves and for him. He loved them so much.

***

Felix stood at the base of the stairs, looking up at the only entrance to the basement. There was a two-by-four held by a pair of wall brackets blocking the doorway. He hoped it would be enough as a last line of defense.

He held the shotgun at his side. Not hearing any commotion yet, there was no need to take aim. Felix felt both relieved and emasculated that Steve had assigned him to the basement. He didn't want to be out there in the fray, as it were. But it would have been nice to be asked.

Instead he was the guardian of the women and children. He was the lone shepherd protecting the flock from the pack of wolves they knew were coming.

"Do you think our dads will stop them?" asked Sloane. She was sitting in a beanbag chair behind Felix, her stuffed bear on her lap.

"I do," said Felix. He said it with more certainty than he truly felt. "They're strong men," he added. "They're smart. They'll protect us."

He turned around, his back to the stairs. Sloane's brother, Max, was sitting on a sectional sofa. He was between his mother and Connor Driggers. Connor and Max were talking to each other softly.

Michelle Kelly was at the other end of the sectional with her daughter, Molly. She was chewing on her cuticles, staring at the coffee-colored Berber carpet that ran wall to wall.

Molly was leaning on her mother's shoulder, feet tucked underneath her. She couldn't get close enough, Felix observed. As if, somehow, she wanted back in the womb: warm, protected, senses muted from the harsh reality outside.

Leigh and Kosia were sitting opposite the sectional at each end of a worn love seat. Neither of them were talking. Both of them had their eyes closed. Felix believed Kosia was praying silently. Leigh, he thought, might be asleep.

His gaze drifted to the corner of the room and an old rocking chair. Gently pushing her toes against the floor, cradling herself back and forth, was his beloved Denise. She was as beautiful as the day they met, forty-eight years earlier.

She was out of his league. They both knew it. But he worked hard to gain her affection and then build a life for the two of them.

Real estate was a hard job, long hours, flaky clients.

"Buyers are liars." Felix would come home, dropping his briefcase by the back door at the end of a particularly long day of carting around house hunters. "You can't trust them as far as you can throw them."

"What about sellers?" Denise would ask, putting the finishing touches on a homemade chicken pot pie or slab of pork chops. "Do they lie?"

"No," Felix would answer. "They can't lie. Their house is their truth. And you can't hide the truth when it's getting inspected six ways to Sunday."

They'd never had children. Not that they didn't try.

Felix leaned the shotgun against the wall adjacent to the stairs and crossed the room to his wife. He knelt down in front of her in that chair, her toes still pushing up and down. Up and down.

Denise looked at her husband and smiled. He was a good man, a little short-tempered and prone to believe the latest, greatest conspiracy, but a good man who she knew loved her. She reached out as he touched her knee, putting her hand on his.

"I love you." Tears welled in his eyes. "I want you to know that."

"You don't have to tell me, Felix," she said, swallowing back her own inclination to cry. "I know. And I love you too."

In the distance, above them and outside the house, was a large metallic explosion. It was beginning.

***

"They're in three groups of three," James said to Felix. "One man is by himself."

"So there's ten of them," Steve responded. "Ten total?"

"As far as I can tell through this scope." James could see the groups assembled at the fence line. They hadn't crossed the threshold into the yard.

"Tell me when!" Steve said. "Tell me when!" He punched his screen, bringing up the power control function on the security application.

"Okay," said James, his right eye hovering at the end of the scope. He was tracing their movements. "They're about to move."

"Tell me when!" Steve was whispering as loudly as was possible. His finger was hovering over the tablet.

"All right." James saw one of the groups set to move. They were at the main gate. "Get ready." The group moved across the fence line. "NOW!"

Steve hit one of the power buttons on his tablet. It sent a signal to a wireless adapter plugged into a GFCI outlet in the garage, closing the circuit and supplying power to an air compressor.

In that same instant, the compressor forced just enough air through forty yards of plastic tubing and into two of the buried cans at the main entrance. The air puffed into the cans, blowing the corn flour into a cloud. But nothing happened.

"Did you push it?" James asked, his trigger finger ready to pull if necessary.

"Yes!" Steve pushed the button again. Nothing. "It's not working!"

"Try another one." James saw a second group of three men start across the opening. They were headed toward the garage. The first group was heading for the parking circle. "Do it now!"

Panicking, Steve hit each of the other power buttons in succession, triggering every remaining can simultaneously. This time it worked.

In seven of the eight cans, the cloud of ball-bearing-laced corn flour exploded when blown into the lit candles, the result of the stored chemical energy in the flour reacting with the heat of the candle flames. Though they were relatively small, they were violent.

The ball bearings found their way into two of the men headed for the garage. They fell to the ground, rolling in pain.

To James, they were green heaps undulating against the earth. He took a deep breath and exhaled before pulling the trigger twice.

Thump! Thump! The suppressed bullets, traveling at twenty-six hundred feet per second, buried themselves in one of the men before James had released the pull. The green blob wasn't moving anymore.

He shifted the Versa-Pod and found the other target. He took a deep breath, exhaled, and pulled twice more.

Thump! Thump! He was true again. Both slugs found their mark, putting an end to the man's searing pain.

"Holy—" Steve looked through his scope.

"I know." James couldn't believe it either. He licked his lips and tried to focus on the mission, disregarding what he'd just done.

***

Berger was knocked to the ground, his side catching a few ball bearings. But he quickly regained his feet and kept moving to the garage.

His ears were ringing and he was disoriented. He looked over his shoulder and saw his two men on the ground. They were screaming for help that wasn't coming.

Berger could have sworn, as he glanced back, he saw a pair of muzzle flashes in the sky. He convinced himself it was the afterglow of the explosion.

Was it an explosion? What exploded? Am I still headed in the right direction?

He stopped halfway between the gate and the garage and bent over at his knees. Closing his eyes to fight his lack of equilibrium, he composed himself and stood up. Readjusting his weapon, he deliberately walked to the garage. He had his rifle waist high, sweeping it from left to right as he swiveled his neck, looking for another booby trap.

There was nothing. Straight ahead was the garage. The entrance was facing southwest, parallel to Route 4024. To its left was a parking circle. But it was dark, and as Berger followed the driveway closer to the garage, he heard a clicking sound and then the high-pitched rev of a small motor.

His hearing compromised, he couldn't distinguish from which direction the sound was coming. But it was getting louder. He swung to the right and saw nothing. To the left, he could see a truck parked in the circle. Was someone in the truck?

No! It wasn't the truck.

***

Mike Kelly couldn't get the engine to turn over. As soon as he saw, and felt, the explosions throughout the grounds, he tried starting the ATV.

That was the plan, crank it when the attackers were disoriented and unable to distinguish one sound from another. He kept pushing the start button, but all it would do was answer him with a weak clicking sound.

I'm screwed! Mike thought. But he kept turning the key and pushing the start button.

Finally, as he was about to abandon his post, the engine revved. It surprised Mike, almost knocking him from his seat. But he recovered, pulled a pair of night-vision goggles over his eyes, and spun the throttle with his right hand.

He didn't see anyone at first. There were hot spots from the explosions glowing as tiny orbs in his goggles. But then he saw him. A man, dazed and off balance, walking toward the garage. Mike was surprised to find only one man, but he was relieved.

He cranked the throttle more, accelerating the ATV over a small mound in the yard, bouncing toward the man. Mike could see the man was armed. The dark shadow of his rifle stood out against the green glow of his body.

Mike closed the distance quickly, closing his eyes as he whirred past the man, missing him by inches. He couldn't tell if the contraption had worked until he heard the thud, the grunting, and felt the tug of two hundred and forty pounds of muscle dragging on the ATV.

Attached to the side of the ATV, just in front of the rear wheels, was a piece of iron reinforcement bar. The rebar caught the attacker at the shins, knocking him off his feet and into a large vinyl-mesh net that was attached to a tow bar on the back of the four-wheeler.

Mike sped toward the tree house, without his headlight on, pounding across the open space of the yard, past the cottage house to the southwestern corner of the property.

"I got him!" Mike called up to Steve and James.

James stood from his perch, pulled the .308 semiautomatic into his shoulder, sighted the catch still writhing in the net, and fingered the trigger twice.

Thump! Thump!

The man in the net screamed once and then was silent.

Three down, thought James. *Seven to go.*

***

Kepler and his team felt the explosions behind them and saw five more blow in front of them. He yelled at his team to get down. They threw themselves into the grass and dirt, assessing the situation.

"What was that?" asked the man to Kepler's right.

"Some sort of IED," Kepler cursed, standing up. "Who *are* these people?"

"Should we quit and go back?" the man suggested, climbing to his feet. "Give up? Try later? I could—"

Kepler put his rifle into the man's chest and held the trigger, shredding him with a dozen bullets. "We're not quitting! Are we?" He turned to the man to his left, who shook his head and started marching for the cottage ahead of Kepler.

Both men reached the cottage door at the same time. Kepler tried the handle and the door opened. He burst into the dark room and unleashed another torrent of gunfire, spraying indiscriminately. Winded, he reached with his right hand and found a light switch, which he flipped.

The room alit in a bath of yellow light from the ceiling fixture. Kepler and his sidekick waded through the lead-splintered debris and found nothing of value.

"There's nobody here," he snarled. "It's empty."

"What do we do next?" asked the sidekick. "I'm with you."

"The barn," said Kepler. "Reggie's got the house. Berger has the garage. We go to the barn."

The men exited the cottage and turned left toward the path leading toward the barn. At the edge of the cottage they made another left, marching northwest. The sidekick was two paces ahead of Kepler, jogging between the cottage and the rear of the house when the sidekick screamed.

"My eye!" he yelled. "My eye!"

Kepler lowered his weapon and took one more step before he felt a tug at his cheek, another at his neck. He tried to move away from the pressure but couldn't. He was caught. The more he struggled, the worse it became, until whatever had embedded itself in his cheek tore its way free.

"I can't see!" The sidekick was flailing. "Help me!"

Kepler realized, amidst the pain, he was tangled in something. He dropped his weapon and tried to work his way free. He couldn't. He was trapped in fishing wire. Hooks were catching his shirt, his pants, his arms.

With every movement, it got worse. "AGGGGHHHH!" he yelled in frustration against the din of the sidekick's squeal.

Who are these people?

Then he saw them emerge from the darkness beyond the cottage.

Three of them. All of them with night-vision goggles. One of them with a rifle leveled at his head.

He heard both thumps that silenced the squealer. He only heard the first of the two that hit him.

***

Frederick joined Reggie and his men as soon as the cans exploded. The four of them waited a beat before moving across the threshold into the yard.

They moved past two men dead in the yard to the left. Quickly, they moved to the right, around the far side of the garage.

"I'm taking us straight up the middle," Reggie said to his group. "They'll expect it. Follow me."

Crouched low, he slowed his pace at the sound of a high-pitched whirring motor. It whined and accelerated past them and to the left, zooming past the garage and toward the parking circle at the middle of the property.

He waved his men between the garage and northern fence, all four of them gliding to the right side of the house. Reggie stopped the four of them there, near the generator.

"Do you hear that?" Reggie asked. "Is that Kepler yelling?"

"I hear someone crying like a girl," whispered Frederick.

"What's next?" one of the other two men asked, his back pressed against the house. "Where do we go?"

"Calm down," said Reggie. "We're fine. They've blown their wad. They don't know we're here."

"You sure?" asked Frederick.

"We're golden," he snarled. "We're gonna get ours. Don't worry."

"What's the plan?" asked the nervous one.

"You and your partner there"—Reggie pointed his gun at both guys he didn't know—"you go around the back of the house. Try the windows. Look for a back door."

"And me?" Frederick shrugged.

"You and me are going around the front," instructed Reggie. "Same idea until we find our way inside."

"Then the barn?" asked nerves.

"Then the barn," said Reggie, moving to the front of the house.

***

James was alone at the back side of the house. Mike and Steve went to the cottage to grab a pair of shotguns from under the bed. They were the backup/emergency weapons. And James knew they might need them.

There were still four men alive. And as James lay belly down in the grass, he saw two of them. They emerged from the opposite side of the house, near the generator. Both of them were armed and they were moving cautiously. One of them approached a back window on the first floor and then backed away from the house. But they were too close to the home for James to risk taking a shot. He could miss and a bullet could hit the gas generator, or worse, he could put a bullet through a wall and hurt someone on the inside. The women, children, and Felix were supposed to be in the basement. But he couldn't be sure.

Think! James. Think!

James knew the men couldn't see well. Clouds had covered whatever moonlight might have helped them. They also didn't know there was a pool between them and him.

James pulled himself to one knee and leveled the rifle so he could see through the scope. The men were still checking the house, but they'd moved into just the right spot.

"Help!" James screamed. "Help me! They got me. They got me!"

The men turned and started running toward James, their rifles at the ready. They couldn't see him. But they could hear him.

"Help!" he cried again, just as the first of the two men stepped off the deck and into the pool. The second man followed a step behind.

James marched to the opposite edge of the pool, moving to his left and away from the sound of his voice. He stood silently, in the dark, as the men emerged from the water, stunned and gasping for air.

Neither of them found it before James fired four more shots.

Thump! Thump! Thump! Thump!

"Eight down," James murmured. "Two to go."

***

Reggie and Frederick ignored the scream for help and the splash of someone falling into a pool or pond. They were focused on getting inside the house.

"The fewer brothers left," reasoned Reggie, "the more we keep."

Frederic nodded in agreement.

"Try that window!" Reggie motioned to what look liked a half-open window next to the front door. "I'll help you up." He clasped his hands together, and Frederick stepped into them, lifting himself up so he could push up on the bottom of the wooden sill.

"It's open!" Frederick looked down at Reggie and then dropped his knees onto the sill to climb in. As he did, two large shards of glass split the skin and drove their way into the joints. As he let loose a blood-curdling scream, he lost his balance. He tried to catch himself with his hands. But they too found glass, which tore through his palms as he fell backwards onto the ground.

Shaken, Reggie stepped back from Frederick and watched him shudder with pain. Then, thinking better of it, he swung his rifle around, pressed its barrel into Frederick's forehead, and fired once.

Incensed, Reggie stepped to the front porch and aimed his rifle at the front door. He opened fire, torching the deadbolt, freeing the door from its hinges.

He was in.

***

In the basement, they could hear the explosions, the crack of rifles, and the occasional scream or call for help. They couldn't do anything about it but wait.

Then they heard the front door bang open.

Someone would knock at the door at the top of the stairs. Someone would be alive and would come for them.

The question each of them wondered privately, to themselves, was who that someone would be.

"I think we should turn off the lights," Leigh suggested. "That way, whoever comes to the door won't be able to see us."

"I don't want the lights off," whined Sloane. "I don't want to be in the dark."

"I think it's a good idea, Leigh," said Felix. "But I'm afraid it'll only cause more problems. We either stop them at the door. Or we don't."

Everyone agreed with Felix. He was in charge.

Kosia grabbed her shotgun from beside the love seat. Mitch grabbed his.

The two of them joined Felix at the base of the stairs. Waiting.

They could hear banging and cursing overhead. Someone was looking for them. And it wasn't their husbands.

Sloane recoiled against every loud noise from above. Max pulled her onto his lap and held her. He whispered in her ear to calm her.

They could follow the footsteps above as they stomped across the floor, moving from one side of the house to the other. Then they stopped.

"It's too quiet," said Kosia. "I don't like this."

Bang! Bang! Bang! "Open up! Open this door!"

He'd found them.

"I know you're in there," he growled. "Open the door or I'm doing it!"

"What do we do?" asked Leigh.

"Shoot him when the door opens!" said Felix.

Bang! Bang! Bang! "That's it! I'm coming in."

An explosion of wood and metal followed as the man opened fire on the door. He sprayed it from top to bottom, leaving little more than a jagged fence post of a door, which he kicked in, and he started down the steps.

He didn't make it past the first one.

Kosia, Felix, and Leigh all fired at least three shots at him as he took his first step. At the same time, Steve and Mike Kelly hit him in the back and side. They'd burst into the house just as Reggie opened fire.

Full of homemade shotshell, Reggie hovered for a moment before tumbling head over feet down the stairs. He landed awkwardly, cracking his neck on the final step.

Steve and Mike raced down the stairs after him, running to find their families. They met them with strong embraces, crying in each other's arms. James appeared at the landing, rifle in hand. He dropped it and ran to meet Leigh and the kids.

None of them noticed, until Denise did, that Felix was sitting on his knees facing the stairs. He was having trouble breathing.

"Felix?" Denise wrapped her arm around his shoulder. "Are you—oh no, Felix! Felix!"

Felix turned to his wife and looked in her eyes before he closed his and collapsed into her lap. Blood leaked from the hole in his chest onto her pants.

"Oh no! Felix!" Denise said over and again. "No!" She sobbed, holding her husband's head in her lap. She was rubbing his face, rocking him back and forth. "Noooo!" she wailed.

They tried comforting her. They tried resuscitating Felix and worked to stop the bleeding. None of it helped.

"He died a hero," James told Denise, holding her hand as she rocked back and forth unable to let go of her husband. "He really did."

"Thank you," she whispered. "But everyone was a hero tonight."

CHAPTER 51

EVENT +218:00 Hours
Sweet Valley, Pennsylvania

"You don't have to leave." Steve leaned on the driver's side window. "You can stay as long as you like. You earned it."

"I appreciate that," said James, his hands gripping the wheel, "but we need to get home. We have to see what's left."

"I understand," said Steve. "But it's not safe out there."

"It's not safe anywhere." Leigh leaned toward the open window.

"I know." Steve sighed. "But it could be tough to get home. You could run into a lot of problems along the way."

"Nothing worth having is easy." James tried to make light of it. "We'll be careful."

"You've got plenty of food," Steve said. "Lots of gas. A supply of weapons."

"We can't thank you enough," Leigh said. "You and Kosia have been so wonderful to us."

"We owe you our gratitude." Steve placed his hand on his chest. "For all you did *that* night, to the cleanup afterward. Plus your help with Felix's memorial…"

"Is Denise going to be okay?" James asked.

"Except for visiting the grave behind the barn, she hasn't come out of the cottage since we put it back together," he said. "I imagine she'll want privacy for a while."

James looked past Steve at the front porch. Mike was jogging toward them, waving.

"Hey!" he called as he got close. "I was just listening to the radio."

"And?" Steve asked. "What are the Canadians saying now?"

"The feds are setting up zones." Mike joined Steve at the truck window.

"What does that mean?" asked James.

"They're calling them TRZs," Mike explained. "Temporary Recovery Zones. They've got these areas up and down the East Coast, from Maine down to Virginia. They even stretch into New York."

"What about Pennsylvania?" asked Steve.

"We're in TRZ 4," said Mike. "At least that's what they're saying. They're doing it to control access, keep order."

"You said down to Virginia?" asked Max from the backseat. Sloane was buckled in next to him, Noodle on her lap.

"Yes." Mike nodded. "I think Maryland is TRZ 5."

"So we'd have to cross zones," said Leigh.

"Yeah," Mike agreed. "I don't know what that means, though."

"It's probably not a good thing," James suggested.

"Not too late to stay." Steve cocked his head and smiled. "Just because you already said your goodbyes doesn't mean you have to go."

"It does," James said. "We need to take our chances. We have a home. And we've made it this far." He shook Steve's hand and then Mike's and rolled up the window.

James shifted into drive and circled away from the main house and through the opening at the front gate. He paused at the intersection of the driveway and Route 4024.

"Which way?" he asked Leigh.

"Whatever you think, Rock." She took his left hand with both of hers, pulling it into her lap. "I trust you."

PART 3

ADVENT

CHAPTER 52

EVENT +1 Week, 3 Days, 15:42 Hours
University Park, Maryland
Temporary Recovery Zone 5

James Rockwell stood over the body, straddling a thickening pool of blood on the tile floor. The candles on the kitchen counter cast a macabre, flickering glow over the fresh corpse.

James's neighbors, Jacob "Sonny" Lawrence and Grant Wood, stood together on the opposite side of the counter. Both of them were armed. Neither fired the deadly shot, but they watched James in stunned silence as he hawked his prey.

James looked behind him, past his neighbors, assured nobody else was coming down the stairs from the second floor, and knelt down to look into his victim's eyes.

They were open and full of life just thirty seconds earlier. Their bright blue was fading into a dull gray. The pupils were blown and fixed. James brushed back the wisps of her jet-black bangs so he could better see them.

"You shouldn't have killed her," said Grant, straining to whisper. "You could have wounded her or knocked her unconscious. Too many people have died already."

"That wouldn't have worked." James stood and leaned across the counter. "Wound her and she has a chance to fight back. Knock her unconscious? She saw me from across the room. I had to fire."

"But you killed her!" Grant protested. "We didn't come here to kill women!"

"Look." Sonny Lawrence put his hand on Grant's shoulder, his dark skin glowing in the candlelight. "It's regrettable. But it was unavoidable. We came here knowing the risks, Grant. We came here to help James, whatever that meant."

"If you want to leave"—James pointed toward the front of the house—"then walk out! We have a job to finish. You've done your part. You saved my life once already. You're good."

"That's not it," Grant softened. "I want to help. I just can't believe we killed her."

James knew Grant wasn't game for the mission from the beginning. Grant was a good man, but he was not cut out for the world post-*event*. His wife, Emma, goaded him into it. So he'd tagged along, armed with a Smith & Wesson revolver and a healthy dose of skeptic fear when they'd left Sonny's house an hour earlier, just after dark. He'd surprised James when it mattered and did what had to be done. Still, as they neared the final push, he was a reluctant participant, and from the beginning he'd second-guessed every morally questionable move.

They'd approached the house from the backyard, hopping a fence that separated the property from the busy street that ran behind it. James could see the candlelight glowing from the family room on the first floor and the master bedroom above it. The backyard sloped steeply upward from the fence line to the house, such that the basement, not visible from the front elevation, looked to be the first floor from the rear.

They had crouched low at the fence line, sitting in silence for a moment to be certain no one had seen or heard them land hard in the grass. Satisfied they were undiscovered, James led the men slowly and deliberately toward the basement entrance.

They'd stopped at the large cedar play set, hiding behind the large plastic yellow slide. On his knees, James checked his rifle, a Bushmaster 300 AAC Blackout. It was light and compact, and though it didn't have a sight or a scope, James knew he likely wouldn't need either.

It was a semiautomatic killing machine with sound and flash suppression. Only the person at the other end of the barrel would know he'd pulled the trigger.

James and his compatriots had crossed the short distance from the play set to the concrete slab abutting the back of the house. Above the slab was a large wooden deck that extended off the first floor. James looked up at the slivers of light peeking through the slats between the pine boards and then pulled a pair of paperclips from his pocket, handing them to Sonny.

Sonny leaned his own rifle against the wall adjacent to the basement door and knelt down to check the clips. He'd bent both of them with a pair of needle-nose pliers. One of them was formed into an "L" shape, with part of the clip bent back over itself. The second clip was straightened and then bent at a ninety degree angle. The end was bent into a series of forty-five-degree angles, creating a rake.

Sonny, a retired police officer, had taken the rake and slipped it into the lock. He'd rocked it back and forth until he felt a series of clicks pop the interior pins. Then he'd inserted the "L" shaped clip on top of the rake, turning it clockwise and then counterclockwise to figure out the direction of the lock. He'd felt it twist and pop.

With the lock picked, Sonny had put the clips into his pocket, grabbed his Bushmaster, and slowly turned the doorknob. He'd pushed gently with his shoulder and then used his foot to swing the door open fully.

James moved in first with his rifle leveled at his chest. He'd swept the dark room, his eyes slowly adjusting to the lack of light.

To their right was a storage closet and to their left were a washing machine and clothes dryer. There was a small plastic sink hung on the wall between the two. Grant had quietly closed the door behind them and stepped further into the basement. Standing at the center of the room, the stairs leading upstairs extended twenty steps up to their left. The door at the top of the stairs was closed, light from the family room glowing under the gap between the bottom rail and the floor. James turned his back to the steps and saw the large open shelving unit, which held bottles of cleaning supplies and boxes of detergent.

They'd walked to the wall opposite the basement door and found a worn sectional sofa to one side and a gun safe to the other.

James's eyes fully adjusted to the darkness and he'd knelt down to check the safe. It was intact. That was a good sign, he'd thought, before crossing the distance to the stairs. He didn't need anything out of the safe for the mission. And if he failed, he didn't want anyone having access to the weapons inside.

"Are you ready?" he'd asked his neighbors before ascending the steps one at a time. Carefully, the men moved to the door.

"The family room is to our immediate left," James had whispered. "The kitchen is catty-corner to our left. There is a hallway to our right."

"I'll take the hallway," offered Grant.

"I'll take the family room and stairs," said Sonny.

"The kitchen is mine, then," James had agreed before throwing open the door onto the first floor and immediately affixing his gaze on the kitchen, stepping toward it as he focused.

Standing behind the counter, at the sink, was the woman of the house. She was slender, her cheeks drawn, small circular scabs on her chin and forehead. Her jet-black hair was thinning and shoulder length. James had seen her before she saw him. He'd pulled the trigger on the Bushmaster without thinking about the consequences, unleashing a single thirty-caliber slug into her chest. The only sounds had been the suppressed thump of the rifle firing and the sickening thud of the woman collapsing onto the kitchen floor.

James knew as he'd pulled the trigger it had been his only option. Now standing with his neighbors, he privately questioned himself.

Another death…

"What now?" Grant asked. "What do we do now?"

"We finish the job," Sonny suggested, nodding toward the stairs behind him. "Then we can go home."

Grant sucked in a contemplative breath and agreed. "Fine. Who goes first?"

"I will," said James, looking both of his partners in the eyes. "This is my fight. You follow me."

James glanced back at the stairs and saw a tall, dark figure emerging from the shadows halfway up the stairs. It was already too late.

CHAPTER 53

EVENT +1 Week, 2 Days, 9:17 Hours
North of Lancaster, Pennsylvania
Temporary Recovery Zone 4

Watching a man's head explode wasn't on James Rockwell's bucket list. Neither was drilling holes into necks or torsos with thirty-caliber bullets.

But James did what was necessary to protect his family, even if it meant chipping away at his own soul in the process. In nine days he'd killed ten men.

He'd dropped three of them to the bottom of Casco Bay, Maine. The others, he shot to death at Camp Driggers. In the days that followed, he shoveled their graves and rolled their rotting corpses into the holes.

"I killed them," he'd told the others. "I'll bury them." With each shovel stroke, he prayed about what he'd done.

Was it forgivable? Was his soul redeemable? What lessons could he learn from this?

James wasn't necessarily a religious man. He didn't wear a cross or go to church on Sundays. But he held a deep faith in God, the Golden Rule, and that sin was punishable. He was also a disciple of science, a physics teacher who believed in the coexistence of a miraculous God and the intellectual study of structure and order. In the days since the *event*, he questioned the reality of both.

James looked at his wife, Leigh, in the passenger seat of their stolen truck, and thought about what they'd survived, what lay ahead. She was leaning against the window, her eyes closed, head bouncing gently with the movement of the truck along a stretch of US 222 between Ephrata and Brownstown, Pennsylvania. Despite everything, she was strikingly beautiful, a beacon in a sepia-dipped world.

He rested his hand on Leigh's thigh and glanced in the rearview mirror. Daughter Sloane was asleep. She was resting her head on her stuffed bear, Noodle.

Max, James's son, was staring out the window, his cheek pressed against the glass. He had a distant, steely look in his eyes, James thought. Max wouldn't be the same kid he was just two weeks ago. He'd seen too much blood, lived too much on the edge of death. Max was hardening into a man too soon, James knew, forged by the harsh environment in which they now lived.

James took a deep breath, inhaling the sadness of his realization, and put his full attention back on the road ahead. It was just in time. Seeing two men standing in the middle of southbound US 222, he slammed on his brakes, fishtailing for an instant before the antilock mechanism kicked in and thumped the truck to a stop.

The men were armed. Both of them carried semiautomatic rifles against the camouflage ghillie suits. They were wearing wool beanies on their heads despite the warm late August temperatures. James had seen men like this before. They were bad news.

"What is it?" Leigh awoke from her nap, stretching in her seat. "Who is that?" She blinked her eyes into focus.

"I don't know," said James, trying to move his lips as little as possible. "Max, you good back there?" He checked his son in the rearview.

"Yes, sir." Max nodded. "I'm good."

One of the two men signaled for James to roll down his window as he approached the driver's side. James kept his hands on the steering wheel.

The man sidled up to the window and rapped his knuckle on it. "I need you to roll down the window, sir."

"I can't do that," said James. "I need to see some identification before I do anything you ask of me. We've run into some rough characters. Just being careful. I'm sure you understand."

"I understand," said the man. He had a three-week-old beard that gave him the appearance of a Navy SEAL. "But I need you to comply with my instructions. Roll down your window." His grip tightened around the rifle.

James looked ahead at the second man, who stood astride the dotted white line in the middle of the highway. He took a step forward, his eyes fixed on the truck.

"Yeah," said James, turning to look at the man outside of his window. "That's not gonna happen. So it seems we're at an impasse."

"We're with the Pennsylvania State Guard," the man announced, pulling his shoulder back as he said it. "We're in charge of all traffic through Brownstown."

"And?" James wasn't budging.

"Sir"—the proud guardsman rolled his eyes—"I'm aware of the danger out there, of the militias claiming authority. We're a resurrection of the Reserve Defense Corps from World War Two and the Korean War."

"So you're a militia," James interrupted.

"Yes," the guardsman acknowledged, "but we're authorized by the state's National Guard. They're overrun. We're assisting, deputized by the governor."

"I believe him, Rock," Leigh said under her breath. "It might be better to roll down the window."

James nodded and looked back at his children before pressing the button to roll down the window. He turned off the ignition and pulled the keys from the column, slipping one of them between his index and middle finger. If things went south, he could use it as a weapon to buy time.

"Thank you, sir." The guardsman leaned on the door panel. "We have a couple of options here before you can get on your way."

"I immediately regret rolling down my window," James replied. His muscles tensed. He was ready to strike.

"Just listen, please." The guardsman stood and stepped back from the window. "Let me explain our procedure."

"Go ahead," Leigh leaned over and said. "We're listening."

"We can't have weapons enter Brownstown," he began. "So if you have any weapons—guns, knives, explosives—we're gonna need to know that."

James said nothing, his eyes fixed on the guardsman in front of the truck, blocking the road.

"I'll guess by your relative hostility, sir"—the guardsman tightened his grip on his weapon—"you are armed. I'd expect it. If I had a family and I were traveling under these circumstances, I'd be armed too."

"You are armed." James's patience was worn through.

"Given that you're carrying weapons"—the guardsman ignored him—"you can turn around and find a way around Brownstown. We can confiscate them and allow you to travel freely through the town. Or you will allow us to escort you through the town, leaving you free to travel once you've exited."

James grabbed his chin with his left hand and rubbed the scruff. It itched. He looked at the guard outside the window, gauging his ability with the rifle, before returning his attention to the one standing in the middle of the road. He came to his conclusion.

"We'll take the escort," James said. "I'm not giving up what little protection I have for my family, and I'm not lengthening our journey given what little fuel we have."

"Understood," said the guardsman. "We'll ask that you keep the vehicle off until we have a PSG escort available for you. It'll be just a few minutes."

The guard turned and walked to his partner. The two of them talked, motioned at James and then at the road behind them.

"I thought you were going to get us shot," said Leigh. "Why are you so combative?"

"Seriously?" James raised his voice, turning in his seat to face his wife. "The last time we ran into this sort of thing, we were nearly executed. I don't trust other people with guns and uniforms. That's it."

"I get it." Leigh held up her hands in surrender. "But you might want to dial it down a notch. Everybody is tense. Everyone is trigger-happy. No need to incite something."

James grumbled and shook his head.

He hadn't incited anything, he reasoned. Leigh didn't truly understand what was at stake, he thought.

He was his family's salvation, if there was to be any. If it meant becoming trigger-happy or edgy or violent, he would become it. Whatever it took to get his family home, to reclaim their lives in this new world, he would do it. If he had to condemn his soul for the sake of theirs, he would give it.

Pure and simple.

CHAPTER 54

EVENT +1 Week, 2 Days, 10:00 Hours
Brownstown, Pennsylvania
Temporary Recovery Zone 4

Brownstown, Pennsylvania, was a dying town before the event. As children grew into adults, they left the Turkey Hill Minit Market and the Sonic Drive-In in the smoke of their burning rubber tires.

A population of eight hundred and fifty at the turn of the century shrank to seven hundred and thirty a decade later. The average income was less than twenty grand. And the biggest news to come out of the stoplight town was the jackknifed tractor trailer that closed Route 222 in 2014 and the sixth-grade teacher at the elementary school murdered that same year.

The Rockwells didn't know any of that history as they slowly drove through the heart of Brownstown, PSG Jeeps leading and trailing their truck from Route 222 onto South State Street toward Stone Quarry Road. The guardsman told the Rockwells they'd closed the highway at the northern and southern end of the town. They wanted to tightly control the traffic.

They explained that in the hours after the event, the town was overrun with people fleeing Pittsburgh, Harrisburg, and Philadelphia. They were seeking off-the-map safe places, and though many of them were well intentioned at first, the neighborly, benevolent behavior deteriorated quickly.

Squatters took over empty houses, they broke into stores and businesses, and terrorized Brownstown's residents. The guard moved in and settled things, but not without violence.

The evidence of that battle was everywhere. The homes lining South State were boarded up with ragged sheets of plywood. Some were spray painted with warnings or lamentations. The side of the road was littered with abandoned or stripped cars and trucks. A couple of them were bullet-riddled.

There was trash in the yards, the charred ash of impromptu fires in driveways. It looked to the Rockwells like a war-zone.

"What *really* happened here?" Max asked, his nose pressed to the glass. "It looks like something from *Call of Duty*. I mean, like World War Two, you know?"

"I know," said James, noticing the armed guards on alternating street corners. They passed Main Street and continued south. "This was bad."

"What did he say about the squatters?" Max plopped his back against his seat. "What did they do?"

"He said they showed up looking for safe places to stay," James explained. "But they made things dangerous for the people who already lived here."

"How?" Sloane was awake, sipping from a bottled water. "Was it like the bad men who tried to kill us at Camp Driggers?"

James glanced at his daughter in the rearview before catching Leigh's eyes. She was hurting. He knew it. He shouldn't have snapped at her. It didn't do anyone any good. Hearing his daughter talk about what they'd experienced with such nonchalance was like a stick to the eye, unexpected and instantly painful.

"Yes." No point in sugarcoating it. "When people are desperate, they do desperate things. They take what doesn't belong to them; they hurt people they shouldn't hurt."

"Is that why we took this truck?" asked Sloane, rubbing her hand on the backseat armrest. "We're desperate?"

"Yes," Leigh answered. "But the people to whom this truck belonged didn't need it anymore."

"Because they're dead." Sloane shrugged.

"Yes." Leigh turned in her seat to look at her daughter. "We're not desperate like the people who have nothing. We have food and water and each other."

"And love." Sloane uncapped the water to take another sip.

"And love," echoed Leigh.

The caravan slowed as it approached Stone Quarry Road, preparing to turn right and head west toward the highway. To the left was a low-slung, single-story brick home. It sat at the end of a long driveway, deep green stretches of grass on either side of the concrete. Just beyond the driveway and the grass was a narrow, muddy river.

"Dad"—Max noticed it first—"do you see the house? The one to the left?"

James looked at the home, or what was left of it. Strewn across the grass were belongings he imagined once decorated the interior: a chambray-colored sofa, a walnut coffee table, a couple of televisions, a wrought-iron headboard from a bed, and a dozen or so lawn bags full of who knows what.

There was no door leading into the home, just the open frame where the door once hung. Two of the home's four front-facing windows were shattered. A hole in the roof produced a wispy trail of white smoke dissipating into the air.

On the driveway, there was a dark spot akin to an oil leak from a car. But it was larger, tinged with red. Splatter surrounded the spot.

Just as they made the turn, a figure appeared in the front doorway. A tall, beefy man, shirtless and in boxers, leaned into the frame. He produced a cigarette and took a long drag before offering the passersby a weak salute. James instinctively averted his gaze to Stone Quarry Road.

"What happened there?" Max turned back to keep his eyes on the house. "Did you see the smoke and the driveway?"

"I saw it," James admitted. "It didn't look good, did it?"

"Do you think that guy was a squatter?" Max asked, gripping the top of James's seat and pulling himself closer to his dad.

James considered the man's oddly muscular physique, the condition of the home, its proximity to two major roads in town. "I don't know, Max," he said. "Could be. But whether he's a squatter or the owner, I wouldn't want to be him."

"Neither would I," said Max. "That place was a disaster."

James feigned a smile and accelerated to keep up with the Jeep leading them west toward Route 222. To their left was brown farmland, the crops long harvested with nothing new on the way. They passed the entrance to a neighborhood on their right, two uniformed guardsmen standing watch. The Jeep slowed ahead of them as they approached the intersection with the highway. The driver waved them forward and James pulled even with the Jeep. Leigh rolled down her window.

"This is where we leave you," said the driver. His eyes were deep set, bracketed by crow's feet on either side. The line running along his nose and past his mouth gave his cheeks a droopy appearance. "You'll head south on the northbound lanes until you cross the Conestoga River. A couple of our guys will direct you back into the southbound lanes and you can head on to wherever you're headed."

"Maryland," Leigh offered. "College Park."

"Oh." The driver nodded. "I think Highway 30 is in good shape. You could take that west, north of Lancaster, and then hit the gate for Zone Five when you cross New Freedom. It's just north of the border."

"Zone Five?" asked James.

"Yes, sir," said the driver. "You're in Temporary Recovery Zone Four. TRZ Five is most of Maryland, south to Norfolk, Virginia. Delaware is a mess, though. You can't get there. It's restricted access."

"But we can get to College Park?" Leigh asked.

"I think so," said the driver, pushing his boonie cap back on his forehead. "That's what the National Guard told us in a briefing yesterday, before we deployed here."

"Thank you." Leigh waved. "Be careful."

"You be careful," said the driver, twisting his hands on the wheel. "This town is just like all of them, from what we hear. Anywhere that *was* safe isn't anymore."

CHAPTER 55

EVENT +1 Week, 2 Days, 14:14 Hours
New Freedom, Pennsylvania
Northern Gate Alpha Checkpoint 1, Temporary Recovery Zone 5

"I don't like doing this at night," said James. He was motioning to the back end of the same Mercedes S-Class sedan at which he'd stared for the last two hours. "It's not as safe."

"Nothing's safe." Leigh leaned her head back against her seat and closed her eyes. "Remember?"

"I remember." James sighed. He thumped his hands on the steering wheel, anxious to make his way to the front of the line and through the security checkpoint. He rolled up his window to dampen the rumble of the generators powering the large, bright lights shining into the vehicle.

The Mercedes inched forward to an armed, helmeted soldier positioned on the driver's side. Beyond the Mercedes, James could see a pair of concrete highway barriers set just far enough apart for a vehicle to slip past.

James watched the body language of the soldier, the way he gripped his M16. He was all business but in control. The soldier directed the Mercedes to the right. It did not go through the barriers. Instead, two other soldiers approached the car and ordered the passengers out of it. There was yelling that James couldn't hear. Two men and a woman climbed from the vehicle and were forced away from the Mercedes while the soldiers rifled through it.

"Rock," said Leigh, "it's our turn."

James turned his attention to the soldier in front of them. He slowly pulled up to the guard and rolled down his window.

"Sir," said the soldier, who James imagined couldn't have been more than nineteen or twenty years old, "who are you and where are you headed?"

"My name is James Rockwell. This is my wife, Leigh, and our children, Max and Sloane. Our home is in College Park, Maryland." James forced a smile. "We were on vacation in—"

"I'll need some identification, sir," replied the soldier without expression. "We need to validate your right to enter this zone."

"I don't have any identification," started James. "As I was expl—"

"Sir," interrupted the soldier, "I cannot let you enter this zone without proof you live or own a business inside this zone."

"I don't have any identification," James repeated through his teeth. He felt Leigh's hand gently squeeze his thigh. "Is there an alternative way to prove our right to be in the *zone*."

"Do you have a registration for this vehicle that might show your address?" The soldier walked to the rear of the truck without awaiting a response and then returned to the window. "There are Vermont plates on this truck, sir."

"Yes," James began, his hands white-knuckling the steering wheel. "I can explain everything—"

"Sir." The soldier raised his hand to stop James from speaking. "Without identification, I cannot allow you to pass into this zone. This is a primary checkpoint. If I let you through here without the proper documentation, you'll be stopped at the next one. So—"

"Hang on, soldier." James had long since lost his patience and his wife's tighter grip on his thigh did nothing to restrain him. "You get me a superior. I have every right to be here. If you had any clue what we've been through to get to this point…to be this close to home…you'd get behind the bumper of this truck and push us there."

"Sir." The soldier squared his jaw. "I am the superior as far as you're concerned. You need to turn your car around and head north, or we'll be happy to confiscate your belongings and offer you a free, comfortable ride to the FEMA camp we have set up just the other side of the barrier."

"You—" James started before Leigh cut him off.

"Sir?" Leigh leaned over her husband and smiled at the young man. "Could I please speak with you? I'm a little less stressed than my husband is at the moment."

The soldier looked at Leigh, glanced back at James, the kids in the backseat of the truck, and nodded. "I'll come to your side, ma'am. Sir, please shut off the ignition."

James cranked the key and the truck coughed as the engine stopped. The soldier nodded and moved around the front of the truck to Leigh's side. Her window was down.

"Yes, ma'am," said the soldier. "You have something to add? As I've already told your husband, we cannot let—"

"I understand you are doing your job," Leigh said softly. "And I can only imagine how much pressure you're under, how tough it must be to be away from *your* family while guarding this gate."

"Yes, ma'am." The stoic soldier flinched, his eyes blinking rapidly for a moment.

"Please give me the courtesy of explaining to you our predicament"—Leigh smiled—"as I'm sure you'd want for your mother or young girlfriend."

"Yes, ma'am." The soldier relaxed his grip on his M16.

"We were on vacation," Leigh began, "when whatever happened, *happened*. We barely survived a tsunami. And that was just the beginning." Leigh went on to explain every last detail of the previous nine and a half days. She told the soldier her husband nearly drowned and then almost died of pneumonia. She relayed the unlikely escape from the church in Acton, Maine, and the heroic stand at Camp Driggers in Sweet Valley, Pennsylvania. She went so far as to tell him about the pandemic six years earlier and the deaths of four family members, including their eldest child.

The soldier didn't interrupt her once. Instead, he empathized, telling Leigh about his father's death from the Jakarta flu and how he'd been the one to take care of his mother in the weeks and months afterward. They had only each other. She was staying not far from the checkpoint. He'd brought her with him from Delaware, a restricted zone into and out of which there was virtually no migration.

"Look." He sighed. "As I instructed your husband, if I let you through, you will be stopped at the next checkpoint and immediately sent to a FEMA camp. You'll lose your belongings, and there is a possibility you'll be separated from your husband."

"So what do we do?" Leigh pleaded. "I'm praying you'll have a workable solution to this."

The soldier bit his lower lip and then held up his finger. "Let me see what I can do, ma'am." He walked over to a pair of soldiers standing at the Mercedes. He pointed back at the Rockwells and the soldiers glanced at them. One of them, a sergeant, shook his head, but the soldier kept talking. The sergeant looked back at the truck again and followed the soldier to the truck.

He stopped at Leigh's window. "Private Jorgensen tells me you're *distant relatives*?" The sergeant had one eyebrow raised higher than the other.

"If that's what Private Jorgensen says…" Leigh flashed a smile.

"We have what's called a status exemption for the relatives of our soldiers here," explained the sergeant. "Each of us gets two."

Private Jorgenson looked down at his boots as the sergeant explained the particulars of the exemption. The private used one of his allowances for his mother. He was prepared to use the other for them.

"The exemption is a piece of paper," said the sergeant. "It's worth its weight in gold. We give you the exemption and you can travel freely across the boundaries for the zone to which it applies. You need to get into Zone Five?"

"Yes, please," Leigh said.

"You're awfully quiet." The sergeant leaned on Leigh's window, directing his comment at James.

"It's better that way," Leigh explained. "He tends to get frustrated in these kinds of situations."

"Who doesn't?" The sergeant laughed incredulously. "So, if you're prepared to accept Private Jorgenson's lone remaining status exemption, I'll get you the paperwork. You'll show it at every checkpoint connected to Zone Five. You'll pass through."

"We accept," said Leigh. "Thank you."

The sergeant nodded and walked back toward the Mercedes, disappearing around the corner. Private Jorgensen approached the window.

"You remind me of my mom." He smiled. "She'd want me to help you."

"Thank you, Private Jorgensen," said Leigh. "Your mom would be proud."

CHAPTER 56

EVENT +1 Week, 2 Days, 15:32 Hours
White Hall, Maryland
Northern Gate Alpha Checkpoint 2, Temporary Recovery Zone 5

The Rockwells approached the familiar-looking concrete barriers on Interstate 83. The line was nonexistent, with most of the traffic not passing through the first checkpoint or being diverted to a FEMA encampment in Stewartstown, Pennsylvania, on Highway 851.

James slowed to a stop and showed a pair of soldiers his status exemption. They checked the paperwork and waved them through the maze of barriers, placed like checkers to keep cars at a slow roll. It prevented drivers from speeding past any given checkpoint.

"Rock," Leigh said, staring out the window at the barbed wire, temporary fencing, and altogether bellicose arrangement of the checkpoint, "I think we're gonna be okay."

"I think so," James said, his blood pressure having dropped significantly during the slow but easy drive between New Freedom and White Hall. "You really worked your magic back there." It was the first he'd acknowledged her successful navigation through the first checkpoint.

"Is that a 'thank you'?" she said coyly, turning to face her husband. "If so, you're welcome."

"I was wrong," James admitted. "I should've stayed calm. But that's getting more difficult for me to do. I find myself…just…reacting. I don't even think about it."

"I get it, Rock," Leigh said. "But everybody is on edge, right? Everybody feels the same way you do. The military, the militias, the good people, the bad…"

"That doesn't help." James accelerated around another barrier and then swung the wheel back to exit the checkpoint.

"I'm just suggesting cooler heads prevail," Leigh stressed. "Kill them with kindness."

"Poor choice of words, Leigh." James looked over at his wife and then back to the highway. They were clear of the checkpoint.

"You know what I mean." She smirked. "Speaking of which…" She turned to look at the children, assuring they were asleep. "How are you doing with everything?"

"I don't know what you mean." James kept his eyes straight ahead, relying on his headlights to see the road. Beyond the checkpoint, they were the only lights aside from the dim bluish glow on the horizon as they headed south. To the left, the blue blended into purple and then reddish-orange. It reminded James of the *event*. He'd never look at a sunrise or sunset the same way again.

"You know what I mean." Leigh kept her voice low. "You've had to be strong this whole time. You've had to—"

"You've been strong too," James interrupted. "You saved my life and kept it together when I was useless."

"Rock." Leigh put her hand on his shoulder. "I haven't had to kill anyone. I know you well enough to see what's going on behind those eyes of yours."

"Now's not the time." James pushed the accelerator and adjusted his grip on the steering wheel. "We can talk about this when we get home. Once we've had time to process it and get back to normal."

"Normal?" She squeezed his shoulder, massaging it gently.

"Whatever normal turns out to be." James checked the fuel gauge. It was at a quarter of a tank. They'd burned a lot of gas sitting at the first checkpoint, but they should be good to make it home.

"I won't nag you," she said, dropping her hand to his leg and shifting to face forward.

"Too late." James laughed, trying to change the mood and the subject.

"Ha!" Leigh said, slapping his thigh.

"Get some sleep," James suggested. "We should be home in a couple of hours, assuming traffic isn't bad once we get to College Park." He slowed the truck, pushing hard on the brakes to swerve around a car stopped on the edge of the road. Its hazard lights were flashing but dim.

"I love you, Rock," said Leigh, closing her eyes and folding her arms across her chest.

"I love you too," James said, checking his speedometer. He was cruising at forty miles per hour. That was the fastest speed at which he felt comfortable driving at night. There were too many hazards, even on the highways.

As they'd driven south from Maine, the major roadways became less congested and less dangerous. There were more stalled vehicles dotting the landscape, especially near exits, and James had to pay attention for people walking in groups along the shoulder, but it was still an improvement.

He wondered what they would find when they finally pulled into their cul-de-sac. Was it the war zone he feared? Or had his neighbors done a good job of holding down their respective forts.

There were six houses encircling the cul-de-sac at the end of Fletcher Road. Each sat on pie-shaped, quarter-acre lots. They weren't huge pieces of property, but they were plenty big.

James pulled on his high beams and considered how the neighbors might have weathered the last nine days. He knew some of them were prepared and some were not.

Moving clockwise around the circle, there were the Whistlers, Neil and Abbey, who'd lived on the street longer than anyone else. They were empty-nesters in their late fifties. He was an English professor at the University of Maryland. She sold homemade jewelry on Etsy.

Next to the Whistlers lived Grant Wood and his wife, Emma. They'd lived in the house a couple of years and had three children, all of them in elementary school. They seemed nice enough, but Leigh knew Emma better than James knew Grant.

Sonny Lawrence lived at 809 Fletcher Road. He was single. His wife died a year after the pandemic. She survived the flu, but it damaged her lungs, and she succumbed to pneumonia. Sonny was a retired police officer and a great neighbor. He was as close to being a "prepper" as there was on the street. James knew he had a wall armory in his basement, where he also stored a lot of canned goods.

Stuart and Susan Gilbert lived between Sonny Lawrence and the Rockwells. Both of them worked at the Maryland Technology Enterprise Institute. James imagined they wouldn't have much to do after the electromagnetic pulse.

On the other side of the Rockwells, in the last house on the cul-de-sac, lived Jack and Lee Pollock. They were a reclusive couple. Jack telecommuted for an energy consulting firm and Lee was a librarian. They didn't have children. And really all James knew about them was that his Leigh spelled her name differently than Mrs. Pollock and that Jack religiously walked five miles every morning.

James couldn't wait to be home. He checked the speedometer and pushed harder on the gas pedal. He set the cruise control at forty-five miles per hour.

CHAPTER 57

EVENT +1 Week, 2 Days, 17:16 Hours
College Park, Maryland
Temporary Recovery Zone 5

The reddish-orange glow pulsating on the horizon was the first indication all was not well in College Park. The farther south the Rockwells traveled on US 1, the more they could see of the black smoke pluming skyward. The belly of the smoke plumes were singed red and orange. Whatever was burning was fully engulfed.

"Is that the university?" Leigh asked James. "It looks like the fire is right there on campus."

"I think you're right." James was looking southwest, to the left of US 1 as it cut through College Park on its way to Washington, DC. "That's the campus."

James took the exit, heading west, onto Highway 193. They'd drive along the University of Maryland's western edge, right by the campus golf course, on the way to their neighborhood.

"Dad," Max piped from the backseat, "this doesn't look like home."

"Can we camp out too?" Sloane pressed her face and fingers against the glass, looking at the tents dotting the golf course to their right.

They were alit by trash cans doubling as bonfires. There were at least a dozen of the fire cans, people huddled around each of them. It looked like a scene from a depression-era film reel, but in living color.

"I don't think so," said James. "We're much better off being in our own home, in our own bed."

"Mmmm." Leigh closed her eyes and pressed her lips into a cheeky smile. "That sounds amazing. Doesn't it, kids? Our own beds?"

The children agreed with their mother. James was too focused on the road ahead to have heard her. In the dark, and without any lighting other than the pale yellow beams from the truck, it was difficult to navigate even what were familiar roads just two weeks earlier.

"You okay, Rock?" asked Leigh.

"Yeah." He nodded, vaguely aware of her question. "Just concentrating."

"We're almost there," she reminded him.

James didn't respond. He leaned forward in his seat, both hands on the wheel as he turned left and accelerated onto Adelphi Road.

Adelphi was lined with trees; the streets branching off into small enclaves were dark. James had no sense of how the neighborhood surrounding his had fared.

"I wish we were getting home in the daylight," said Max.

"Me too," echoed Sloane, gripping her stuffed bear, Noodle. "I can't see anything. It's too dark."

"Me three," said Leigh. "It's totally different with the streetlights working. I would have thought we'd have power by now, being so far south."

"I didn't," James admitted. He'd privately held his belief much of the country, or at least the Eastern Seaboard, was dark. An electromagnetic pulse, or pulses, was the culprit. He was sure of it. And while he knew the EMP couldn't account for the tsunami they'd survived on Peaks Island, Maine, he was sure it was a central part of whatever had imploded their world on the final day of a summer getaway.

"There's your school, Dad." Max pointed across his sister as they passed the sprawling parking lot of Northwestern High School to their right. "It's dark too."

James glanced to the dark, open expanse between clumps of tall evergreens and oaks. He'd worked at Northwestern for ten years and was a proud Wildcat. He loved most of the twenty-two hundred students, and enjoyed telling people he worked at the same school where Kermit the Frog was born. Jim Henson, the Muppets' creator, attended Northwestern in the early 1950s. He knew more than ever, as he reconciled the likely end of that career, at least for the time being, it wasn't easy being green.

James turned left onto Underwood and into the tangled web of shaded streets that made up University Park. They didn't technically live in College Park. Their address was University Park, but they typically told people College Park. It was more familiar because of the university.

James slowed the truck as they wound their way closer to home. A left, another right, and a final left put the Rockwells on Fletcher Road. James could feel the sledgehammer of his pulse in his neck. The closer they got to the end of the street, the more apprehensive he felt.

"The homes look okay," Leigh offered. "I mean, from what little I can see. There are no fires. No burning trash cans. That's good, right?"

"Right." James knew his wife wanted reassurance more than anything. "I think everything looks good so far." He neared the cul-de-sac and slowed to make his way to the right, past the Pollocks' house.

"We're home!" Sloane exclaimed as her father pulled into the driveway at 819 Fletcher. Their house, a tasteful blend of white HardiePlank siding and faded red brick, sat patiently at the end of their driveway. Nobody responded to the nine-year-old's cheer. Something was wrong.

There was a small Chevy Camaro at the end of the driveway, close to the single, double-bay garage door. It had West Virginia plates. James felt the sweat on his palms against the wheel as he noticed a faint glow emanating from an upstairs bedroom. It danced against the window as would candlelight.

"There's someone in the house," he said, pulling the truck as close as he could to the Camaro without hitting it.

"What?" Leigh asked. "Are you sure? One of the neighbors could be parked in our driveway. That doesn't—"

"They're West Virginia plates." James indicated the car with his hand. "And there's candlelight in Sloane's bedroom. Somebody is in our house!"

"What do we do?" asked Leigh, her eyes widening.

"We get it back."

CHAPTER 58

EVENT +1 Week, 2 Days, 17:48 Hours
University Park, Maryland
Temporary Recovery Zone 5

James left his family in the truck, the doors locked, and walked the short concrete path connecting his driveway to the front stoop of his home. He quietly stepped up the two brick pavers onto the stoop and raised his hand to knock on the door. He'd considered trying the doorknob, but decided against it. Whoever was inside his home could be armed. He'd rather not surprise them.

"I wouldn't do that," a voice called from the street.

James spun around, his hand still poised to knock, and saw a dark figure standing at the curb in front of his house. He didn't recognize the person, but he knew the voice.

"Sonny?" James called after stepping off the porch and into the front yard. His ankles told him the lawn hadn't been cut since he'd left. "Is that you?"

"It's me." Sonny Lawrence stepped into the grass to greet his longtime neighbor and friend. "I can't believe it's you, James." Sonny wrapped his arms around James and hugged him. "Where are Leigh and the kids?"

"In the car." James pointed back to the truck.

"New truck?" Sonny squinted, trying to better see the vehicle in the driveway.

"Sort of," James said. "What's going on? Who's in my house?"

"Before I explain," Sonny said, leading James back to the curb, "you might want to move that truck. Bring your family with you and crash at my place."

"I don't—"

"I'm telling you"—Sonny raised his finger, his tone stern—"get your family and that truck and meet me at my house. It's not safe out here."

James nodded without protesting any further and moved his family two houses down, parking in Sonny Lawrence's driveway. He told Leigh there was a problem, he didn't know how serious it was, but Sonny had warned him to move.

He welcomed Leigh with a warm hug and the kids with bags of freeze-dried Neapolitan ice cream. "It keeps longer than cookies," he explained. Max and Sloane thanked him and found their way to the kitchen. Sonny's bulldog Albert was under the table, hiding from the intruders. Usually, Albert was the first to the door, ready to bound outside. The event had affected him too.

"I didn't know if I'd see you again," Sonny said, helping James with a small bag from the back of the truck. "You were in Maine, right?"

"Yes."

Sonny took Leigh's bag and placed it on the floor next to a small bench in the foyer.

"It wasn't as easy a trip back as it was there."

Sonny laughed and led his guests into the family room. It was comfortable, lit by oil-fed hurricane lanterns, and still carried Sonny's wife's feminine touch. A large black-and-white photograph of her was centered on the mantle above the fireplace. It was the focal point of the room.

"So who's in our house, Sonny?" James plopped into an easy chair next to the hearth after offering Leigh the seat. She declined and sat at his feet on the matching ottoman.

"How long have they been there?" she asked.

"Since the fourth or fifth day." Sonny eased onto the sofa facing them. He winced as his knees protested the depth of the seat. "I'm not sure."

"Who are they?" James repeated.

"As best I can tell"—Sonny leaned forward, resting his elbows on his knees—"they're a pair of brothers, a wife or girlfriend, and a couple of kids. They tried Jack Pollock's place first. He turned them away."

"So why did you tell me not to knock?" James sat up in the easy chair. "If they left Jack Pollock alone, then—"

"They didn't leave him alone." Sonny shook his head. "After they moved into your place, they went back and killed him and Lee."

"Wait!" Leigh shot to her feet. "What? They *killed them*?"

"They shot him in the doorway," said Sonny. "Then they killed her, looted the house, dragged their bodies into the yard, and went back to your place."

"How do you know this?" Leigh dropped onto the ottoman.

"I saw it happen," he said. "I was in my driveway talking to the Gilberts about your house, since they're your next-door neighbors, and we saw the woman and the brothers walk over to Jack's house. She knocked. He answered the door, yelled something at them, and the men shot him. Dead. Right there."

"Oh my…" Leigh covered her face. "Where are Jack and Lee now? Where are their bodies?"

"We don't know." Sonny shrugged. "We think they pulled them into the backyard, back into the house, or buried them. We haven't been over there."

"What else do we know about them?" James leaned into his wife, draping his arms around her from behind. "They're from West Virginia?"

"We can assume that from the plates," said Sonny. "But you're driving a truck with Vermont plates. So…"

"Right."

"What about the Whistlers on the end of the street, and the Woods?" asked James. "How are they?"

"They're both fine," said Sonny, nodding. "Nervous but fine. The people in your house haven't come outside since they killed the Pollocks. Not that we know of, anyhow. We take turns watching them. I was on duty tonight when I saw you pull up."

"Why them?" asked Leigh, her chin trembling. "Why haven't they attacked anyone else?"

"Well"—Sonny shifted in his seat, resting his elbow on the arm of the sofa—"we figured you didn't have much food in your house. You were on vacation."

"True," agreed James. "Maybe canned goods, some rice, pasta, sauces. That was about it. We ate everything else before we left."

"Right." Sonny sighed. "They went through that in a few days and then went after the Pollocks. They knew they were alone, or figured they were. They took their stock. That was two days ago."

"So they'll use up his rations and then attack another house?" Leigh worried.

"That's what we're all thinking," said Sonny. "We figure it's going to be tomorrow or the next day."

"What are you doing about it?" asked James. "Why isn't everybody huddled into one place? There's safety in numbers."

"Sometimes," Leigh mumbled.

"Nobody's willing to do that yet," said Sonny. "We discussed it. People are afraid of the panic, of cabin fever, of giving in to these thugs. We abandon all of the houses but one and they run roughshod over the whole street."

"We can't just sit back and take this," said James. "I want my house back. I want them gone."

"What do you propose?" asked Sonny.

"There's three of them, plus kids." James held up five fingers. "And we have one, two…nine adults. We can take them."

"Are you serious?" Leigh pulled away from her husband. "Despite what we've been through, we are not SEAL Team Six. We can't just swoop in and take out the bad guys." She turned to Sonny. "What about the police? Can't they do something?"

"We have no way of getting in touch with them," said Sonny. "We tried. We have no phones. So 9-1-1 is useless. We've heard rumors they're communicating on short-range walkie-talkies. That does us no good. None of our cars are working. So I walked over to the headquarters on Baltimore Avenue the day they killed Jack and Lee. I know a couple of the guys from my days with Prince George County P.D. Nobody was there."

"What do you mean *nobody*?" Leigh was incredulous.

"I mean nobody." Sonny shrugged. "There was a note on the door indicating the entire force was coping with Baltimore. It suggested anyone who needed help should contact Riverdale or campus police. And being black and armed, I wasn't about to test my luck at a place where I didn't have friends."

"What do we do?" Leigh asked Sonny. "What are you doing?"

"We live with it for now," said Sonny. "We deal with it when they try something again. Take a defensive position."

"No, we don't," said James. "We go on the offensive. I refuse to live in fear. I refuse to let anyone live in my house and terrorize what's left of this neighborhood. We've come too far for this."

"So I'll put it to you again, James," Sonny said. "What do you propose?"

"We get together, all of us," answered James. "We talk this through. All of us together can come up with something before it's too late to do anything."

"We have a planned meeting here tomorrow morning," revealed Sonny. "Will that work?"

"Sure."

"In the meantime"—Sonny pressed on his knees and stood—"you stay here. I've got two empty bedrooms for you. You're here as long as you want to be."

"Thank you, Sonny." Leigh stepped to her neighbor and hugged him.

"Thank you." James joined his wife and patted his friend on the shoulder. "But I don't plan on staying long."

CHAPTER 59

EVENT +1 Week, 3 Days, 03:30 Hours
University Park, Maryland
Temporary Recovery Zone 5

James Rockwell blinked open his eyes, not remembering having fallen asleep the night before. He reached over to his wife, but found empty sheets.

What time was it? How long had he slept?

He rolled over onto his back and stared at the popcorn ceiling, absently trying to identify a pattern in the random bumps until he heard voices downstairs. They dragged him back to reality and he slipped on his clothes before traipsing to the kitchen to join them.

His children were sitting at the bar, drinking juice and eating from ziplock bags of cheerios. At the table, petting Albert the dog, was Leigh. Her back was to him as he descended the stairs, seated next to Emma Wood and Abbey Whistler. Their husbands, Grant and Neil, were in the living room on the sofa, as were the Gilberts. They were all deep in conversation and none of them seem to notice James as he walked into the small space between the kitchen and living room.

"James," said Sonny, who was sitting in the easy chair. "Good morning! You slept well."

"A rare blessing," James said, waving a greeting to the Gilberts, Grant Wood, and Neil Whistler. "So what did I miss?"

"We're talking about how to handle the people living in your house now that you're home," said Neil. "We understand you'd like to take a *proactive* approach."

"That sounds like police talk." James chuckled, giving Sonny a knowing glance. "But I guess it's accurate. I'm not sure why you're content to sit and wait for the inevitable."

"You just got here," snipped Grant. "You haven't been living this. So I don't think it's fair for you to swoop in and judge—"

"Hold on." James waved his hands, stopping Grant from ranting. "I'm not judging anyone. It's just an observation. And as for *living* this? You have no clue what it took for my family and me to get home. You don't want to know, either."

"Nobody was suggesting—" Sonny tried to run interference, but James stopped him.

"Yes, they are," James corrected him. "Grant *is* suggesting I'm trying to bulldoze everyone without knowing the reality of the situation. And maybe I am." James glared at Grant. "My house is occupied by someone other than my family. And the people living there are killers. They did it once. They'll do it again."

"That doesn't mean we need to stoop to their level," reasoned Grant.

"Stoop?" James laughed, his voice rising an octave. He could feel his face growing hot, the desire to clench his fists. "How are we stooping, *Grant*, by making sure these murderers don't kill your family next?"

"Rock!" Leigh put her hand on her husband's back, rubbing it gently. "Calm down," she counseled. "We're all on the same team."

"I think we need to come up with a reasonable plan to prevent another attack," said Stuart Gilbert, his wife nodding in agreement. "It doesn't have to involve violence. I agree with what both of you are saying. We can find a middle ground."

James looked at Stuart as if he were France casting its vote at the UN Security Council, but he said nothing. Standing with his arms folded across his chest, he waited for Sonny to offer a solution.

"Well"—Sonny sighed—"I think that may be the best idea. We can be prepared without being trigger-happy."

"What exactly does that mean?" asked Grant.

"We've been on a rotation," explained Sonny, "watching the Rockwells' house since Jack was…"

"Right," said Grant. "We know."

"We haven't put together a plan about what to do if we actually see anything," said Neil. "Is that where you're going with this?"

James wanted to walk along the length of the sofa and punch everyone in the face. It was as if his neighborhood was filled with ostriches intent on burying their heads in the sand. Their idiocy and lack of recognition was astounding. He squeezed the circulation out of his hands and took a deep, cleansing breath. Leigh kept her hand on his back.

"Yes," said Sonny. "If we see movement, we need to have a plan of action. Does anyone have any suggestions?"

"My guess would be they're coming for your house next," James said softly, directing his stare to the Gilberts.

"Why do you say that?" asked Stuart, his brows furrowed and lips pursed.

"It involves the least risk." James shrugged. "You're next door. It's the shortest distance back to the safety of my house."

"That's a good point," said Sonny. "They did scout Jack's house first, right?"

The gathering mumbled as would the extras in a Broadway play, unintelligibly with overexaggerated shoulder shrugs and nods. They all agreed the Gilberts' home was likely the next target.

"So," continued Sonny, "we should be on the lookout for a scouting trip to Stuart and Susan's place. Once we identify they're targeting their house, we'll have, at most, a few hours to react."

"We'll need to clear the house," suggested James. "We should do it now, actually."

"I'm not leaving my house," said Stuart. "Why would I do that?"

"Because," James explained, "they'll see it. They'll know you're gone. And then all we've done is give them three houses on the street. But if you leave now and make them think you're still home, we have an advantage."

"Go on," said Sonny.

"Well"—James unfolded his arms and started talking with his hands—"we need to trick them into thinking they have the element of surprise. When, in fact, we do. If we stop them at the Gilberts', this will be over. If we don't, our houses will fall one by one."

"How does stopping them at *my* house get your house back?" asked Stuart. "Especially if we're trying to avoid any bloodshed."

"I never said I was going to avoid bloodshed," said James. "I just tacitly agreed to minimize it, to forego a preemptive strike."

"I don't know—" started Grant.

"Hold on, Grant," Sonny stopped him. "James is right. You have to fight fire with fire. We need to be prepared to defend ourselves."

Grant leaned back in the sofa, pouting and biting his lip. He turned to look at Stuart and Neil. They shrugged. Grant sucked in a deep breath and then huffed, "Fine. What's your idea, James?"

"Thanks for asking, Grant." James smiled. "If we all work together, I'm telling you, we get our homes back."

CHAPTER 60

EVENT +1 Week, 3 Days, 10:00 Hours
University Park, Maryland
Temporary Recovery Zone 5

"So you really think it's best we're all living together under one roof?" Leigh asked James. They were sitting on the edge of the bed in their room. Their kids were playing with Albert on the screened porch in the backyard.

"We don't have a choice," he explained. "We can't have everyone moving from one house to the other. There's safety in numbers. Plus, it's easier to take shifts on watch if we're keeping each other honest."

"Grant Wood doesn't seem too keen on this whole thing." Leigh chuckled. "Even though Emma is pushing him to trust you."

"I've never been a huge fan of his," James whispered.

"I know." Leigh rolled her eyes.

"That obvious?"

"Yes."

"I'll have to do a better job of masking my disdain." He kissed his wife on the forehead and stood from the bed.

"As long as we get our house back and everyone survives this"—Leigh took her husband's hand, holding it to her cheek—"I don't care what you mask. When is your shift?"

"A couple of minutes." James brushed Leigh's face with the back of his hand. "We're staggering the move-ins."

"I know." She looked up at him, her eyes wide. She was still the most beautiful girl in the world to him. And she knew he loved the way she looked at him. "The Gilberts are already here. The Whistlers will come by at sundown and the Woods will once it's dark."

"Good," said James. "I know this will work, Leigh."

"Just be careful." She stood, pressing her body against his, her arms sliding around his shoulders to caress the back of his head. "I've almost lost you twice. I can't do this without you."

"I'll be careful," James assured her with a confidence he could tell surprised her.

He knew he was emerging from this post-apocalyptic cocoon a changed man. He was stronger, more decisive, clear of purpose. There was something primal about him.

"You better be, Rock." She kissed him gently on the lips. "Or *I'll* kill you."

The door to the bedroom swung open and Max rumbled into the room. He shielded his eyes when he saw the affection his parents were sharing.

"What's up, Max?" James waved over his mop-haired son, inviting him to join a group hug.

"Nothing." Max shook his head and kept his distance. "I just got tired of playing with the dog. He wanted to go out and kept pawing at the back door. Boring."

"Where's your sister?" asked Leigh, her voice suddenly filled with worry. "You didn't leave her outside, did you?"

"No, Mom," said Max. "She's back in the kitchen, eating some of the disgusting astronaut ice cream. I can't believe she actually likes it."

"Okay." Leigh relaxed. "Good. So what's up?"

"I'm going with Dad." Max was matter-of-fact. "Right, Dad?"

"Who told you that?" Leigh's eyes narrowed as she pulled away from James.

"Dad."

Leigh's attention snapped back to her husband. "Oh really?"

"It's okay," James assured her. "We're just doing surveillance. We're not doing anything dangerous."

"Since when is anything not dangerous, Rock?" Leigh protested. "I don't like the idea of it."

"Trust me, Leigh." James put his hands on her shoulders. "We'll be okay. If we see anything suspicious, I'll send him inside immediately. Okay?"

Leigh looked at her husband and then at her son, his hands grasped in prayer. "Fine," she relented.

"Yes!" Max curled his hands into fists and pumped them in the air. "When do we go?"

"A few minutes," James said. "It's you, me, and Sonny."

"Cool." Max offered his dad a high five and then spun to bolt downstairs. "See you downstairs."

"He needs a little time with me, Leigh," James explained, pulling her into his chest. "He's been a trooper."

"I worry about him," said Leigh, "and Sloane."

"I know." James palmed his hand on the back of her head, tousling her hair. "Life is going to be different."

"It's not just that," Leigh explained. "I worry about what they've seen, what they've experienced. It would be enough for a child to have survived a car wreck, a tsunami and homicidal pirates in the same day, but add all of the *stuff* that's happened since then…"

"Kids are resilient," James offered, gently resting his chin on Leigh's head. "They seem okay at the moment."

"That's what bothers me, I guess," she countered. "They shouldn't be okay. They should be curled up in the fetal position, their knees pulled to their chests, rocking back and forth in a corner."

"That's how I feel," James joked.

"It's not funny." Leigh pulled away. "I'm serious. Long after our world returns to some sense of normalcy, if and when that happens, are kids are going to be scarred, Rock. Sloane can't rationalize what's happening. Max is probably compartmentalizing it, avoiding the emotion of it."

"I don't—"

"No." Leigh folded her arms across her chest. "Wait a minute. Let me finish. He's twelve and he's excited about doing surveillance with his dad, trying to keep tabs on some homicidal squatters who've stolen our house and killed our neighbor!"

"Would you rather him curl up?" James argued, trying to keep his voice low. "Would you be happier if he were a blubbering, incoherent mess?"

"No."

"Then do what you can to comfort him," counseled James. "Ask him questions. Get him to open up. Do the same with Sloane. We can't control what's happened, whether it's an asteroid or an EMP. We can't control the outside world. It'll collapse and rebuild itself. All we can do is...maintain our sanity."

Leigh pulled her hands to her face, cupping them over her nose and mouth, and fell into her husband's arms. She sobbed quietly as he held her. It was just the second time she'd cried since the event. The first was as a man shoved a pistol into her husband's mouth and promised to execute her entire family.

"We'll be okay," James promised her, trying to convince himself.

CHAPTER 61

EVENT +1 Week, 3 Days, 11:41 Hours
University Park, Maryland
Temporary Recovery Zone 5

Despite the trees blocking the line of sight to the Rockwells' front door, Sonny's roof was as good a spot as any to keep an eye on the squatters. The gables on the second-floor windows provided good cover, as did the sun. On a cloudless, late-summer afternoon, it shone directly into the Rockwells' west-facing house. There was a slight chill from the northerly breeze blowing through the trees.

They'd been on the roof for more than an hour. Armed with two pairs of binoculars and a rifle scope, they'd seen no movement from inside their home or in their front yard.

"How long are we up here?" Max's initial excitement had long since melted into the hot composite shingles. "I mean, if we don't see anything?"

"Until sundown," said Sonny. "Then Neil and Stuart take a shift."

James pulled the scope back to his eye and focused it through the foliage toward his front stoop. He scanned to the right and then swept back to the left, slowly checking for any signs of movement, any opportunity to get a good look at the—

"Dad!" Max said, pointing toward their driveway. "There!"

James jerked the scope to the right and moved it in small tight circles until he saw her. A woman with long dark hair, wearing a white T-shirt and cutoff jean shorts, was leaning against the back of the Camaro.

She was smoking a cigarette, or maybe something else, James thought. She took too long a drag for it to be a Marlboro. The woman was barefoot and was scratching her cheek with her free hand.

"Good eyes, Max," James commended his son. "You see her, Sonny?"

"I do." Sonny's eyes were pressed against his binoculars. "She's smoking a joint."

The woman shifted against the Camaro, crossing one leg in front of the other. She ran her finger through her hair and then took another hit, closing her eyes as she held in the smoke. She exhaled, blowing out a trail of smoke, which she fanned from her face.

"I'm assuming that's the one who helped kill Jack and Lee Pollock?" James kept his eye on her, the way she fidgeted as she stood there. She was an addict. No doubt.

"That's her," said Sonny. "No doubt. She's wearing the same clothing. Her hair's the same. I know that's her."

"So we're still at three adults and a couple of kids, then?" asked James.

"As far as we know." Sonny nodded. "We haven't seen anybody else."

"Is she the wife of one of the men?" asked James, noticing a thin silver-colored band on her wedding finger.

"We guess so," said Sonny. "There's no way to know. She might belong to both of them."

"Or both of them might belong to her," James joked. "She looks pretty hardened."

"She has to be," Sonny explained. "She dragged Lee Pollock into the yard herself. No remorse. She even stepped on her body and kicked it as—"

"I gotcha," said James, nodding over at Max. His son's eyes were wide, as were his ears.

"Oh." Sonny blushed. "Sorry. I forget sometimes. Days of being a cop, you know."

"It's okay." James patted Sonny on the back. "He's probably been through worse these past two weeks than you could describe to him."

"Oh great!" Sonny sighed, the binoculars still at his face. He wasn't looking at the woman. His attention was elsewhere.

"What?" asked Max.

"Albert got out of the house," he said, pointing to the grass on the center island of the cul-de-sac.

"You gonna get him?" James offered, watching the dog waddle through the grass island in the center of the cul-de-sac. Albert was sniffing around, looking for a place to lift his leg.

"Not yet." Sonny shook his head. "He'll do his business and come back."

James looked at the dog through his scope and then back at the woman. She wasn't leaning on the car anymore. She was standing at the end of the driveway, her attention toward the center island. She squatted and clapped. Her lips were pursed, as if whistling. James couldn't hear anything, however, over the gusts of wind. He felt goose bumps pop on his arms and neck. But he sensed it wasn't from the chill. Something bad was happening. He shot Sonny a look.

Sonny pulled his eyes from the binoculars and bit his lower lip. He scratched his head and then rubbed the back of his neck.

"I don't like this," he said. "But I'm not going over there, exposing myself to them. They already know I saw them kill Jack Pollock."

Albert was in view, now just a few feet from the end of the driveway. The woman was working hard to call him toward her, to get him close enough to pet him. The dog was wary. He moved toward her, but cautiously. He'd take a couple of steps, wag his tail and sniff the air, and then he'd inch closer.

The dog took another step to the woman before turning back to look at his owner. His tail wagged and he started back to Sonny when the woman called him or whistled or did something that gained Albert's attention.

He reached the edge of the driveway and the woman knelt down, offering the back of her hand for Albert to sniff.

The woman slipped her fingers inside Albert's collar. He responded to her at first, licking her hand and wagging his nub of a tail. But something caught his attention and he tried to pull away. Albert strained against his collar to turn around, but the woman strengthened her grip and looked up, farther down the street.

James pulled the scope away from his eye and leaned forward, looking into the street between the front of Sonny's house and the center island. He nearly jumped from the roof when he saw what had captured their attention; Sloane was alone, walking toward her house, and Albert, and the homicidal woman.

CHAPTER 62

EVENT +1 Week, 3 Days, 11:50 Hours
University Park, Maryland
Temporary Recovery Zone 5

James threw open the window and hurdled the sill into the house. He raced down the hall, almost stumbling over his feet as he bounded down the stairs and out the front door.

He sprinted into the street and looked east toward his house. Sloane was at the end of the driveway, petting Albert. The woman's free hand was on his daughter's shoulder, her eyes on Sloane until she glanced up to see James hurriedly moving toward her.

A smile wormed its way across her thin, cracked lips as James broke his stride just feet from the end of the driveway. She kept her hand on Sloane's shoulder, gripping it with her fingers.

"Sloane," James huffed, his heart pounding against his chest. His lungs burned from the quick dash, still recovering from the infection. "Sloane!" he barked. "Come here, please!"

"Hi, Daddy." Sloane spun around, freeing herself from the woman's touch. "I came to get Albert. He got out."

"Come here, Sloane." James spoke to his daughter, but his eyes were on the meth fiend in front of him. The picked scabs on her face and neck were giveaways, if the gaunt, witchlike structure of her face wasn't enough to betray her demons.

"But, *Daddy*." The woman giggled in a throaty, raspy voice. "We were just having some girl talk."

James took a step forward and gently pulled Sloane to his side. He glared at the woman but said nothing.

"Seems you got a little party over there," the woman said, gripping Albert's collar as he struggled against it. "And you ain't invited us."

"Go home, Sloane," James said, gently nudging his daughter toward Sonny's house. He didn't notice Sonny, Leigh, Max, and the Gilberts were on the street and nearing the island.

Sloane obliged and skipped obliviously back to her mother, who stepped from the crowd to grab her daughter's hand and lead her back inside the house. Max and Susan Gilbert followed them. Stuart Gilbert stayed on the street with Sonny.

"We was just talkin', Daddy," she twanged. "Ain't no cause to be rude, now."

"Who's *us*?" James asked.

The woman stood from her crouch and stuck out her chin, letting go of Albert after a final yank that forced a yelp from the affable dog. He shook off the choke and trotted back to Sonny, and the woman took a step toward James and stuck her thumbs into her pockets. She gurgled a laugh and smacked her lips.

"I asked you a question." James could feel the tension in his neck. "Who is *us*?"

"I was talkin' to your girl there." She nodded over James's shoulder, toward Sonny's house. "She's a real cutie. She told me you used to live here."

James choked back the urge to attack the woman and waterboard the information out of her. But he clenched his jaw and didn't respond.

"I can tell by the fire in your eyes that's the truth," she quipped. "Thank you for leavin' it in such fine shape. I mean to say it's first class." She narrowed her eyes. The smile disappeared. "Love what your wife has done with the place."

"Don't get comfortable," James said.

"I was just gonna say the same thing to y'all." Her drawl dripped with smug condescension. "We *love* us some parties." The woman was a caricature of herself, drawn from some C-rated Steven Seagal movie and perfectly cast.

The woman's eyes widened again and she laughed, a phlegm-coated, smoker's laugh. She winked at James and turned around, swinging her nonexistent hips as she walked back to the house. Peeking out from her waistband, framed by a green-inked winged tramp-stamp, was the grip of a nine-millimeter handgun. It was black with a silver inlay, which caught the sunlight as she moved. The woman reached the stoop and turned.

"Finders, keepers," she said, blowing a kiss. "Ain't that right, *Rock*?"

James stood at the end of the driveway, *his* driveway, dumfounded. He wanted to rush the woman, knock her through the door and use the gun against her and everyone inside. She'd managed to push every last one of his buttons. But he did nothing. He said nothing. Instead he watched her open the door to his family's home and disappear inside.

James took a last survey of the house before he left, taking note of the two boys peeking through Sloane's window. The older was a teenager, James guessed, maybe thirteen or fourteen. The other was half his size. He was a six- or seven-year-old.

James waved at the boys, offered a smile, and walked back to Sonny's house, meeting Sonny and Stuart at the island.

"What in the world was that?" Stuart asked. "What did she say?"

"She threatened us," James said, walking swiftly past his two neighbors as they quickened their pace to keep up.

"They're not afraid of us," Stuart reasoned.

James stopped short at the curb in front of Sonny's house and looked back at his house. Then he turned to Stuart and said without any hint of emotion, "They should be."

CHAPTER 63

EVENT +1 Week, 3 Days, 12:30 Hours
University Park, Maryland
Temporary Recovery Zone 5

While Leigh berated herself for letting Sloane slip out of the house, James tried to ascertain exactly what his daughter revealed to the enemy. He sat on the floor next to the kitchen table while Sloane stuck her nose against Albert's, baiting him to slather her face with kisses.

"Sloane," James said, his hand on the small of her back, "tell me again what the woman asked you."

"She told me how pretty I am and how much she loved dogs." Sloane pecked at Albert. He snorted. "And then she asked me how many people were at our party."

"And you told her what?" James rubbed her back, trying to sound more curious than interrogatory. "What did you tell her about our party?"

"I told her it wasn't a party." Sloane turned to look at her dad, and Albert snuck a disgusting lick across the side of her face. "Alllberrt!" She giggled.

"What did you tell her it was?"

"A sleepover." Sloane looked over to her dad. "I heard you talking about it. You said *everyone* was staying here."

"You told her that?" James swallowed hard.

"No, Dad." She rolled her eyes. "I told her we were having a sleepover because they were in our house. That was it. I didn't say anything about a party. The *lady* said that."

"What did you think of that lady?" James asked the question in the wake of a sigh of relief.

"She was scary." Her brows arched, her eyes narrowed. "She was like a witch or something. But I didn't want her to know she scared me. So I acted like Momma and pretended everything was okay."

From the mouths of babes…

James reached over and hugged his daughter and pecked her forehead with a kiss. "Play with the dog, Sloane." He smiled and pushed himself up.

Sonny crossed the family room, his lips pursed, the deep line running across his forehead more evident than James remembered it. He put his hands on his hips expectantly.

"She didn't give anything away," James explained. "She told them we were staying here. But they may have already known that. The woman recognized me."

"How?"

"Family pictures probably," James guessed. "There are a bunch of them on the refrigerator. She probably recognized Sloane before I even walked over there."

"Does this change anything?" Sonny asked. "Do we need to move up the timetable?"

"I don't think so." James scratched the growing, uncomfortable beard on his neck. "The Woods will be here in a couple of hours. Then the Whistlers once it's dark. I think we keep an eye on the neighborhood and stick with what we've got."

"Grant is up on the roof now." Sonny looked up at the ceiling as he spoke. "He's by himself right now. I'll join him in a couple minutes. But I wanted to show you something first."

"Okay." James looked over Sonny's shoulder at his wife. She was on the sofa, rocking back and forth, biting her cuticles. "But let me talk to Leigh for a second."

"She's killing herself over Sloane," said Sonny.

"I know." James frowned.

"Meet me in the basement when you're finished up here." Sonny patted James on the shoulder.

"Got it." James smiled and walked the few steps to the family room sofa, dropping next to his wife, who seemed too deep in thought to notice him. "Leigh?" he said, putting his hand on her leg.

Leigh looked over at her husband, her eyes heavy and framed by dark circles. The faint laugh lines at their corners were etched with worry. Her index finger was in her mouth, the edge of her nail between her teeth.

"Leigh," James repeated softly, "Sloane is fine."

Leigh blinked back tears, her eyes welling until the lids couldn't hold the pool and they streamed down her cheeks. She wiped them with the back of her hand without saying anything.

"She is fine," James said a third time, praying it was the charm. He needed his wife's strength. "She's nine years old. You can't expect to know what she's doing twenty-four seven."

"Yes I can," she whimpered, sucking in breaths like a child on the backside of a tantrum. "I'm her mother. She's my responsibility. I should have known. I should have stopped her."

"Nothing happened," James reassured her, inching closer to her and softening his voice. "She's here. She's unfazed."

"Oh, Rock!" She laughed, snot spraying from her nose. "Unfazed?! Do you really believe that? Our children are *fazed*. Don't kid yourself. They're not the same."

"My point is," he tried to clarify, "we've done nothing but protect them the best we can. We've done nothing to harm them."

Leigh wiped her nose with the back of her hand, sniffling. "It's not what we've done or haven't done. It's that we can't protect them forever."

"That was the case before the world turned upside down," James argued. "There were always dangers."

"But now they're amplified," she said. "Now they're everywhere, around every corner. And I don't know, Rock. Even if we get our house back and these horrible people are gone, who's to say another threat doesn't appear right after them."

"You're right." James nodded. "*When* we get our house back, the outside world is still the outside world: chaotic, treacherous, short of electricity and food but long on weapons and criminals."

"That's my point." She grabbed the sides of her head with her hands. "What's the point?"

"The point is"—James took a deep breath, as much to gather his thoughts as to lament his wife's malaise—"nothing worth having is ever easy. We will survive this chapter. And we will thrive in the next."

"You can't promise that." She shook her head, her eyes searching for comfort James imagined her mind was willing to accept.

"Tomorrow is never promised to us, Leigh," he offered. "But that's no reason to give up on today."

She folded her arms across her chest and lay her head back against the sofa. She closed her eyes and clenched her jaw. She was shutting down and James knew it, so he grabbed her hand.

"Look at me, Leigh," he said, his tone firm and direct. "I need you. The children need you. We cannot have you retreating into that head of yours, intent on defeat and darkness."

Leigh looked at James, focused on his message. She picked up her head and turned her body toward his.

"Get over yourself," he said. "Focus on what needs to be done *now*. Be strong for your children. Be strong for me. When I get us back into our house, you can collapse in our bed, wrap yourself in a blanket, and hide for a week. But now you need to man up."

"Ha!" It was a genuine laugh. "Man up? You're ridiculous."

"Maybe," James smirked, "but I'm serious."

"I get it," she said, taking his hand. "I just…"

"Just what?"

"Needed a good cry," she said. "I'll be okay." Leigh drew her finger into her mouth and gnawed on the cuticle.

James knew his wife. He knew she was placating him. She was on the verge of a breakdown. He'd seen it when their daughter Nora died. She drifted away from him, from Max and Sloane, from the functioning world.

He'd pulled her back by forcing her to participate, by pushing her to get out of bed in the morning and stay up late with him at night. He'd decided the only way to live was to push themselves beyond their limits.

That's when they began the extreme adventuring. That's when he bought guns and learned how to hunt. He took cross-fit classes, became a certified SCUBA diver, took sailing classes. He dragged her along for the ride until she could drive herself literally and figuratively.

He couldn't let her slip into the morass again. This time, he knew he'd lose his grip and they'd both sink beyond redemption.

CHAPTER 64

EVENT +1 Week, 3 Days, 13:11 Hours
University Park, Maryland
Temporary Recovery Zone 5

Sonny's basement was unfinished, blanketed in the pink insulation exposed between the pine wall studs. It was dank, with a cold, veined cement floor. Sonny had always talked about making a man-cave out of it: a bank of flat panel televisions, Ravens and Orioles memorabilia covering the walls, a popcorn machine in one corner, a full bar in the other. When his wife died, he'd abandoned the plan.

"The whole place is man cave now," he'd lamented. "No need to escape anywhere on Sunday afternoons."

Where the popcorn machine would have stood was a large metal shelving unit. On it were canned vegetables, containers of rice and flour. There were large gallon jugs of water, vinegar, empty mason jars, and cooking oil.

Adjacent to the shelves, on the floor, were warehouse-size packages of toilet paper and paper towels. He had enough to last at least six months, maybe a little longer. There were also a couple dozen bottles of hydrogen peroxide.

"You'd be amazed by the uses for the stuff," he'd bragged to James the first time he showed him what he called his "prepper shelf". "It's a great disinfectant and cleaner. It's good for mouthwash, getting out bloodstains, and killing mold or fungus."

"You could spray it on your hair and give it a natural, golden tone," James had joked.

"Because a brother like me wants to look like that," he'd laughed, running his hand across his head.

James thought about that day as he crossed the room to where the bar should have been. Instead there was a large gun safe and a small drop-in freezer. James pulled open the freezer and found it empty.

"There's nothing there because I ran out of gas to run the generator," explained Sonny. "We had to eat what food I had in there on day four and five. There was chicken, a few fish filets. I really wasn't as prepared as I planned on being."

"More prepared than me." James closed the freezer and looked at the open gun safe. It was an identical model to the one in his own basement. The contents were different.

"I think these'll work." Sonny pulled out a pair of Bushmaster 300 AAC Blackout semiautomatic rifles. "They're super light." He handed James one of the rifles. "Magpul ACS stock, takes any AR-type ammunition. It's pretty nasty looking, right?"

"It is." James held the rifle as if aiming it across the room. He adjusted the stock to fit his arm length. "You have two of them?"

"I have four." Sonny nodded toward the safe. "I buy the same weapon because it breeds familiarity. I'd rather be super proficient with one type of weapon than have some crazy cache of weapons I don't know how to use."

"Makes sense." James thought back to Camp Driggers in Pennsylvania and Steve's employment of the same philosophy. "Any handguns?"

"A couple of Smith & Wessons," Sonny said. "Nothing fancy."

"Are these going to be noisy?" James asked, holding the weapon up to his cheek, noticing the lack of a sight. "I mean, do we lose the element of surprise after the first trigger pull?"

"No." Sonny smiled. "These have noise and flash suppression on them. We'll be about as quiet as we can be with this kind of firepower. Not dormouse quiet, mind you, but pretty close to it."

"Cool." James handed the rifle back to his friend. "Hey, I can't thank you enough. You've been really good to us."

"It's nothing, James." Sonny put both rifles back in the safe. "You and Leigh were so kind after…" Sonny choked on his words and shrugged. James knew he couldn't say her name, couldn't talk about what happened, couldn't delve into the pain he suffered in the wake of her death. "I just…especially when you were coping with your own loss…I could never repay you. But this is a start."

"You've more than repaid us," James said. "Despite the awful bean soup we've eaten three times already."

"There's only so much I can do with a pot and a gas cooktop." Sonny laughed. "Like I said, the meat's gone. Beans are good for the fiber."

"They're good for something else too." James patted his stomach and winked. "In fact, we might not need any smoke grenades after another helping of the soup."

"Speaking of which!" Sonny held up his finger. A cartoon lightbulb might as well have appeared over his head. "I've got a couple flash grenades. Some SWAT guys gave them to me after the pandemic. They've got a ten-year shelf life." He reached into the safe and pulled out an army green cylinder, handing it to James.

"I'm guessing this is a metal oxidant mix of magnesium and aluminum plus an oxidizer of ammonium perchlorate or potassium perchlorate." James examined the flash grenade. It was embossed with white lettering that read "2 BANG 1.5s DELAY".

"Hell if I know." Sonny laughed. "You're the science professor! I just know it knocks someone silly long enough to get the upper hand."

"Teacher," said James. "I'm not a professor."

"Whatever you say." Sonny chuckled. He took the flash grenade from James and put it back in the safe. "We'll come back and grab these when we need them. I don't want the kids having access to them."

"Good idea," said James.

"So it's back to surveillance." Sonny pushed shut the safe door and spun the combination lock. "Wanna join me until the Woods show up?"

"Sure." James followed Sonny up the stairs. "I think Max is up there with Stuart already. He wants to be part of this."

"He's turning into quite the young man," said Sonny, talking over his shoulder. "Despite everything, or maybe because of it, he's got a maturity about him I didn't notice before."

"It's probably both," James acknowledged. "We've all seen and done some things that'll make anyone age."

"Leigh's having a tough time." Sonny stopped at the top of the steps, waiting to open the door to the main floor. It was an observation more than a question.

"Yeah." James pursed his lips. "We all are. I'll fill you in on everything once we've had some distance from it." He let the response hang in the air until Sonny forced a smile and pushed his shoulder into the door. They could hear Grant and Emma Woods in the kitchen, talking about what they brought for dinner. James was about to tell Sonny how relieved he was to avoid another bowl of bean soup when Max met them in the hallway. He was out of breath.

"Dad," he gasped, "Mr. Lawrence, you gotta come quick! Mr. Gilbert says there's a problem." Max waved both men to follow him and raced up the steps two at a time.

They reached the window and climbed out onto the roof. Stuart Gilbert was crouched behind the gable, looking in the wrong direction. The binoculars pressed to his eyes were facing west when they should have been on the Rockwells' house, facing east.

"What's the problem?" James asked. "Max said you told him to come get us."

Stuart lowered the binoculars, revealing a man who'd just seen a ghost, or something worse. He blinked against the sun, which was hanging low against the horizon, ready to sink behind the trees, but he said nothing.

"What is it, Stuart?" Sonny waved his hands in front of Stuart's face, trying to snap him from the haze.

"I think the Whistlers are dead."

CHAPTER 65

EVENT +1 Week, 3 Days, 13:46 Hours
University Park, Maryland
Temporary Recovery Zone 5

James listened to Stuart repeat himself slowly. His face was pale, his forehead beading with sweat. What he explained was almost too hard to believe.

"I had my eyes on your house," he said, gulping past what must have been a thick knot in his throat. "I think Max was looking over at my house. That was the plan. Look east. That was the plan."

"Yes." James tried to soothe his neighbor with his voice. "That was the plan."

"So I was looking toward your house and the woman came outside," said Stuart. "There was a kid with her. A boy, I think. He was young. And she was scolding him, making a scene."

"What kind of scene?" asked Sonny.

"She slapped him across the face and then grabbed his arm," he explained, his hands gesticulating wildly. "She was yelling at him. The kid shrank from her when she raised her hands. It was bad."

"It was bad, Dad," Max echoed. "Both of us were watching it."

"But then she stopped." Stuart's gaze was distant, as if he were watching a replay as he described it. "She shoved the kid toward the stoop and then looked up, straight at us, and pointed."

"She pointed at you?" James looked at Sonny, his brow furrowed. "What do you mean she pointed?"

Stuart sat on the roof, one hand gripping the edge of the gable. He was mumbling something unintelligible.

"No!" said Max, picking up the baton. "She looked at us but pointed down the street at Mr. and Mrs. Whistler's house. She was telling us to look there."

"Then what did she do?" asked Sonny.

"She went inside." Max shrugged. "We both turned to look across the street. I didn't see anything, but Mr. Gilbert did. Then he told me to come get you."

"Stuart." James took his neighbor by his shoulders and shook him gently, drawing Stuart's eyes to his. "What did you see?"

"Nothing at first," he said, shaking his head, his eyes drifting downward. "But then it was a flash. At first I wasn't sure what it was. But it was a flash. And then another flash. Like a small explosion or something. I don't know. I thought maybe they were taking photographs. You know, to remember their house as it was before they left. I don't know."

"The light wasn't from a camera, was it?" James already knew the source of the flashes.

"No." Stuart shook his head and buried his face in his hands. "It wasn't."

"They were shot," James said.

Stuart nodded. "I saw one of the men at the window. He pulled back a curtain and stood in the window. He had a gun in his hand. He waved at me. He stood there with the gun and waved."

"They knew we were watching them?" Max asked. "How could they know? How did they slip by us? We were always watching?"

"First," James explained, his hand cupped around the back of Stuart's neck as his neighbor mourned, "we don't know how long *they've* been watching *us*. Second, they clearly set us up. Her beating on the kid was a distraction. It was a sick distraction, but one nonetheless."

"But how did they get to the Whistlers without us seeing them?" Max asked again, but with more urgency.

"They could have traveled backyards," suggested Sonny. "They could have gone either direction to the Whistlers, knowing we'd be looking in the wrong place."

"Why the Whistlers?" asked Max.

"They're older," answered James. "They live alone."

"Easy targets." Max understood.

"Something we haven't asked you," added James, turning to Stuart. "Are they still in the house? Have you seen the men since one of them waved at you?"

"They're still in the house," said Stuart. "I mean, I think they are. I haven't seen them leave."

"It's been less than ten minutes, Dad," said Max. "We could go get them. We know where they are. They won't be expecting us."

"That's not happening," said James. "You're not going anywhere. But I do think the rest of us should pay the Whistlers' house a visit."

"That's suicide," said Stuart, looking up from his stupor.

"So is waiting for them to come here," countered James.

CHAPTER 66

EVENT +1 Week, 3 Days, 14:01 Hours
University Park, Maryland
Temporary Recovery Zone 5

"Stuart's in no condition to go with you," Leigh stressed, having lost the brief fight to keep her husband within the walls of Sonny's home. "He's essentially catatonic up on the roof. I don't know that it's a good idea for just you and Sonny to sneak up on the Whistlers' house."

James watched Emma and Grant Wood talking to each other through their teeth. They were standing off to the side of the room, close to the mantel. His hands were on his hips, hers were crossed over her chest. From the hunch in his shoulders, James could tell Emma was winning the argument.

"Did you hear me, Rock?" Leigh waved her hand in front of her husband's face. "I said I don't like the idea of the two of you going alone."

"I don't think you have to worry about that," James whispered, acknowledging his wife. "I have a feeling Grant's going to be coming with us."

Leigh followed her husband's gaze to the corner of the room. She agreed with James that Grant was likely being conscripted into service.

"I've got two rifles," Sonny announced, emerging from the basement. He had a small pack slung over one shoulder. "One for both of us," he said, offering one to James. "I've got extra magazines in the pack, along with two flash grenades."

"We're going to need another rifle," James said under his breath. "I have a strong feeling Grant's coming with us."

"I'll go get one." Sonny started back down the hall when Grant stopped him.

"Sonny," he said, running a hand through his thinning comb-over. Grant was forty going on fifty. His paunch added at least five years to his balding head, which added five to the gray of what was left. "I'm coming with you. But I don't want one of those rifles. I wouldn't know how to use it. I could end up hurting one of us."

"No problem." Sonny winked at him. "I have just the thing for you." He disappeared downstairs and came back with a Smith & Wesson revolver. "It's loaded. It's got six shots. You're an emergency gun, okay?"

"Okay." Grant took the gun and held it as if it were a snot-soaked rag.

"Hold it like this." Sonny grabbed his hand and molded the gun to fit his grip. "The business end always points toward what you want to shoot. If you don't want to kill someone, don't point the gun at it. Got it?"

Grant nodded.

"We need to go," James suggested. He turned to his wife. "You know how to handle a weapon. Go downstairs and get the rifles. Both of them are already plugged with loaded magazines. Use them if you need them, understood?"

"We better not need them, Rock." Leigh stepped to within an inch of her husband. "I'm counting on you to stop them out there, or get back here before they do."

"I'll do my best." He leaned to kiss her forehead, but she pulled back.

"Rock." Her eyes searched his without any hint of humor. "I'm not kidding. I know you're not Rick Grimes, or whoever the hell that guy was in the zombie show you watched on Netflix, but kill these motherf—"

"I got it." He kissed her lips, fully convinced his wife had dived head first into the deep end and was digging deeper still. As much as she worried about the children, and the long-term effect of the end of the world as they knew it on them, he was already peeking glimpses of what it was doing to her.

"Lock the door behind us," said Sonny. "Pull the curtains and stay in the same room together. I'd like to tell you Albert would bark if anyone tried to break in, but he won't."

"Stuart's still on the roof," said James. "He's our lookout. Since he hasn't alerted us to anything, we have to guess the squatters are still in the Whistlers' house."

"He's not altogether there," counseled Sonny. "So we can't be sure his intelligence is accurate."

"It better be." Grant frowned before reluctantly kissing his wife goodbye.

James made sure to hug his son and his daughter, told them how much he loved them, and then led Sonny and Grant out the back door through the screened-in patio and into the backyard.

The sun had dipped below the visible horizon, but a faint orange glow hung above the trees. The gusty winds brought with them clouds, which would make it more difficult to see once the sunlight completely faded.

James walked purposefully across Grant's backyard. The grass was thick under his feet as he marched toward the fence that separated Grant's property from the Whistlers'.

Sonny was to his right, carrying the rifle in both hands. His pack bounced on his back as he walked, making the faintest metallic "clicking" sound as the contents slid against each other.

Grant trailed a step behind. He was a mouth-breather and stumbled to keep pace across the short distance. James wondered if he was going to be a problem. Actually, he already knew the answer.

They reached the six-foot-high cedar-plank fence and James handed his rifle to Sonny. He gripped the cap just above the top rail and hoisted himself, belly first, onto the cap. He lay there for a moment, looking toward the Whistlers' house. He couldn't see anything, so he dropped himself into their yard and landed flatfooted into the ankle-deep grass.

Sonny placed James's rifle on the cap and James retrieved it before Sonny joined him in the Whistlers' yard. Surprisingly Grant managed to heave himself up and over with little trouble. Though he was decidedly out of breath by the time he landed next to his neighbors.

"Hang on a second," he pleaded between labored breaths. "I need a second."

"Not gonna happen, Grant," whispered James. "We don't have a second."

"Seriously?" he complained. "Why?"

"Because I see movement inside the Whistlers' house," James explained. "The squatters are still inside."

CHAPTER 67

EVENT +1 Week, 3 Days, 14:13 Hours
University Park, Maryland
Temporary Recovery Zone 5

Sonny took the lead en-route to the back of the house. He'd been on raids, served warrants, and conducted high-profile takedowns during his years as a police officer. He knew the right way to approach a volatile situation in which there was limited information about the suspects, how they were armed, and where in the structure they were in relation to the entry door.

Back in the day, if he suspected two armed men were in a home and that they'd killed somebody, he'd have called for additional assistance. He'd have waited for a Special Weapons and Tactics team or even a set of hostage negotiators. He didn't have that luxury.

A step behind, heart racing and mouth dry from stress, was Grant. He didn't want to be there. His wife, with an overbearing conscience, forced him to join what he worried would be an ill-fated, fatal attempt at stopping a trio of psychopaths.

"We're not soldiers," he'd stressed to his wife. "We'll get killed. Where will that leave us?"

"If you go," she'd reasoned, "you'll give them a chance. And if you don't go, the squatters will come after us anyhow. It's better to try."

"You're essentially sending me to my death," he'd hissed through his teeth. "You're killing me."

"I'm asking you to save us," she'd snapped. "Me and our three children."

"You want them to grow up without a father?" It had been his final volley.

"You want them not to grow up at all?" she'd spiked back into his face. "I don't *want* you to go. I don't want *any* of you to go. But I understand *why* it has to be done. I can't believe you don't."

As he stepped through the grass, feeling it brush against the sides of his legs, he wished he'd thought to suggest she go instead of him. But as soon as the thought crossed through his mind, he knew it would have been the absolute wrong thing to do. It was the wrong thing to feel. He was as angry with himself for not having the instinct to protect his family as he was with Emma for pushing him to do it.

In the rear was James, a man who'd seen more than a lifetime's share of death and misery in the last ten and a half days. The idea of killing or maiming someone for his family's sake had become so familiar, it didn't faze him. He was almost on autopilot, laser focused and of a singular purpose.

He crouched low, the Bushmaster pointed at ten o'clock and toward the ground as he moved. His trigger finger was unwavering, his heartbeat steady, as was his breathing. James felt good. It was almost as if he relished the anticipation of the coming fray.

The slight slope of the Whistlers' backyard was much less inclined than the others in the cul-de-sac. They didn't have a basement. So as the trio approached the house, they were at the main floor of the two-story house. Across the rear of the home was a large wooden deck. At one edge of the deck was a well-worn charcoal grill, at the other a wooden A-frame bench swing, and in between them a picnic table. Beyond the deck furniture, centered on the back of the house, was a large glass-paneled pair of French doors. The glass panes were covered by curtains affixed to the top and bottom of the doors. But they were sheer, and through them James could see the faint parabolic beam of a dying flashlight dancing around the kitchen.

The men stopped and dropped low behind the picnic table. James whispered to Grant, telling him to breathe through his nose to reduce the noise. Grant nodded and compromised, breathing in through his mouth and out through his nose.

"That's the kitchen," James reminded his compatriots. "On the right, where the squatter is. He's probably loading up on supplies."

"The dining table is there at the double doors," added Sonny, "if I remember correctly."

"I think you're right," agreed James. "But I don't think we're smart to enter here. What would you do, Sonny?"

"I think we split up," said Sonny, "take both sides of the house. There's bound to be an unlocked window, or at least a better entry point."

"Who goes with who?" Grant huffed. "I don't want to be the odd man out, here."

"You go with James," Sonny instructed. "I'll go by myself. I'm the only one with experience with this kind of thing, anyhow."

"And once we find a way inside?" asked Grant. "What then?"

"First we have to find the Whistlers," suggested Sonny. "On the off chance one or both of them are still alive, we need to help them and, if possible, get them out of the house."

"We know the squatters are there, though," Grant countered. "What do we do about them?"

"Whatever you have to do." Sonny shrugged. He gave the men a salute and slid off into the darkness around the right side of the house.

"It's you and me," James whispered to Grant. "Let's go."

James moved from behind the picnic table, stopped for a beat at the bench swing, and then sprinted around the left side of the house. Grant was a couple of steps behind him, imitating James's movements until they both stood with their backs pressed against the clapboard, a window to their right.

James motioned to Grant and then he ducked beneath the chest-high window to move to the other side. It was dark enough outside that, unless the flashlight beam hit him directly, whoever was inside the house wouldn't be able to see him peeking through the window. Grant stayed frozen in position as James pivoted to his left and looked into the house.

James's eyes adjusted quickly to see the interior of the house. He was on the far side of the family room, looking past the dining area into the kitchen. The layout was similar, but not a duplicate, of Sonny's house. James pressed his face closer to the glass, trying to see a wider view of the interior of the house. There was nobody in the kitchen or the dining area or, as he swept left, any movement at the front of the house near the stairwell.

He backed away from the window and then placed his free hand against the glass, applying gentle pressure upward.

It was unlocked!

James nodded to Grant and handed his partner his rifle. He pressed both palms flat against the glass and pushed slowly, and quietly, to raise the window high enough for him to enter. James stuck his head through the opening and got a better sense of his surroundings. Grant shot James a look of disbelief as the high school physics teacher pulled himself onto the open sill and waved for his weapon as he tumbled inside.

CHAPTER 68

EVENT +1 Week, 3 Days, 14:20 Hours
University Park, Maryland
Temporary Recovery Zone 5

The instant he dropped to the carpet inside the Whistlers' home, James Rockwell knew he'd made a mistake. He wasn't sure, in that split second, whether it was hair standing up on his neck or the strong odor of ammonia and chicken soup that told him he'd been played.

But no sooner had he balanced himself and tried to grip the weapon, he felt a jarring blow to the center of his back, right between his shoulder blades, followed by the weight of someone pushing him forward to the floor, ejecting the rifle across the carpet.

James, winded by the hit and stunned by the tackle, still managed to turn onto his side and thrust his left elbow backward. It caught the attacker in the ribs and the man grunted and cursed as he tried to regain control.

But James, now high on the adrenaline, struggled onto his back and connected with a fist to the man's chest. It knocked the attacker back long enough for James to land another punch in the man's groin.

But the attacker was undeterred, fully straddling James at his waist, punching him in the face twice before slipping his hands around his throat. James grabbed the man's wrists and pulled at them as he felt the force of his grip around his neck. As he shifted his body, trying to gain any leverage against the attacker, one of the men who'd stolen his home, he got a good look at his face. Even in the darkness, he could see the crazed, vacant look in the man's eyes.

His face was drawn, like the woman's, and what was left of his teeth was rotting. His breath was rancid, overpowered only by the thick dank body odor.

A familiar sense of dread washed over him as James's mind flashed to Peaks Island and their escape from the fire tower. His daughter, Sloane, wrapping her hands around his neck. He knew then as he knew now he was about to lose consciousness. This time, he knew there was no reprieve.

Pow! Pow!

The pressure around James's neck released and the man slumped forward against the echo of the gunshots, his head dropping to the floor next to James's. His eyes were fixed wide, his tongue hanging from between his lips.

James pushed himself away from the head and from under the man's body. He grabbed his throat and coughed against the thick dull pain in his neck.

Grant dropped from the edge of the windowsill, the Smith & Wesson in his hand. He knelt beside James and put the gun on the floor.

"Are you okay?" he asked, his hand on James's leg. "Are you all right?"

James nodded, not sure if he could talk and not wanting to try. Instead he patted Grant's shoulder and forced a thin smile to thank him.

Grant offered his hand and helped James to his feet. "That was close," he whispered. "I just…I just…can't believe I killed someone."

James tried to swallow, but it hurt too much. He winced against the pain and squeezed his eyes shut.

"Should we go back?" Grant asked. "I think we should go back. We don't know where the other guy is. That was too close, James."

James opened his eyes and shook his head emphatically. "No." His voice was hoarse and guttural, as if he'd stepped out of the Mojave. "We're not doing that. We need to find Sonny."

Grant sighed and nodded, muttering under his breath. James thanked him again for saving him and then found his rifle on the floor. Both men stood, bent at their waists, and slowly maneuvered their way toward the front of the house.

As he approached the foyer, James saw a shadow move against the front windows. Somebody was there, maybe fifteen feet away. James raised his rifle. His finger was poised against the trigger. He squinted against the darkness, trying to make out who it was at the front of the house.

He stopped and held his arm out, signaling Grant to pause his advance. Both men crouched down behind a small end table. Somehow, the shadow hadn't seen them.

And then he did.

The shadow jerked his head to the left, instinctually looking to where he heard. He raised a weapon and stepped cross-legged into the family room. He was exposed. James considered taking a preemptive shot.

The shadow moved to within three feet and then turned, walking past James and Grant and toward the kitchen. James pivoted and looked behind him.

He recognized the shadow.

"Sonny!" he whispered, drawing the shadow's attention. "It's James and Grant."

The shadow lowered his weapon. He stepped to the table as James and Grant stood to greet him.

"I heard the shots," Sonny said. "I was on the other side of the house. There's nothing there. Are you both okay?"

"Yes," James said. "Grant saved me. We're good."

"Okay," Sonny said, adjusting his hold on the Bushmaster. "Did you get both of them?"

"No," Grant offered. "Just one."

"I haven't seen anything," Sonny said. "Except…"

"Except what?" Grant asked.

Sonny nodded toward the front of the house and led the men to the formal living area adjacent to the foyer and the stairs. There, they saw what they hadn't hoped to find.

CHAPTER 69

EVENT +1 Week, 3 Days, 14:24 Hours
University Park, Maryland
Temporary Recovery Zone 5

Neil Whistler was on his back. His eyes were squeezed shut, the anticipation of his death frozen on his face. His legs were splayed across his wife's torso, as if he'd fallen back across her as he was shot.

"They killed her first," James said, crouching near the bodies. "They made him watch."

Abbey Whistler was on her side, her head resting on an extended arm. Her eyes were open, her lips curled into what looked like a smile. In the dark, James couldn't tell exactly where they'd been shot. There was too much blood and he didn't want to examine either of them to find out.

They were dead. That was the bottom line.

"They were good people," said Grant. "Good neighbors. Abbey would take care of the kids if we wanted a night out. Neil mowed our lawn for us a couple times."

"He mowed my lawn too." James rubbed his neck and tried to swallow again. "Abbey was always great at Halloween. Remember she would dress up for the kids?"

"She gave out full-sized Snickers bars," Sonny recalled.

"Yeah," said James. "I would always tell Max and Sloane to hit their house first to make sure the candy bars weren't gone." He silently prayed for their souls before refocusing.

"Did you hear that?" asked Grant. "I think I heard something."

"Where?" James didn't hear it.

"Upstairs." Sonny pointed to the stairs with the revolver. "I heard it. I think it's up there."

"All right," said James. "Let's check it out. You stay down here."

"By myself?" Grant reached for James's arm. "I don't—"

"Seriously, Grant." James was still hoarse, his voice filled with gravel. "I need you to keep an eye down here. I'll only be a second."

Grant nodded and checked his grip on the revolver. He walked to the base of the stairs and then stood guard.

James looked up the stairwell, where dark became darker. He wrapped his left hand more securely around the Bushmaster and climbed the steps one at a time, listening for any sounds coming from the second floor. Sonny was a step behind him.

They were halfway up when James heard a creak followed by a thud. It stopped him cold and he waited, hoping he would hear it again over his intensifying pulse. He stood there, his neck throbbing with a dull ache. His lungs burned with each shallow breath and he suddenly felt an acute pain in the back of his leg and wondered if he'd reopened the wound he suffered in the rising water of the tsunami on Peaks Island. The book of Job came to mind.

Creeeaak. Thump.

James looked over at Sonny, who nodded, and down the stairs at Grant, but could only make out a dark shadow pacing back and forth. He turned back to the stairs ahead of him and quietly took another step. Then another. He was almost there.

If he remembered correctly, from the one or two times he'd been upstairs in the Whistlers' house, there were two bedrooms to the right of the stairs. The master bedroom was to the left. James took another two quick steps. He was on the landing.

He listened for the noise again but didn't hear it. He motioned for Sonny to work the left side of the floor. He moved to the right, toward the two secondary bedrooms, walking the hall from vague memory. He couldn't see more than three feet in front of himself. James turned back to Sonny. It was too dark. He couldn't see him. But he heard the noise again. It was coming from a room at the end of the hall.

He slowly stepped heel to toe along the hallway until he came to the room. The door was cracked open, but the sliver of darkness inside revealed nothing. James pushed open the edge of the door, widening the dark expanse with the barrel of the rifle. He followed his weapon into the room, trying to adjust his eyes. As he stepped inside, he could make out the shapes of furniture. There was a twin bed to the right and a small armoire on the wall opposite. Straight back, centered on the exterior wall was a window. James walked to it and lowered the rifle to his side. Outside the window was a large oak tree. Its branches were swaying in gusts of wind, occasionally scraping against the glass.

He stood at the window, looking past the tree into the abyss beyond. The night was a far scarier place without power. He pressed his hand against the window just as a thick oak branch, a couple of inches in diameter, slammed against the house.

James jumped back at the noise, startled by the percussion. But at least now he knew what was causing the noise. He inhaled deeply and let it out and tried again to swallow past the ache in his throat.

James turned and left the room, dragging his hand along the hallway wall to maintain some sense of direction. He met Sonny coming out of the master bedroom.

"There's nothing in here." Sonny shook his head.

"There's nothing back there," James offered. "It was a tree branch."

"So where is he?" Sonny wondered and they walked to the stairs.

"I don't know." James shrugged. "You think he's still in the house?"

"I never saw him—" Sonny was interrupted by a bright flash filling the stairwell beneath them and the thunderous crack of a bolt-action rifle followed by an explosion of splintered wood.

Pop! Pop! Grant was returning fire. He had two bullets left.

Both men rounded the corner to the stairs, almost sledding down the steps on their heels as they raced toward the gunfire.

James took the final couple of steps on his behind as he came to a stop next to the demolished front door. He saw Grant lying prone on the floor, covering his head with one hand while aiming the Smith & Wesson blindly with the other.

Pop! He had one shot left.

Pow! Another blast from the rifle shattered the sidelight glass adjacent to the door, spraying shards of glass everywhere.

James rolled over onto his stomach and crawled on his elbows, as he'd seen military recruits do in action movies and recruiting commercials. He slid next to Grant, putting himself between his neighbor and the oncoming blasts.

Pow!

James saw the flash of light coming from the dining area an instant before he felt the whiz of a bullet screaming past his right ear.

He settled himself, braced the rifle, and pressed his finger into the trigger.

Thump! Thump! Thump! Thump!

A quick volley of bullets gave Grant enough time to crawl to the relative safety of the stairwell, out of the line of fire. Sonny was now at Grant's side.

Thump! Thump! Thump!

Both of them were unloading bursts down the hallway into the dining area. James could hear the bullets shredding furniture and shattering glass.

Thump! Thump! Thump!

Sonny held up his hand, signaling James to withhold his fire. James nodded and listened. He didn't hear any movement coming from the dining area. He couldn't see anything that far away in the darkness.

"What do you think?" he whispered to Sonny.

"I don't know." Sonny shook his head. "I wish I'd bought IR scopes for these things. Big mistake."

"You live and you learn." James smirked.

"You hope to live so you can learn." Sonny inched forward on his elbows and then pulled himself to his knees. He pulled the rifle to his chest and scanned the narrow sweep of the hallway.

Pow! Another shot from the rifle narrowly missed James, buzzing over his head and into the drywall behind him. James couldn't believe the shot missed Sonny. But in the flash, he saw the squatter. He was standing just outside the house, the French doors open, his feet on the threshold.

"He's outside!" James yelled at Sonny. "He's outside the house!"

James knew if they lost him, if they let him get away, the squatter would take his rifle straight to Sonny's house, straight to Leigh and the kids.

He couldn't let that happen.

CHAPTER 70

EVENT +1 Week, 3 Days, 14:32 Hours
University Park, Maryland
Temporary Recovery Zone 5

Unsure if the squatter was still in the doorway, James got to his feet and bolted down the hallway toward the rear of the house. As he skirted past Sonny, he leveled the Bushmaster and pulled the trigger, paving a path with short bursts of gunfire.

He ran into the side of an armchair and almost lost his balance, but skated to the dining room, climbing over the table and landing in the doorway. He looked to his right and saw the faintest outline of someone on the fence line.

James pushed his way past the picnic table and ran to the right, toward the fence separating the Whistlers' yard from Grant's. He was feet from the fence when he tripped on an exposed root, flying helpless into the high grass, losing the rifle as he fell face first.

James's neck was throbbing, the back of his leg pulsing, his lungs screaming for air that wasn't coming quickly enough. Stunned, he blindly grabbed clumps of the grass with his fists and squeezed. He was spent. But he couldn't let the squatter make it to his family and the others before he did.

"James." Sonny slid into the grass beside him. "Get up. Are you okay? Get up."

James rolled over onto his back, seeing two Sonnys beside him and a pair of Grants standing over him. "I'm okay." He coughed and offered his hands for his neighbors to pull him to his feet. Where's my rifle?"

"I got it." Grant picked up the Bushmaster and handed it to James. "Here you go."

"We gotta go," James wheezed. "That guy…is on…his way…to your house…Sonny."

Without saying anything, Sonny put his rifle on the top of the fence, climbed into Grant's yard, and ran after the threat. Grant went next, despite his fatigue. James, using every bit of strength he could muster, heaved himself over the fence. He hit the ground and started running again, praying he wouldn't hit another root.

He was faster than Grant and passed him as they reached the next fence, the one leading to Sonny's property. Sonny was already over the fence when James got there.

James listened for a beat, but heard nothing but Grant huffing behind him, before he climbed the fence, using a loose board to propel one foot over the top. He hit the ground and grabbed his Bushmaster, running to the back porch. Grant was close behind.

"I'll go around front," Grant said. "Make sure he's not there. That way we're covering both entrances."

"Good idea." James pulled on the screen door and inhaled as deeply as he could, suppressing a cough as he tried to regulate his breathing. As he entered the porch, he saw the door to the house was wide open.

He crossed into the house, his rifle sweeping left to right as he entered. Past the darkness of the short hallway, he could see the yellow flicker of the candles illuminating the kitchen. He passed the door to the basement and stepped into the living area. It was empty.

But as he looked left, on the dining table were half-eaten plates of food. One of the chairs was toppled over. He looked to his right. A July issue of *People* magazine was on the floor, as was a thin cotton blanket.

Behind him, James heard a noise coming from upstairs. He spun around and placed himself between the bottom step and the hallway, his pulse quickening, when Sonny appeared at the top of the steps.

"Nobody's here," James said.

"The upstairs is empty," Sonny said, descending the steps to the main floor. "Where's Grant?"

"He's out front," James answered, "checking the front of the house."

"I haven't checked the basement," Sonny said.

James's eyes widened with the sudden realization that everyone was likely downstairs. "I didn't even think about that," he admitted. "What am I thinking?"

He turned to pull on the basement door and opened it. It revealed more darkness. James had grown tired of dipping into black holes, unaware of what might be waiting for him. He and Sonny stood to either side of the doorway, their backs pressed against the wall.

"It's us," James called down the stairs into the basement. "Sonny and James!"

From the darkness, he heard a collective sigh and footsteps bounding toward the stairs. Max was the first to emerge, throwing himself at his father when he reached the top of the steps.

"Dad!" he cried, his voice muffled against James's torso. "We thought you were all dead." He squeezed tighter, causing James to wince against the pressure.

James put his free hand on the back of his son's head and tousled his hair. He stepped back, pulling Max with him as Leigh, Sloane, and Susan Gilbert climbed the steps to the hallway. Leigh's eyes were swollen and red, and as she stepped to her husband, she collapsed into him. She wrapped her arms around him, sandwiching Max between their bodies. She put her lips to James's ear and whispered.

"You scared the living daylights out of me," she said breathlessly. "We heard the gunshots. We thought…"

They moved into the living room, standing in the space between the sitting area and dining table. Emma Wood and her children joined them, her eyes darting around the room.

"Where's Grant?" she asked. "He's not…he didn't…"

"No, no, no," Sonny assured her, putting his hand on her

shoulder. "He's fine. He's in the front, looking for one of the squatters."

"By himself?" Her face stretched with fear. "He's not equipped for that. I never should have bullied him into going. I just—"

"I'm okay." Grant walked into the living room from the hallway, joining the others. "I didn't see him." He looked at James as he spoke. "He must have gone back to your house."

James nodded and looked around the room. "Where is Stuart?" he asked.

"He's still in the basement," answered Susan. "We all ran down there when we heard gunshots. We didn't know who shot who or what happened."

"We had the guns ready, Dad," explained Max. "We were all together down there. We were ready for them."

"What happened?" asked Emma.

"One of them is gone," said Sonny. "We took care of him. But the other one got away. We chased him, but lost him."

"And the Whistlers?" asked Stuart. He was standing behind everyone, in the hallway. His arm was draped around Susan's shoulder. "Are they…?"

"Yes." Sonny lowered his head. "Both of them."

"James"—Leigh's forehead shortened, her brows arched with concern—"what happened to your neck. It's bruised. It looks horrible, even in this light." She reached out to touch it, but stopped short.

"It's nothing." James dismissed her. "I'm fine."

"You're not fine," she said. "It looks swollen. What happened in there?"

"Nothing," said James. "I'm good. Grant helped me out of a jam."

Leigh looked at her husband in such a way that James knew they'd be talking about it later. She wasn't going to take his answer at face value. He also knew she understood there were more pressing issues at hand. She dropped it.

"So what now?" Stuart asked, closing his eyes. "What do we do now?"

"The plan hasn't changed," James said. "We're getting rid of these people. And it's happening tonight."

CHAPTER 71

EVENT +1 Week, 3 Days, 15:01 Hours
University Park, Maryland
Temporary Recovery Zone

"We can't wait for him to come back," argued James. "If we do, we're at a huge disadvantage. We need to take the fight to them."

The seven adults sat around the kitchen table, with James standing behind Leigh with his hands on her shoulders. The five children were feet away in the living room, playing with Albert. James knew Max was listening to the adult conversation, even if he was pretending to focus on the dog.

"I'm not so sure." Stuart, whose fog had lifted, shook his head. "From what you just told us, you almost got yourselves killed at the Whistlers' house. Aren't we better off defending ourselves here? We have the weapons to do it. And it's just one man now."

"I agree," echoed Grant. "We're pressing our luck every time we try to engage them."

"We can sleep in shifts," Stuart added. "Like we originally planned. There are seven adults. Three can sleep, four can stay awake. Then we can swap. We'll always have him outnumbered."

"I disagree," said James, trying to maintain his cool. He felt Leigh reach up to grab the fingers on his left hand. She squeezed gently. "And here's why," James responded, slowing the cadence of his speech. "We need the element of surprise. He will not be expecting us to come after him *right now*. He's back at my house telling that woman what happened. They're getting more incensed by the minute. The longer we give them, the more time they have to plan an attack on us."

"I don't—" Grant started.

"Let him finish," Sonny interrupted.

"You're right," James acknowledged, "when you say we have them outnumbered. We have seven adults. They have two. But we also have five children sitting over there."

"I'm not a *child*," Max called from the sofa, confirming James's suspicion.

"We have four children and a young man," James obliged his son. "And if they come here, if we allow them to attack us, we put our children at risk. I'm not willing to do that."

"I'll go with you," said Sonny, looking at Grant and then at Stuart. Both men averted their eyes.

"I think he's right," said Emma, drawing an explosive glare from Grant. "I don't want our kids in danger."

"I agree," said Susan. "We can't let them gain the upper hand."

"Who's to say they don't have the upper hand now?" Grant snapped. "They've already killed four of our friends. They're in your house." He pointed at James and Leigh. "They've got the upper hand."

"Not right now," Sonny disagreed. "They're panicked. I'm telling you. We killed one of them. The other two are grieving and coping with the shock of it. If anything, they're blinded by anger and aren't thinking clearly."

"Which is dangerous for us," countered Stuart, not realizing he was bolstering Sonny's argument.

"And exactly why we need to attack *them* now!" James said. He polled the table with his eyes. Some nodded. Others didn't.

"I guess I'm in, then." Grant rolled his eyes and relented. "It's better that you have three." He dropped his elbows onto the table and ran his hands across the top of his head.

"Thank you, Grant," James said. "Stuart, you stay here. That way—"

"Don't even say it," Emma Wood interrupted. "Just don't say it."

A pall swept across the table. James knew each person was meditating on what this meant, on what could happen. As dangerous as the last venture was, this was worse. They were tempting fate.

But James rationalized, as a man of science and of faith, that the odds were always mathematically better when one accepted God's will, while at the same time forging a path of self-determination.

As he looked at the faces of the men and women considering their own fates, James knew his family would not have survived everything they had in the last ten days only to die at the hands of a backwoods, meth-addicted squatter. He had faith God had bigger plans for him. And while killing was not among the sins easily forgiven, he also knew all sins were the same. And the people who stole and coveted and lied were no more likely to find heavenly favor than he.

Men often find God as they reconcile their own mortality. For James, the faith was nothing new. But it was acute as he considered the danger, the violence which lie ahead.

What would be, would be. God's plan was his plan, whether James understood the reasons for it or not.

But damned if he would let that fate come to him. He was going to meet it head-on and with a semiautomatic rifle in his hand.

CHAPTER 72

EVENT +1 Week, 3 Days, 15:32 Hours
University Park, Maryland
Temporary Recovery Zone 5

The breeze was stronger than James remembered it. It carried a mist, which added a milky hue to the darkness. The grass was wet and slippery under his feet as he, Sonny, and Grant made their way across the Gilberts' backyard, moving toward 819 Fletcher Road.

The men were quiet, trudging carefully to the far northeast corner of Stuart's property. Conveniently, there was the ladder to a play-set slide adjacent to the fence, which made climbing up for a better view more feasible.

Sonny, carrying a pair of binoculars, climbed to the top of the slide and pulled the lenses to his eyes. He gripped them with his free hand, spinning the focus dial with his finger. His rifle was at his side on the small platform between the ladder and the slide.

"I see candlelight," he said, his voice barely audible underneath the breeze and its whistle through the trees. "On the first floor and on the second. I think one of the lights is in the family room."

"Anything in the basement?" James asked. His house, on a steep upward slope from the back fence line, had an exposed basement entrance.

"Not that I can see." Sonny dropped the binoculars. "I think we're clear there."

Sonny climbed back down the ladder, grabbing his Bushmaster, and moved to the fence. He pulled the binoculars from around his neck and placed them on the ground, next to the play set.

"Won't need these," he reasoned. "Better to travel light."

"All right." James led the huddle. "Our plan stays the same. We enter through the basement. Then we head upstairs. Good?"

"Good," Sonny and Grant answered simultaneously.

"Sonny," suggested James, "you lead the way."

Sonny nodded, handed his rifle to James, and climbed up the fence, heaving himself over to the other side. Grant followed with some difficulty. James was last.

He found himself in his own backyard, looking at the faint glow emanating from a pair of windows in the house he'd called home for a decade. He'd lived in that house when one child was born and another died. They'd mourned and rejoiced inside those walls, in the pie-shaped expanse of their backyard.

But it may as well have been a moonscape for James. It felt cold and unfamiliar. The sanctity of the space was defiled. He felt violated.

He stood there for a moment, lost in the surprise of the emotions seeping into his skin with the mist, and lamented what would never be.

"James," Sonny called to him, apparently noticing his friend's sudden disengagement. "James!"

James blinked past the wave of melancholic anger and joined Sonny and Grant at his family's own play set. It sat on a small plateau in the steep drop of his backyard.

"So far so good," Sonny observed. "You ready?"

"Yeah." James nodded, suppressing a cough.

"You got what I need?" Sonny's left eyebrow arched higher than his right. "If you don't, we're pretty much S.O.L."

"I got 'em." James patted his pocket. "We're good to go."

Grant wiped the sweat from his forehead and then pinched the front of his T-shirt, picking it away from his chest to fan himself. His breathing was labored and Sonny reminded him to use his nose rather than his mouth. Grant grunted something and ignored him.

Without warning, Sonny crossed from the play set to an unfinished concrete slab that abutted the back of the house. Grant followed, huffing his way under the large wooden deck extending outward a floor above.

James was last, cursing himself as he approached the slab, that he'd never taken the time to cover it with brick pavers as Leigh had asked him to do. He looked up through the slats of the deck, seeing the faintest hint of candlelight from the family room illuminating the cracks. The deck needed a fresh coat of weather-resistant stain. It was three or four years since he did it last.

Refocusing, James dug into his pocket and pulled out a pair of manipulated paperclips. He handed them to Sonny.

"Here you go," James said with a hint of a smirk. "I didn't forget them."

Sonny worked the paperclips with aplomb, and inside of forty-five seconds, the door was open and the trio was inside the basement.

James checked his gun safe. It was locked and secure. That was a good sign.

"Are you ready?" he asked the men. They acknowledged they were as ready as they would ever be.

They ascended the stairs toward the first floor. They assembled at the top of the steps, James's hand on the door.

"The kitchen is mine," he said, after Grant agreed to take the hallway and Sonny the family room and stairs.

James sucked in a deep breath and opened the door.

CHAPTER 73

EVENT +1 Week, 3 Days, 15:41 Hours
University Park, Maryland
Temporary Recovery Zone 5

She saw James an instant after he rounded the corner. He knew she did. She was standing at the sink, her hands pressed against the stainless steel edge. She was leaning in, her elbows locked. Her jet-black hair, hued red from the candlelight, draped at her shoulders. It was thin and stringy, like and old frayed grease mop.

She turned almost imperceptibly, to pick at her cheek, when he knew she spotted him with those blue eyes. Her eyes narrowed as James calculated she was trying to rationalize what she was seeing. As her brain processed the intrusion of three men, James put just enough pressure on the Bushmaster's trigger to unleash a single bullet.

A slight thump and whoosh were likely the last things she heard as the rifle slung the thirty-caliber bullet into her chest. Her mouth opened as the force of the slug knocked her off balance. She dropped with a thud onto the tile floor.

James looked over at his neighbors. Both of them were okay, their areas of responsibility clear of danger. James moved to the kitchen and stepped behind the counter.

The woman was still alive. James saw fishlike gasps for air, her head jerking slightly with each breath. He stood over her, watching the depth of those attempts at air lessen in strength and frequency. The jerking stopped. The flow of blood from the gaping wound beneath her collarbone looked like oil leaking from a can.

James stood over the body, straddling the thickening pool of blood. He felt an unexpected smile creep outward from the corners of his mouth.

Except for the blood on the tile, which he knew he'd need to clean before Leigh saw the mess, this was good. God would forgive him as James knew the world, as frail as it was, was a little stronger without that woman in it.

Two down.

Grant protested and Sonny rationalized James's quick trigger pull. None of them was watching the stairs. Then James turned and noticed the shadow cast along the wall leading up the stairs.

He leveled the Bushmaster, ready to fire again, but something stopped him. He hesitated. It was just enough of a pause for the figure to emerge.

"What happened?" asked the boy. He was in a T-shirt and shorts, his hair matted from sleep. His hands were empty. He was the older boy James had seen in Sloane's window. He looked much thinner now. "I heard a noise."

James looked for help from Sonny and Grant. None was coming. So he handed Sonny his rifle and walked to the bottom step. He spoke softly, but clearly.

"Your mother is dead." James wasn't one for candy-coating things with his children, why should he be that way with those belonging to meth-addicted squatters.

"I know." The boy's brows arched, shrinking his forehead. "She died nine days ago."

James took another step closer to the boy, resting his hand on the bannister. "What do you mean?"

"Our mom," repeated the boy, crossing his arms in front of himself, gathering his shoulders, "died the day after the power went out. How did *you* know she was dead?"

"What about the woman who brought you here?" Sonny interjected.

"She's not my mom!" The boy backed up a step, his face slipping from the light.

"Who is she?" James asked.

"The devil."

"What do you mean?"

"She's not my mom," the boy repeated. He was scratching at his elbows with both hands. "He's not my dad."

The other squatter!

In the haze of the gunfire and the boy's appearance, all three of the men had forgotten about the squatter, the man who escaped the Whistlers'. James's eyes widened. He felt his pulse skip into his throat.

"Where is that man?" James tone was forceful. "The man who's not your dad."

"I-I-I don't know." The boy shook his head. "He left with his cousin a while ago. They said something about getting food and they left. That's all I know."

"So he's not here?" James pressed.

"No."

"Then he's…" James felt flush. He spun and yanked his rifle from Sonny and ran toward the front door. His family was in danger.

CHAPTER 74

EVENT +1 Week, 3 Days, 15:49 Hours
University Park, Maryland
Temporary Recovery Zone 5

James couldn't see more than a few feet in front of him as he raced across the cul-de-sac toward Sonny's house. He tripped on the curb separating the street from Sonny's front yard, but regained his balance as he galloped awkwardly to the front door.

He felt the bullet tear through his skin, searing its way into his waist from his back before exploding out the front. Then he heard the shot from somewhere behind him as he collapsed against the door, grabbing at the bleeding, jagged hole while struggling to find the source of the gunfire.

Another bullet zipped past his head, boring through the front door. James inchwormed his way onto his back, grunting against the pain.

He knew he was bleeding, but he had no concept of how serious the wound might be. He lay flat on the ground, moderately confident the squatter couldn't see him well enough to hit him.

Pow! Zipppp!

Another bullet, this one to his right, but just inches above his face. James knew he couldn't stay in the doorway. He quickly laid the rifle on his chest and crossed his arms over it tightly. He logrolled away from the door and into the grass. Against the front windows to the right of the entry door was a row of boxwood hedges.

James managed to maneuver himself between the hedges and the house. It was a narrow space, maybe two feet wide, and didn't provide much room for maneuverability.

James rolled onto his back, releasing the rifle, and pressed his hand against his shirt, just above the outer edge of his ilium. It was warm and wet. There was a lot of blood. At least it felt that way. He knew he was bleeding from his back too. It wouldn't be long, he imagined, before he'd begin to lose focus. And that was assuming he didn't suffer any organ damage.

James closed his eyes, listening for any sounds coming from the street. There was nothing. The breeze had stopped. The mist was gone, leaving behind a palpable thickness. He could feel the sweat under his arms and on the back of his neck. It was as much the pain as it was the humidity.

He opened his eyes and looked into the sky. The clouds had given way to a beautiful starry night. There were so many twinkling, shimmering white dots above him.

They sat there, hanging in their spots, burning balls of gas held together by their own gravity. James winced against the pain and refocused on the incandescent spots. He was looking into the past as his eyes danced from one to the next.

Even at the speed of light, one hundred and eighty-six thousand miles per second, they were so far away, the specks of brilliance emitted from the stars took thousands, or even millions, of years to reach earth. The energy that left a star a million light years away had traveled 99.9999972 percent of its journey when James's world shifted on its axis. It was a time machine, a concept he loved explaining to his high school students.

"Time travel is possible!" he would begin the lecture. "All you have to do is look up!"

James stared at a lone star, absent a constellation. It was dim, its flicker like a dying candle. He considered that three hundred and sixty-four million, nine hundred and ninety-nine thousand, nine hundred and ninety days from now, someone might be looking at the same sky and see the light that left the star the day his family survived a car crash, a tsunami, would-be pirates, and a bloodthirsty militia.

He pressed his eyes closed again and rolled over onto his stomach. From his position behind the boxwood, he might be able to see the squatter advance before the squatter spotted him again.

James brought the rifle into position and rested it on its magazine. It was awkward, but he didn't have the strength to hold it properly as he lay prone in the wet mulch.

Pow! Zipppp!

The squatter's bullet found its way into the glass above James's head, shattering it. James's plan didn't work. The squatter knew exactly where he was. He'd eventually hit him. James was pinned. And despite his effort to see past the sting of sweat in his eyes, he couldn't make out the squatter's position.

Figuring he had nothing to lose, he adjusted the Bushmaster and pulled the trigger, holding it for several seconds.

Thump! Thump! Thump! Thump! Thump!

He felt the recoil pound against his shoulder as he fired. He hadn't pressed the butt of the rifle tight enough against his body. He released the trigger and listened. Still nothing.

James pressed his finger to the trigger again, ready to pull, when above his head he heard the familiar sound of a suppressed Bushmaster 300 AAC Blackout.

Thump! Thump! Thump! A quick burst and then another.

Thump! Thump! Thump! It was coming from the second floor of the house. Somebody was helping him!

Pow! Pow!

Thump! Thump!

James finished the pull and let loose another volley.

Thump! Thump! Thump!

Then from his left, close to Stuart's house, Sonny opened fire.

Thump! Thump! Thump! Thump!

And then the shots came from above again, but this time the shooter was on the roof.

Thump! Thump!

It sounded to James like what he imagined a firefight in the midst of war might be. It was a four-piece orchestra of Sonny's Bushmasters blistering the squatter with bullets.

James thought they'd succeeded in stopping the squatter. He was certain there was no way the man could have survived the onslaught of semiautomatic fire from four weapons at once. But he was wrong.

James heard the squatter before he saw him. As he pushed himself to his knees, leaving his weapon in the mulch, the man was already just feet from him. He screamed and bellowed something unintelligible as he left his feet, his dark figure lunging at James.

It was a final, primal attempt to finish off the man who'd come home and taken back his neighborhood. But it was futile.

Thump!

A single shot caught the squatter mid-leap, stopping the man as if he'd hit a wall. The bullet, coming from a steep angle downward, killed the man instantly. He was dead before his limp body hit the boxwood.

James fell back against the house, sinking against the wall, the adrenaline leaking from his system. As he slipped into unconsciousness, he was unaware it was his wife, Leigh, who climbed onto the roof through the gable with the rifle in her hand. And he would not find out until he awoke, it was his son, Maxwell, who armed himself without the adults' permission and fired the fatal headshot that saved his father's life.

CHAPTER 75

EVENT +2 Weeks, 1 Day, 5:00 Hours
University Park, Maryland
Temporary Recovery Zone 5

James stood in the middle of the cul-de-sac, his arm around Leigh, as they visited with Sonny for the first time in two days.

"How are the boys?" Sonny asked. "Are they adjusting?"

"As best they can." Leigh sighed. "It'll take them a while to trust us. I think they already like Max and Sloane. And Max has really taken on the role of protector. He feels strangely empowered by what he did."

"So," Sonny said, shoving his hands into his pockets, "tell me again what happened to them? I only caught pieces of it."

"You mean because you were busy sewing me up?" James patted his hip. "Making sure I didn't bleed out?"

"You were lucky," Sonny acknowledged. "That bullet went straight in and straight out. If you had any real organ damage, you'd know it by now. Back to the kids…"

"Yeah." Leigh nodded. "They still don't talk a lot about it. But the best I can tell is that the three adults were a pair of cousins and a girlfriend. Somehow, they carjacked the kids and their mom in the Camaro near Richmond, Virginia. They were on their way home to Bluefield, West Virginia."

"They killed the mom," said Sonny.

"Yes," answered James. "But they kept the kids. They abused them, made them their slaves, essentially. The older one seems to think they used them to fool the guards at the TRZ checkpoints. He said the woman told the guards that the kids were hers and they let them through. The men threatened the kids to stay quiet or they'd kill them too."

"Poor kids." Sonny shook his head. "It's good of you to take care of them."

"What else are we going to do?" reasoned Leigh. "We can't kick them out, make them fend for themselves. They're sweet kids."

"We'll figure it out," James added. "How's everybody else? We've all retreated into our private quarters the last week."

"The Gilberts came over last night," Sonny said. "We talked about setting up a neighborhood watch."

"Really?" James asked.

"Yeah." Sonny nodded. "I already talked about it with Grant and Emma Wood. They're game."

"So we're the final vote, then." James laughed.

"Not really," Sonny admitted. "It's already a done deal. Majority rules. But we do want you to be the captain."

"No way." James shook his head. "You're the cop. You're the one with the experience."

"True," Sonny acknowledged. "But I'm not you."

"What does that mean?" James asked.

"I saw you in action, James," Sonny said, a sadness in his eyes. "Something happened to you. Or something came out of you, something buried deep inside. I don't know what it was. But this is, somehow, your world. This dystopia…you were meant for it. It's like *this* was your fate."

"I'm not sure—"

"There was a look in your eyes when you stood over that woman's body, James," Sonny interrupted. "I'm not judging you. Don't get me wrong. But there was something unearthly about you. You're a survivor. You'll do whatever it takes to survive."

"What's wrong with that?" James asked, sensing Sonny's

discomfort with a conversation he must have felt was necessary.

"There's nothing wrong with it, James," Sonny answered, "when the world has gone to hell. Nothing wrong with it at all."

James clenched his jaw. He didn't like what Sonny was telling him. He didn't want to be who he'd become. But maybe Sonny was right. Maybe it's what he was always meant to be.

He would protect his family and the ones he loved regardless of the cost to himself. He was unafraid of the personal consequence if it meant saving others.

James Rockwell was home the moment he awoke to the burning glow two weeks ago. He was home the instant the power died and his world was cast into uncertainty. He was home every time he pulled the trigger, threw a punch, or lit a fuse.

It was a revelation he only now understood.

TOM ABRAHAMS
THE ALT APOCALYPSE
ASH

GET THE FIRST THREE BOOKS OF THE SERIES
THAT STARTED IT ALL

"MAD MAX MEETS
THE GOOD THE BAD AND THE UGLY"

BEGIN YOUR JOURNEY WITH THE TRAVELER SERIES

EXPERIENCE THE STORIES THAT INSPIRED PILGRIMAGE

FROM USA TODAY BESTSELLING AUTHOR
STEVEN KONKOLY

38140550R00199

Printed in Great Britain
by Amazon